"I became aware of Tom Burke years ago when a character of his named Worm insisted on being called Whurm. This moment has stood proud in my brain ruined by thirty-four years as a schoolmarm teaching writing. *Eastbound Into the Cosmos* is so odd it feels like Worm insisting on Whurm."

PADGETT POWELL, author of *Edisto*

Praise for *Eastbound into the Cosmos*

"*Eastbound into the Cosmos* is a big-hearted and funny novel about youthful folly, youthful grief, and the intricacies of an international mushroom smuggling business, among many other intriguing things. Thomas Burke has fashioned a winning narrator in Everett: witty, self-deprecating, honest, and always searching the darkness for human wisdom. And you never know where you'll find it."

SAM LIPSYTE, author of *Hark*

"Imagine a modern-day cross between Alexander Portnoy and Frederick Exley and you just might have Everett, the titular heart-on-his-sleeve, slacker hero (anti-hero?) of Tom Burke's hilarious debut. Reading *Eastbound into the Cosmos* conjures that feeling so many of us have in the Trump era: How did we get to this point and when exactly did everyone around me go certifiably insane? In his case, Everett returns to the American suburbs from time poorly spent in China to find his parents marriage fallen apart and his life at an undignified dead-end. A hilarious, riveting read you'll want to ride all the way to the surprising end."

JEFF PARKER, author of *Where Bears Roam the Streets*

"Tom Burke's accomplished debut novel *Eastbound into the Cosmos* is riveting, fast-paced, and full of heart. The prose is careful, and the story is often hilarious. Tom Burke is an author to keep an eye on."

JEFFERY RENARD ALLEN, author of the novels *Song of the Shank* and *Rails Under My Back*

"Thomas Burke's splendid new novel is at once a darkly comic international caper and a remarkable investigation of grief and spiritual longing. In these pages you'll encounter a delightfully loathsome guru, a recently deceased father, a persecuted cult-like sect, and a profoundly misguided mushroom-selling venture. Do yourself a favor and dive in."

DAWN RAFFEL, author of *The Strange Case of Dr. Couney*

"Full of energy, intelligent, fast-paced, darkly humorous and poignant in the vein of a cross of sorts between David Sedaris and the late great Soviet/Russian/Abkhazian writer Fazil Iskander."

MIKHAIL IOSSEL, author of *Notes from Cyberground: Trumpland* and *My Old Soviet Feeling*

"*Eastbound into the Cosmos* is a lively exploration of spirituality, desire, and loneliness. Tom Burke expertly blends action with introspection, the bewildering present with the pained past."

CHRIS BACHELDER, author of *The Throwback Special*

"Everett returns from China in *Eastbound into the Cosmos* to mourn his father, and surprise! a crystal-laden mother. Until you get to "Mom's weird apology-baptism thing," you aren't sure whether the hero will survive re-entry. Indeed, he even makes a quick and harrowing return trip. From a fight over homemade icicles to flying turkeys to the cultish Xuan Gong and a (non-hallucigenic) mushroom bust, Thomas Burke effortlessly takes the transparent and makes it 'dark and spiky.' Lose yourself in *Eastbound into the Cosmos* and cheer for Everett."

TERESE SVOBODA, author of *Great American Desert*

E A S T B O U N D   I N T O   T H E   C O S M O S

Thomas Burke

MADHAT PRESS
ASHEVILLE, NORTH CAROLINA

MadHat Press
MadHat Incorporated
PO Box 8364, Asheville, NC 28814

The Library of Congress has assigned
this edition a Control Number of
2019937249

ISBN 978-1-941196-89-2 (paperback)

An excerpt from this book previously appeared
in the spring 2009 issue of *Matrix Magazine,* titled "Closet."

Text by Thomas Burke
Cover image: *Paper boats sailing on the dry soil*
by Jelena Jovanovic
Cover design by Marc Vincenz
Author photo by Hamilton Poe

www.madhat-press.com

First Printing

For my family

CHAPTER 1

I had been home from China for two days when I stole a crystal from my mom. The crystal was gray, the size and shape of a pinecone, but not very different from the other crystals in her collection. She kept all of them on top of her Federal secretary in the bedroom she'd shared with my dad until his death five months before.

This was unchartered, my mom's new-age hoodoo altar in a house that was otherwise calculated to the point of sterility. The objects on Mom's desk seemed out of place: dozens of crystals, incense cones in dusty bags, bundles of sage, assorted candles, and five small brass urns holding ashes, pebbles, and sand.

The items were of dubious purpose in my mind, which was why I wrote the theft off as a mere family infraction as the chunk slid snugly into the front left pocket of my jeans. It helped that I had a distinct memory of Mom snooping around my bedroom when I was younger in search of what I might have kept sacred, her fingers prying behind and underneath my furniture, extracting my assorted contraband and piling it at the center of my rug.

Stealing the crystal wasn't premeditated, but I had seen that same crystal in a dream the previous night. It'd apparently stuck with me from the day before, when I'd done a perfunctory sweep of the house, taking inventory of all we'd need to do before we sold the house.

Standing in Mom's room, I wondered about the true catalyst

of her new bent. The simple explanation was my dad's death. An event like that could spin someone into patchouli-scented oblivion, no question, but I suspected those roots had been there all along. Truthfully, I only had vague suspicions; I'd barely been home in two years. I'd completely missed her acquisition of spiritual knickknacks, a collection that now rivaled a semi-respectable rock shop.

Despite my reservations, it all seemed to be helping her somehow. She looked healthier and more attractive than she had in decades. It was just that the contrast between this Mom and the old Mom was so stark.

Mom was raised Presbyterian, after all, and raised me that way, too. Her father had been the assistant to the deacon at the Fourth Presbyterian Church of Rochester, a detail Mom repeated to me most Sunday mornings of my childhood, usually in response to pillow-muffled whimpers for some additional shut-eye. And when Mom was feeling especially unworthy for whatever reason—usually this was in the car on the way home from church—she'd go on about how "My family had the minister over for supper every third Sunday of the month. Our lack of hospitality is disgraceful." On the Sundays that Dad was in town, he'd swerve to the curb and threaten to pull a U-turn so she could ask whomever the hell she wanted to our nonexistent Sunday smorgasbord.

But forget Sunday suppers. Mom taught Sunday school to the kindergarteners, worked on the flower guild, and helped with the annual church rummage sale. She had the moral tenacity to call people "good Christians" when being a good woman or good man didn't quite cut it. And she would sometimes sing hymns, the timing of which would often infuriate me, like a windows-down "Onward, Christian Soldiers" as she drove me to school.

In short, I'd never had reason to question Mom's faith.

Plucking the crystal off the secretary and slipping it in my pocket was reactionary, mechanical, and I didn't reflect on it, didn't have time to, because just as the crystal dropped plumb against my thigh, I heard Mom behind me.

"What are you doing?" she asked. She was standing in the doorframe wearing flip-flops, black leggings, and a wool sweater-jacket with a belt.

"Hi, Mom," I said. "Just checking out the crystals. Just trying to assess the house, the move, and saw your crystals."

It wasn't like I had churned through my youth perfecting the art of lying, but the cover-up flowed from my mouth smoothly and naturally. In my twenty-five years, Mom's hunk of quartz—while not the most valuable item I'd ever stolen—did likely constitute my most meaningful heist. Maybe the gravity in that fact gave me courage; that and the unfamiliarity of it all, the eeriness, made it unreal, and therefore easier. Still, it was just bearable.

"Are you okay?" Mom said.

"Why wouldn't I be?"

I imagined invisible waves of negativity transmitting into the world from the pocket of my jeans like a field stone plopped into the middle of a pond.

Mom hadn't yet looked at me. Her eyes seemed focused on a crease where a strip of crown molding met and kissed another. "You can keep it," she said.

"Keep what?"

"I want you to have it."

I was indignant. "Have what?"

Mom put her arms in front of her and appeared to be pressing all ten fingertips toward an invisible point about four inches in front of her navel. It was some breathing exercise, which I, with difficulty, tried to keep from watching.

My heart fluttered. I considered my next move, and the phone rang.

These days, the ring of a phone causes my mind to cycle through the possibilities of what news awaits on the other end. The day Dad died, I was getting ready to leave for work when the phone began to ring. For no good reason, I didn't answer it. I just let it go on and on. Then, almost as an afterthought, I picked up the receiver just before I left. It was Mom. She told me Dad had taken a turn for the worse. I asked if I should come home, and Mom said yes, but that I probably wouldn't make it in time. Mom said Dad wasn't able to talk anymore. She said I should think good thoughts about him.

I went to teach my oral English class, but I couldn't keep anything straight in my head. The lesson plan had something to do with "The Jabberwocky," but it unraveled mightily. My eyes welled up and wouldn't stop leaking, which led to an impromptu crash course on allergy vocab.

When class was over, I headed back to the apartment and called Mom. She picked up right away, and she told me Dad was gone.

Back in Mom and Dad's bedroom now, I watched Mom open her eyes. She walked over to the cordless next to her bed, but I stayed where I was. "Hello?"

"Just a moment," she said and handed me the phone. It was my first call in the US since coming home. Not like this made the cut for the CNN news ticker, but it was monumental for me.

"Hello?" I said.

It was Dino, my roommate in China. Dino had left China four months before I did, and he was back in Chicago, too. We'd e-mailed since but hadn't spoken. Hearing his voice made four months feel like less than a week, in a good way.

"Dino, hold on a minute." I offered Mom a meek wave goodbye and walked down the hallway and halfway down the stairs to the landing. I planted myself on the top step where I

4

could survey the foyer. It was a spot I'd occupied for hours at a time over the years, even entire nights, most often in darkness and wrapped in a blanket, on the lookout for burglars or, idiotically, for my out-of-town dad coming home unexpectedly.

"Are you maintaining?" Dino said.

"I suppose. I haven't slept since I've been home."

"Exactly."

"Are you at home?" I asked. Dino lived forty minutes away in a western suburb of the city.

"I am. How're things on your end?"

"I'm not sure how long I can take it."

"You'll be fine, champ. By the way, do you remember that guy we hung out with in Guangzhou, the cop from Wisconsin? Ron. You remember him?"

"I have no idea what you're about to tell me."

"You remember him?"

"I do."

"Ron wrote me an e-mail saying he's looking for a business partner. Something about selling dried mushrooms to upscale grocery stores. Lots of money to be made."

"You gave that guy your email?"

"Ron gets mushrooms by the kilo for almost nothing. All we've got to do is bring them back through customs. That's the only complication. Everything else is profits."

"Sounds like a drug-running operation. Total scam."

"It's not a scam. Ron's the police. Easy money."

It was a ridiculous proposition, granted, but I had no other gigs in the works—I had no gainful employment on the horizon, and my bonus from teaching wouldn't last long—so I agreed to meet Dino for lunch in Chinatown the next day.

When I got off the phone with Dino I didn't move, and Mom didn't disturb me. She was understanding—if not overly laissez-faire—about my need to be weird right now. I appreciated this, but it also felt a bit indifferent, and that hurt. It reminded me of her relationship with Dad my last two years of high school, the last time all three of us lived under the same roof. By then, they hardly ever pursued anything beyond practicalities. I wondered if that was in store for me.

CHAPTER 2

Later that night, Mom and I were in the kitchen, she finishing dinner, I searching for mine, when I broached the subject of the guru. "What's the deal with Tucky?" I said, as I opened the refrigerator.

"What do you mean?" Mom was licking the plate she'd used for her cinnamon-toast dinner.

"Who is he? Where'd he come from?"

Mom's posture changed from casual to yogi-debutant, and she snorted, a noise I think was meant to roadblock me, so I rephrased. "Can you just explain it to me? The changes seem positive. Maybe it's something I should look into."

"Tucky's my adviser."

"In what sense?" I sat down at the counter with Mom and began slicing a hunk of cheddar into wedges.

"A guide, a mentor. He's helping me establish clarity and control in my life."

I said, "That sounds like something Tucky told you to say," which I regretted.

"It's what Tucky does. He helps people on their journeys, not so much as a guide, but as a companion."

"So is he ... you know ..." Mom looked at me funny, so I said it outright—and I didn't mean to sound accusatory—I was mostly just curious, and only partially potentially resentful—"Is he your boyfriend?"

Mom didn't flinch. "I don't ask about your sex life," she said.

That wasn't what I'd expected. I figured she'd squash that idea outright. I came in from another angle. "How much does it cost?"

"Tucky charges on a sliding scale, not that it matters."

"And what are the sessions like?"

"We meet twice a week for meditation, counseling, and subconscious self-awareness exercises." Mom squinted, better defining her crow's feet. She'd always had a pretty face: big brown eyes, a soft smile. She hardly ever wore makeup.

"What's a self-awareness exercise?" It felt like we were entering dark territory, and even though my insides were beginning to twist up, and my heart was doing its tightening thing, I aspired for outward casualness. I rested my elbows on the granite countertop and rotated a salt shaker in my fingers.

"Now's not a good time to get into it, but in short, it's a type of hypnosis."

"Hypnosis for what?"

"What I just told you."

When I think of hypnosis, it's along the "look into my stopwatch pendulum" lines. But now: Mom in the lotus position centered in a room thick with sage smoke, her retinas pointed toward her gray matter, maybe some whispering in tongues.

"Does he put you under?"

Mom said, "Today's society effects such significant suppression of emotions and needs in individuals through its unrealistic expectations and debilitating limitations that most of us are deathly afraid to even attempt to process what lies in the subconscious."

"What are you talking about?" I stared at Mom, and she gave me death eyes right back.

The condescension wasn't intentional. Mom may have hoped for a slow reveal of her new crazy, but for me, at that moment, I was in a pit and the cement truck was already pouring. I didn't know what I was actually supposed to do with this information. It wasn't digestible. Even in this new Mom, it seemed like a foreign substance. I had a strong urge to wring her clean.

"I'm not dumb," Mom said. "And it's not your job to tell me how to live and what to think. You don't know. You have absolutely no idea what you don't know. I've been a prison for terrible things. I need to release them."

Mom was shaken and looked a half breath from tears. Her mouth opened as if she were on the verge of saying something more, but she didn't.

A prison for terrible things? I bit my tongue. Good or bad, there's never been anything truly remarkable about us. At the risk of being completely heartless, it felt like the set and cast of a bad soap opera had just lowered around me.

She fought it, but Mom started to cry. I sat inches away from her in the kitchen of the house my family had lived in the last twenty-five years, and I didn't budge. And inside I was breaking. I should have run outside and picked her an armload of flowers. But, in my mind, I was constricting and mashing her body in search of the loony squatting in there. And in reality, my feet were sliding my chair backward, increasing the distance between us.

Mom would have never been able to sit there and watch me cry. She would have hugged me and told me things would get better. Some kind of monster, I thought to myself—where had I gotten these hideous genes? I ought to have empty eye sockets and scales covering my face. But I needed space, some time to locate maybe one or two of the freaking puzzle pieces. I got up from the table and began to cry too as I left the room.

Chapter 3

In the morning, despite my lack of sleep, I blinked my eyes awake, and I was up. Standing, I saw the clock: 5:12 a.m. My body sank with exhaustion. But, like I said, I was up, and I headed to the bathroom.

Mom was apparently up too, because I smelled something burning. Not plastic, not wood, not toast—it was a much earthier smolder. I headed downstairs to investigate.

From the landing, I could hear music, the bounce-drip of slow tabla. I stopped to listen. It wasn't very professional sounding, so I suspected a live concert—Mom, an orchestra of one, probably also digging at a bowl of puffed spelt. I continued down the stairs.

It was still dark out. Mom hadn't turned on any of the lights, but my mind never lost the floor plan. I could see the flicker of candles coming from the family room.

But as I rounded the corner, I got stopped at the threshold. In front of me was a scene that required processing.

The first thing I saw, as my eyes adjusted, was the bare back of a man, presumably Tucky. He was sitting cross-legged on the floor. His skin was pasty and his shoulders were hairy, and he had a ponytail that pointed like an arrow to his ass crack, also bare. His knees poked out to the sides, and his elbows wiggled as he batted at his drum.

He was nothing but flesh, and he wasn't alone. There, just a few feet away from him, was Mom, also completely nude.

Her eyes were closed, and she was engaged in some kind of deep backbend. Her head dangled loosely from her shoulders. Her nakedness was overwhelming.

The whole of my body spasmed at once, which somehow produced an airy substance that got pushed up toward my throat and out through my mouth. It was audible, like the last burp of a chain saw shutting down, except that it lasted several long seconds.

I didn't want to look, but I was locked in, tractor-beam-style, and I stood there staring. And suddenly Mom's eyes were wide like dinner plates and square on me.

But she didn't break from her backbend. She maybe even corrected her pose slightly.

On top of that, she didn't look sorry or embarrassed. It was more like she was disappointed, plus highly annoyed at the interruption. As though I'd purposely vanished all the magic from the room, and that that was the real tragedy of the morning—never mind the instant tattoo on my temporal lobe of my mother, candlelit and engaged in a full-on nudie backbend with Prince Shit-for-Brains, right there in our family room.

Next Mom's eyes shifted, and she conveyed a very different but very clear message, like, *unless you're about to peel off that tank top and join me in a backbend ...*

I practically tripped backward getting out of there, and that goddamned smoldering witch's brew was shading the house darker by the second—not to mention its suffocating effect, or how it suddenly had my eyes ultra leaky.

I managed to get to the kitchen, but I felt like I'd been taking Thorazine for a decade. I stopped at the odds-and-ends drawer and fished blindly through a mess of old batteries, loose birthday candles, etc. for the keys to Dad's Cadillac. I found them, stuck a finger through the ring, and made for the back door. The only shoes available were Mom's flip-flops, so I slipped them on and stepped out.

The morning was brisk, and the transition to cool from the heat of the house felt momentarily hyper-dimensional. The sun was just starting to layer the neighborhood in a dim yellow haze, just enough light to see the gloss of dew on the backyard and its contents. Maybe it was beautiful even, in ways unavailable to me then.

In long, clumsy zombie strides, I pressed across the yard and into the garage. I got into the DeVille, and it was again very dark. Too dark, and also too quiet, so I put the keys in the ignition and turned partway. The dash lit up, and Dad's conservative talk radio poured from the speakers. I twisted the radio off immediately. Mom must not have driven the DeVille since Dad died, which was strange. But she had her own car.

I fingered the keys in the ignition and tried to distract myself. Nothing trumped recent events, however. They filled the DeVille and leaked into the garage, touchable, like mountain clouds. And, chomp, the morning consumed me whole, and it felt like the underside of my skin was being tickled by the furry ends of a million old-man ponytails.

I grunted, loudly, and I scratched all over my body—frantic, powerful scratches—for maybe five seconds. (I may have grunted for the duration.) And then, as quickly as it had arrived, the mania passed. I kept scratching, more slowly, with more comforting strokes, self-soothing or what have you. It helped.

Then it became unbearably hot. I rolled down the window and said, "Fuck it," because a window down wasn't doing it. I flung open the door and hopped out of the DeVille. "Man, that guy," I said. And, what? They were still in the house? Still doing that?

I saw a hubcap on the opposite wall, and I imagined banging

it over an invisible head in front of me. Not perfect, a little too *Three Stooges,* but it was something. I looked around for other possible weapons.

Mom had a bucket with a few gardening tools in it: a little hoe, rusty shears, a bag of fertilizer, etc. There was some potential there, but still not perfect.

I spotted golf clubs near the door. I dumped the bag on its side. The irons, yes, a 3 and an 8, those had heft. I also put on a golf glove that was in a side pocket, even though the leather had dried to the point of crunchiness.

With a club in each hand and a glove on one, I felt better prepared for battle, at least physically. I even started toward the door, but I stopped. I'd heard something. An actual voice had spoken to me, like what some people might claim is a guardian angel, though that isn't exactly my style. Whatever its origins, the voice delivered a message: "That outfit isn't exactly military issue, son."

That took me down several pegs. I saw an olive-green rain poncho hanging on a hook near the door, and I slid it over my head. Better, perhaps, but not because it beefed up my confidence any. It was more like relief that the world was now shielded from my flesh. I was that kind of warrior.

At that point, I still had fury in me, somewhere, but my mind was working fast at obliterating whatever courage might have been there. Maybe I'd known all along that I wouldn't be going back in the house, that I lacked the muscles to slug Tucky with a 3 iron. Mostly I was just really sad and upset.

I stood in that same spot for a long time, my brain blank. I didn't move, either, except at one point to pull the hood up on my poncho in an attempt to keep from crying, which made zero sense, even though it sort of worked.

Very slowly, I floated back to awareness. Practicalities. No, the garage was not a suitable place to suffer through my remaining years, and although I had some chickenshit part of me that wanted to crank the DeVille to life and huff myself to sleep in her cockpit, I had a deeper-seated chickenshit in me, too, which removed that plan from the table. So, my feet would eventually need to transport the rest of my body to a different location.

I ditched the golf clubs but kept the poncho, gathered up what gusto I could, exited the garage and crept around to the bushes in front of the house. Being the spineless creature that I am, I was careful not to look through the windows along the way, for fear of what I might spy on the other side of the glass.

From the safety of the front bushes, I scanned the neighborhood until I saw a good hideout. I took off at as near a sprint as flip-flops allowed—the poncho trailing behind me like a cape—to a neighbor's house across the street and three doors down, the one whose landscaping Mom always said ruined the block. Maybe so, Mom, but for a man in a poncho whose intention is to discreetly keep tabs on the comings and goings of our shared home, it was ideal. So I nested myself into the hodgepodge of our neighbor's junipers and giant wheat stalks.

I had no clock with me there in the shrubs, but suffice to say—especially since I couldn't keep a single thought in my head for more than two seconds—that the morning felt neverending. It was like my ass hitting the mulch had pressed a secret button that made the earth stop rotating. I waited.

Tucky and Mom finally exited the front door together. Mom locked up, cool as a cucumber, and when they hit the sidewalk, they stopped, faced each other, put their hands in front of their chests like they were praying, and bowed. Then they got into separate cars and drove off in opposite directions.

However long it'd been since I'd walked in on them, one thing was for sure: Tucky and Mom had had enough time to do the deed in quadruplicate, followed by the kind of shower that unsticks wallpaper.

Chapter 4

I was much more aware of how I looked coming out of the neighbor's front landscaping than I was going in—which is to say, I looked ridiculous, and quite possibly criminal—so I made a quick escape from the shrubbery on wobbly legs and double-timed it back home.

It felt eerily calm inside the house, not like a former battlefield but more like I was walking through a very familiar display window in some department store. I may have been deluding myself, I admit, but I needed to tell myself something in order to pull myself together. I still had an agenda for the day. It felt mostly impossible, but even so, I never once considered bailing on my meeting with Dino. I guess Dino represented hope.

I took baby steps, started with a shower, etc. I found my old backpack from grade school in my closet, complete with a *Highlights Magazine* and a black comb from a picture day. It no longer fit on my back, which meant I had to carry it in my hands by its straps, but it otherwise retained functionality. I stuffed it tight with provisions—clean underwear, socks, a flashlight, three yogurts, the heel of a summer sausage, a toothbrush, the poncho—and I dumped a jar of quarters into a back pocket meant for pencils and pens.

I left the house. I was unsure of when I would next return. Not that I had anywhere else to go.

The train that took me south to Chinatown to meet Dino started out elevated, went underground, and finally dumped me off again aboveground. In that hour the temperature rose about fifteen degrees, so that when I stepped onto the Cermak-Chinatown platform, it was hot. I was perspiring in my jeans and sweater in October, cooling down only in the shade when the lake breeze hit my neck sweat. I had missed this weather, this city. Mobility and heat were doing me well, as was a little adventure. Considering my morning, I felt surprisingly human.

That said, part of me was leery of meeting up with Dino. His latest business idea was absolutely cockeyed, not that that wasn't par for the course. I had learned over two years of living with Dino that he heaves himself into projects, moves swiftly and dumbly through anything he gets excited about. When I arrived in China and initially met Dino, the first thing he did was invite me to join his early morning speed-walking team. Not surprisingly, it was a first at the school. I declined, as did everyone else, so he gave up, or rather, he refocused. Next was perfecting his handmade pork dumplings. That was followed by a miserable six-week crash course on the *erhu*, a two-stringed beast of an instrument. It was during Dino's *erhu* period that I first felt my heat flashes of hatred toward him. After the *erhu*, Dino trolled traditional medicine shops in our neighborhood, compiling a book of remedies for chronic diseases. He taped the resulting four pages to his bedroom door, where they hung for months after he'd moved on from the project. That was followed by a darker phase, during which Dino sampled as many rice wines as our town offered, then drunkenly scribbled about bouquets and acidity into a ratty little notebook. I flipped through that notebook one night while he upchucked. Complete nonsense.

Dino can be very intense. When we first met, our friendship developed quickly, and when it devolved, it was also on a fast track. We were at each other's throats before he left China, had two brawls in our last three months together—more screaming-wrestling than face-pounding, but still. By the time Dino had his life packed and was waving his final *zàijiàn* to our high school, he and I could barely bring ourselves to high-five goodbye. At an earlier point, the high-five had been our much-loved, much-applauded trademark around campus. There were high-fives between classes, high-fives to students, high-fives to cafeteria workers; we double-high-fived Vice-Principal Pu at an assembly once. At its height, Dino and I even high-fived in privacy, like after a quarterly mopping or when Dino came out of the squatter announcing the enormity of a shit.

But on Dino's departure, we slapped hands only to appease the two hundred Chinese students who'd gathered for a proper Dino send-off. Our final high-five was not powered by love.

That said, I didn't envy Dino's position his last few days in China. Saying goodbye to our lives there, preparing for reassimilation, etc., while also negotiating his interactions with me as I dealt with my dad's death. I'd returned from Dad's funeral just a week before Dino headed back to the States. During that last week together, Dino mostly busied himself with packing and the gaggles of students dropping off keepsakes—cards, colorful pencils, photos, and the like, most of which he threw directly into the trash.

But there were also gestures, tiny as they were. He brought me carryout noodles one night. For the first time, I had daily dibs on the bathroom. And on three consecutive nights, Dino sat in my company quietly drinking beer while I processed tall stacks of bootleg DVDs, playing thirty seconds of each to check their quality. I slipped the decent ones into a disc booklet to bring home with me and bent the unwatchable ones in my hands until they shattered.

We never talked about my dad, not like I expected. When

I told Dino, he just swallowed it. No condolences, nothing verbal, no hugs, nothing beyond a nod of recognition. Dino's reaction was undoubtedly married, understandably, to his dad's Parkinson's, but I figured he'd have had things worked out better than I did. A bit more sympathy, maybe. But it occurred to me, during many sleepless nights, that Dino might have been giving me exactly what he'd learned over the years: deal with it, he was saying.

I'd only been to Chinatown once before, nearly two decades earlier, when Dad had brought me along to a business lunch with a client. It was one of the few times we'd gone someplace just the two of us, but I can't remember the circumstances, having been only seven years old at the time. Dad must have been in some sort of predicament, or maybe it was Mom. Someone was perhaps sick, or Dad needed a human shield for business? Maybe one or both of my parents was feeling unusually guilty about my chronic inability to shit anywhere but my pants? What I remember was that Dad and I held hands walking through Chinatown that day. Dad was rarely affectionate, almost never showed emotion. But that day, holding hands, Dad pointed to the tile rooftops we passed and told me that they reminded him of the Forbidden City in Beijing. He also bought me a faux jade dragon statue, which I still have.

In some ways, I think it's possible to trace my two years in China back to that lunch date with Dad.

Not that I wanted it to, but probably because I couldn't shake the image from earlier that morning for more than fifteen seconds at a time, I found myself wondering when Mom and Dad had last had sex.

Growing up, I never encountered anything to suggest my parents had a sex life. There weren't any obvious indicators. I figured they didn't do it because of my brother, Michael, who had died when he was very young; that they had simply removed from the table any possibility of another sperm penetrating another egg.

I only remember Michael through a photo. In it, he's in a diaper on his back on the carpet, smiling, the scar down his chest still raw from surgery.

Sometimes I worry my heart is broken like Michael's, and nobody but me knows it yet. I wonder if Dad thought the same thing, that maybe he walked through each day in constant fear of his heart dying, too. I always figured Dad would die from heart complications, like Michael did, like I probably will.

CHAPTER 5

Dino and I met underneath the red and gold Chinatown gate. I wasn't sure if we should hug, coolly nod heads, or what when we saw each other. Dino didn't have any hesitation. He put his hand up for a high-five, and I obliged.

The same junky trinkets we saw in touristy spots in China were sold here. We even passed several dozen faux jade dragons on Wentworth Avenue, all identical to the one Dad had gotten me all those years earlier. True, I'd seen thousands in China; they were for sale outside practically every pagoda and Buddhist cave in the country, so I was aware mine wasn't exactly unique, but still, it was disappointing to see so many clones in Chinatown. I hadn't expected its further devaluation that day.

"This place is a joke," Dino said, and he hacked up some phlegm and spit on the ground. It wasn't a gesture of disgust, though, and it wasn't related to Chinatown being a joke. Spitting signified to any Chinese in earshot that Dino belonged. In China, spitting was common—I saw grandmas do it, kids, everyone. It never stuck with me, but Dino hack-spit all the time.

"You didn't bring any mushrooms, did you?" I said.

"So you've been thinking about it."

"Not hours at a time."

"You want in?"

"I need something."

"Anything to get back to China."

21

"Not really."

"I wouldn't teach in China again. Or would I? I could do another year."

"Just go back. They'll hire you. They hire anyone."

Dino gave me a tiny version of the evil eye. It was a joke I knew stung, which was, of course, why I said it. Dino didn't have any teaching experience before China. I didn't either, but when I first met Principal Xi and Vice-Principal Pu, and they asked about my background, I referenced some summer camp counselor experience (never mind that I was ninth—and last—in command), and from that point on, Dino—who'd already fortified his top-tier position at Pingnan Middle School, or so he'd thought—was bumped to economy class, and I became the prizewinning thoroughbred import.

It bruised his ego. Whenever there was a choice of whom to assign to mentor the advanced classes, or which one of us to pimp out to a neighboring town's afternoon English language clubs (these were paying gigs), they always picked me, which left Dino perpetually uninvited, rejected, and assigned to the forgotten under-performers.

At the same time, Dino had a great advantage over me because he spoke Mandarin. Dino at twenty-six had studied Mandarin for nine years, and me, none.

Dino now pointed to a decrepit-looking restaurant, the scuzziest joint on the block. "I know," he said as he led us under the drip-rumble of a massive AC unit miraculously balanced on the rusty lintel.

Inside was mainland China—it was Guangdong Province pedestrian, and it was amazing. Square tables along the walls, circular tables snug between structural columns, mirrors on a few of those columns, a television mounted in an upper corner playing a Chinese soap opera, and on the tables, toothpicks and bowls for when we rinsed the orange plastic chopsticks and all-white porcelain dishware at the table with our first steaming pot of tea.

The proprietor was a thin woman with a plump, round face, likely in her late forties. She was excited to see us and addressed Dino by name, at which point Dino launched into some diatribe in Mandarin, none of which I understood. I busied myself with the menu, which was entirely in Mandarin. Of the hundreds of characters, I recognized a few: man, water, the number two, the number four, mountain.

We'd played this scene out dozens of times, and it always made me crazy, which Dino knew full well. I fingered the plastic toothpick container, wiggled a stick out, and began to splinter it with my fingers.

The proprietor and Dino were back and forth like old friends, and after a few minutes, she retreated to the back, at which point the entire restaurant was overborne by the roar and whistle of an intense cooking flame under a wok. I leaned in closer to Dino. "You know her?" I said. "This place?"

"What's weird about that?"

"You wandered into here, of all the dumps in Chinatown."

"It's not a dump, wait until we get the food. And she invited me here. We met at a public gathering a few months ago."

Public gathering? That wasn't Dino speak. It had the familiar stink of Mom's nonsense, and I had a strong physical reaction. Not just my heart doing its crazy dance—everything felt twisted up inside. It made me wonder how long it'd be until I'd have to start replacing my organs with pumps and rivets and other machine parts. I took a breath. "What kind of public gathering?"

"I'm very interested in telling you about it."

I raised my eyebrows.

"I've got a DVD here for you." Dino produced a color pamphlet from his bag and opened it up to show the disc inside.

He knew I was a sucker for free or cheap DVDs. That's the primordial gatherer in me.

"What's this?" I said. And, in a whisper, "Dude, is this porn?" In China, Dino had occasionally gifted me his old *huang se*—"yellow"— porn DVDs after he grew bored with them. It felt like a little piece of the old Dino had returned, and that relaxed me.

"It's a DVD that explains about the Xuan Gong."

"*Huang se* Xuan Gong DVD?" I said. It came out obnoxiously loud, but it's rare to stumble upon an unexplored porn genre, so the bit required a certain resonant power for full effect.

"I hope you'll watch it." Dino was poker faced.

"You're serious?" I said.

"Xuan Gong practitioners are being persecuted in China right now, which is one of the reasons I want to tell you about it."

"You want to tell me about it?"

"I do."

This was strange, even for the sometimes remarkably unpredictable Dino. I didn't know where it was coming from. I was mildly curious on some level, I suppose, but I didn't have the energy for anything more than that. I had no desire to tread in this new water, especially in light of Mom's new cuckoo.

Dino kept talking. He laid out the basic framework of his new adventure, but I found myself barely listening. My mind wandered like it did when I talked with Mom. I thought of a friend from college. We lost track of each other after graduation, but a few years later he had gotten in touch and invited me to invest with him. It was a Ponzi scheme related to do-it-yourself scented candles. Apparently he contacted all of his old college pals and offered them the same opportunity. No one bit. What was sad was that it completely estranged him, and sadder yet was that he may have actually believed in the project—his despicable father-in-law was the one who'd reeled him in and also duped him into shelling out his nascent nest egg.

But Dino wasn't asking for money. I sensed that what Dino was soliciting was a donation of thought to the Xuan Gong, and that felt even more intrusive. There was the suggestion of a collective moral obligation, but who wants those shackles?

I dropped back into the conversation and said, "How involved are you in all this?"

"I'm devoted to it." Dino said.

"Like you go to Sunday morning service?"

"Xuan Gong isn't a religion. It's a way of life, a practice."

"Tai chi?"

"Yes, there are exercises."

"Praying?"

"Meditation. It's not what you think. It's not a religion."

"How's your dad doing?" I asked. The connection between Dino's mania and his dad's illness was so obvious to me. So many of Dino's choices revolved around that need for a constant, a rock, a heavy focus, and I could already see that he'd moved into this Xuan Gong business at a gallop, as per usual, and that he was riding too fast, riding chest-first with his eyes closed and his hands clasped behind his back. I knew how the final chapter would play out, too. Dino is a flake, but even so, he'd keep with the Xuan Gong until he eventually collided with some obstacle, like he always did, and he'd tumble forward, an unbalanced mess, flailing and scraping across gravel until friction stopped him.

Had he had the chance, Dino would have lunged at my college buddy's DIY scented candle scam. Not only would Dino have offered money, but given the opportunity, he'd have stood on street corners distributing pamphlets while wearing a traffic-cone-orange jumpsuit with the company's logo on the chest, one that was the result of a logo-creation contest he initiated and advertised in the local paper. He'd have been the nonessential nut and bolt of that almost organization, its crummy appendix. And he'd have kissed someone's stinking feet for permission to come aboard.

At the moment, Dino was having the good sense not to respond to my question about his dad. The question didn't produce even a sideways glance, which made me doubt whether it had actually come out of my mouth. Instead, Dino offered an abstract parable about self-sacrifice and purity, what it meant to face a personal history of defilement and neglect. "Truthiness, sympathy, and acceptance," he said in summary.

Mom and now Dino—what the hell had happened in the last few months that got everyone hurried up and on board the express train to bonkers?

I tuned out and willed my mind a sieve.

I imagined a man with a sifter for a head, a shiny, conical, stainless steel sieve. Not the kind with the flimsy netting, but professional grade, sturdy. The sifter didn't have eyes or ears. There was nothing human about the sieve itself, except that it was oriented on top of some shoulders. It was a true sieve. The bottom of the cone was loose from the neck so that it still functioned properly. And he wandered the world, this man with a sieve for a head, offering sifting services to the public to pay his way. He operated alongside street mimes and jugglers. Mr. Sieve did, for instance a week-long stint sifting for the crowds underneath the Eiffel Tower. He liked Paris but was saving up dough to relocate down south, somewhere on the coast. Spain, maybe.

Dino pulled me back to the table. He caught my interest by explaining that he denied himself all things pleasurable until they were no longer pleasurable. I didn't understand.

"I don't drink anymore," said the former rice wine aficionado.

"Do you miss it?"

"Not really. But, even if I did, I wouldn't have a drink now because I might enjoy it, so I'll deny myself alcohol until I don't want it anymore."

"Then you'll have a drink," I said.

"Then it won't matter if I have a drink, because I won't want or need it."

"But will you derive pleasure from that drink?"

"If I thought that was possible, I wouldn't have the drink."

We had the same conversation about food as we ate. There was a feast in front of us. To tell the truth, it was the best meal I'd had since China, and I gorged, humming and chomping through the steamy piles of garlicky proteins as Dino carried on about commitment and self-control.

I was disappearing one plate after another, my chopsticks pinching with the precision of appendages. It was streamlined overindulgence. But I realized it was a solo effort. I alone had devoured the *kung pao* chicken and picked our *tang cu* snapper to the skeleton. Dino hadn't eaten any of it. He nibbled on white rice. My mouth full of food, I pointed at his bowl, used my eyebrows to ask, what gives?

"I only want to eat what I need," Dino said. "But please, go right ahead. That's why I ordered it."

Dino looked self-satisfied, and to me, that indicated pleasure. Sure, this particular type of gratification belonged to a different subsection than that achieved by, say, inhaling a deep-fried Twinkie, but they were positively in the same genus.

I had no doubt in my mind that Dino was very happy watching me stuff my face, especially because it was a fine opportunity for him to demonstrate his new resolve. I was sure that it provided a good deal of pleasure, but I didn't call him on it. Instead, I wondered if Dino would make me pick up the tab. According to Chinese protocol, Dino was the one who'd ordered, so it ought to be his wallet, even though I was the one who'd shoveled it all home. And if he was so genuinely Chinese, so *di dao,* and now a bona fide member of the Xuan Gong on top of it, he should follow protocol. Certain sensors and receptors in my head began to buzz, and we hadn't even gotten the bill. That was my trained reaction in Dino matters.

But then I noticed a serenity on Dino's face. It was a unique expression that I'd seen him wear only once before. He had it when I came home a day early from a trip to Hong Kong. Dino was in his desk chair, naked and passed-out drunk. He was apparently at the tail end of a bender. Both of his pillows were on the floor in the bathroom, soaking wet. Beer bottles were everywhere, several of them broken. His mattress was bare, the bedsheets bundled and thrown in a corner. Covering the floor were dozens of low-res titty and crotch shots he'd printed on our ink-jet printer. The look of serenity on Dino's face was disturbing as he slept his binge off naked in his desk chair. It was like watching someone sleep with a television playing their dreams in real time.

"What about sex?"

"I don't," Dino said flatly.

I corrected him. "Don't anymore."

"You're right. I don't do that anymore."

"Just stopped?"

"Yep."

"Procreation and recreation?"

"It takes discipline. I work hard to maintain it."

"But the body has needs. You don't relieve yourself?" I closed my eyes and puckered my face, furiously wiggled my fist up and down in front of my chest.

Based on her facial expression, I think the proprietress, watching us from the other side of the room, would have agreed this was not my classiest moment. I don't often pantomime masturbation, and so wasn't very practiced at it. But I wanted to solicit a reaction; I wanted to laugh with Dino about this, though I would have been happy with disdain, or any reaction, really, any sign of the old Dino, but he didn't budge.

"I might enjoy it if I did. So I don't."

"What happens, it builds up and you're back to having wet dreams like a kid?"

"I'd take pleasure from those, too."

"You can't stop those. The backup has to come out!"

"I wake myself up."

"But what if you can't? What if you sleep through it?"

"I wake myself up, and if I can't, I try harder next time."

The more I learned, the less I wanted to visit this island Dino now called home. "What about a wife? Will you get married?"

"Maybe."

"And will you have sex with your wife?"

"If she wants to."

"But isn't sex pleasurable? Wouldn't you experience pleasure?"

"I would try not to."

"That's impossible."

"I know it's hard to understand, but this is what I do now."

That was enough. I was full to the brim and unable to process anything more. We both must have sensed that. We didn't talk about anything of substance for the rest of our lunch.

Dino paid the bill, and he wouldn't accept any contribution from me. Maybe that was part of his master plan, a little buttering up before we discussed the mushroom enterprise. The gesture did, admittedly, soften me up a bit.

"Let's talk turkey," he said.

Dino made an effort to separate the conversation we'd just had with the one that was unfolding. He shifted his demeanor and his tone of voice. He was practically chipper as he delivered a similar pitch to the one he'd given me over the phone. In truth, I didn't need much convincing. I'd already made my decision when I agreed to meet for lunch, driven primarily by the fact that I was running low on funds. Dino's Xuan Gong bullshit was alarming, but at the same time, I was desperate. There could have been almost anything on offer, I suppose, and I would have bitten. Maybe Dino's impulsiveness had rubbed off on me a bit. So I committed to a trip to Oshkosh with Dino. I didn't, however, ask Dino if I could crash with him for a few nights, or even just one, which I'd planned to do from the get-go. I just couldn't bring myself to do it. I didn't mention my morning at all.

As we left, Dino kept looking at the Xuan Gong DVD in my hand. He didn't really take his eyes off the DVD until I'd put it in my doggie bag. I guess that indicated it would make it home with me, which for Dino meant mission accomplished.

CHAPTER 6

The train rolled slower on the ride back than it had on the way there. It moved slower that I could ever remember a train going. At one point, an old lady on a bicycle seemed to be moving across a vacant lot faster than we were. And, not to put too fine a point on it, but this woman on her bike, if she'd decreased her speed by even a hundredth of a mile per hour, she absolutely would have toppled over and crashed.

Everything on the other side of the train's laminated safety glass felt heavy with impermanence. I recognized this in painted-over white-on-tar-rooftop graffiti. My eyes lingered on small things: a sun-faded beer poster hanging in a storefront, a steel-mesh garbage can with a divot the height of a car bumper, and so many people pacing the sidewalks, all of them seemingly in permanent recoil.

That night I slept in the backseat of the DeVille, parked three blocks from home, though "sleep" may be overstating it. I achieved maybe one to two hours of actual shut-eye. I thought about Dad a lot that night. I wondered if he ever regretted his choices, if he was satisfied with his life at the end. Or ever. Was anyone? I also wondered if Dad ever understood the true depth of Mom's dissatisfaction, or if I did. Was it something they talked about? Was that dissatisfaction what had launched Mom into this nonsense? Was that why she was sleeping with Tucky? She had to be, right?

Back when I was a squirt, I used to think Dad had a secret second family, or that Mom and I were the secret second family, and that the other family got the goods, and we got the table scraps.

They existed, this second family, for my entire childhood. I had a doppelgänger in that other family, and I imagined him in great detail, mostly to see if Dad gave him more than he gave me.

The doppelgänger was very similar to me, except that he always wore lederhosen. They all did, Dad too, their whole team always in their cute lederhosen, which was dumb as shit because the only reason I thought they were German was because of the word *doppelgänger,* like all doppelgängers had to be German because no English equivalent was good enough.

I woke up in the morning to a motorcycle roaring down the street, which made me momentarily furious at American bravado. It was rank as morning mouth in the cab of the DeVille, and five achy hot spots had sprouted on my back during the night, none of which was helping my mood.

It was strange that the sound of a motorcycle could set me off like that. They were everywhere in China: four cylinders, six cylinders, scooters, mopeds, the occasional two-wheeled patched-together Frankenstein machine. Pingnan even had a fleet of motorcycle taxis, the quickest and cheapest way around town.

Sometimes when I got drunk, I'd flag down a motorcycle taxi for a ride, a routinely difficult transaction to negotiate—I suspect those guys didn't get many 3:00 a.m. joyride requests—and none of it was helped by my shit Mandarin. I used hand gestures: "We go to no lights, hicks live here, we go fast."

You could see stars on some nights, once you got away from the haze of the city's fluorescents. Zipping along in the dark on those rides, my fingers clutching the fender rack, the drained swampland and razed villages got erased. In my mind and in my drunken memory, that land we rode through was primeval.

I knew Mom had a yoga class that afternoon—and no, not the private variety, this one was at the YMCA. I staked out the house, parked on the opposite block, and waited for her to leave.

With her gone, and once I was in, I dead-bolted the door behind me for an extra five seconds of warning, got a beer from the fridge, and headed upstairs.

When I was younger and alone in the house, I was an amateur sleuth, sifting through Mom and Dad's things. But a complete disregard for others' privacy made me nervous about my own. In fact, that scenario produced my first real case of paranoia. It got so that I used a pry bar and a hacksaw to create cubbyholes in furniture and beneath floorboards for my especially sensitive possessions, which mainly consisted of pornography, at first, then pornography and cigars, and finally, upon high-school graduation, pornography, three pipes (one corncob, two glass), baggies of pot (shake residue, to be more precise), cans of cheap beer, and pints of liquor in varying states of emptiness.

With Mom gone, I headed straight to her room. I checked out the secretary desktop first. There was an addition. Mom had cut a piece of gray construction paper into the shape of the crystal I'd stolen and placed it there among the other knickknacks. That made me curious, and it also worried me. I considered returning the crystal, but I pressed on into the pink-on-white master bath instead.

I started with the medicine cabinet and its patchwork of orange and white pill bottles, salves and cotton balls, and unlabeled tubes of cream, crusty around the caps. There were over twenty prescriptions, some for Mom but most for Dad. I didn't touch any of them, but I duly noted a small bottle of

Percocet and two bottles of liquid codeine.

I sniffed the wet towel hanging beside the shower, wondered why I did it, then sniffed again and was disgusted with myself. It was a pink towel splotched with permanent stains—blood, makeup, or Lord only knows. How about black towels? Or navy or forest green? I never understood why people preferred the impractical purely because of aesthetics, even in a space as private as the master bath.

I walked over to Mom's altar again. The understudy construction paper crystal really bothered me. If it was purely a message—don't touch my shit—that I could understand. But I didn't think it was that simple. For me it indicated that Mom had crossed a new boundary, not a small one, either, and she'd done it right before my eyes, and likely because of me: the crystals were at the top of the food chain.

I moved across the room to Dad's closet. My guess was that Dad was the last person to touch the doorknob. The inside of the closet was jammed tight with wool suits and pressed khakis. The side shelves were stacked with unopened boxes from the dry cleaners. The floor was completely covered with shoes, including ten pairs of wing tips, wooden forms within like turn-of-the-century toy insects. Mom had told me over the phone while I was still in China that most of Dad's things had already been donated. It was a comforting thought while I was away, but this space was clearly untouched.

Standing with barely my toes past the closet's threshold, I was full of dark ideas, like that I'd waited for Dad to go so I could nab his closet full of expensive clothes. Or that Mom was completely helpless without a caretaker.

I snapped myself out of it, took a sip of beer, and reminded myself that it was a time for practicality. I took a charcoal suit jacket off its hanger and tried it on. It was too tight. Looking in the mirror, I tried to imagine my dad's face where mine was, but it only came in pieces, the bushy eyebrows, the thin nose, a thick, ear-to-ear horseshoe of white hair and the tan freckles on his bald head.

I put my fingers on my left cheek and pulled down on the loose skin beneath my eye, revealing the raw, a chink in the armor. My hairline was receding, too. I had thick black hair coming out of my nose, blond strands from my ears, and a two-inch-long, nearly transparent protrusion halfway down my neck, which I considered plucking but didn't.

I couldn't remember ever touching Dad's face, and I wondered if his felt like mine, and whether he had ever stood in front of a mirror doing what I was doing, and if yes, whether it also made him feel like an idiot.

Removing the jacket required holding my breath for some reason, and I was red-faced by the time I peeled it off. The rest of the clothes were probably all too small, too. It would depend on what Dad had had taken in. He gained weight during my childhood, lost it in the years preceding his death, from diet and exercise at first, and later, I guess, from chemo. I felt in the jacket pockets and found a business card, one side in Portuguese, the other in English. Another pocket revealed a name tag from a conference on marketing strategies in Central America, and in a third pocket, I found a small wad of Mexican pesos, which I slid into the right front pocket of my jeans.

Contemplating the cost of tailoring and what my closet would look like full of these things, I reminded myself that I seldom had reason to wear the one suit I owned, a college graduation present. Dad's suits would merely collect dust. So we needed boxes, I thought, lots of boxes. Mom might have mentioned something about the church rummage sale. The Presbyterians would have boxes. Did Mom still go to church?

And as I thought about boxes and transporting goods to the church carloads at a time, I found my fingers methodically inspecting the jacket and trouser pockets of each garment in the closet. I was imagining Dad's DeVille packed to the gills, driving it back and forth to the church, steeple to Mom, Mom to steeple, while my body became frantic, searching and scavenging. Suit pants and blazers flew off hangers, and I started a pile of booty on the bed: a collage on the down comforter, *Untitled.* But this needed to be done, I knew. Must be done, at some point, no matter what. One can't just donate clothes with the remnants of a dead father still in the pockets.

I did a fine job of transforming a neat, though cluttered closet into a disaster area. The space looked ransacked.

Even with shame setting in, I couldn't leave well enough alone. I stood on my toes and slid several shoe boxes off the closet's top shelf, half an inch at a time, until one by one they toppled onto my head. Three contained old shoes, clunk, spill, but the fourth, that box rained metal discs down onto my head.

They were 8mm film canisters. I dropped to my knees and gathered them together for inspection. Other than their age and distinct metallic odor, they were nondescript, gray, and empty. However, there were three anomalies in the box. One was a presumably watchable reel of film—unlabeled, and the images were too small to make anything out when I held them up to the light. There were also two empty film canisters with *Reunion* and *Bday* written in Dad's script on labels. I put those three items on the bed with the other desirables.

I closed the closet door, assuming that Mom wouldn't have the heart to twist that doorknob anytime soon. My heart slow-pumped four beats and then regulated itself.

There was still the array on the bed to deal with. Along with the 8mm items, there were seventy-nine American dollars (in bills), six American dollars and forty-three cents (in coins), two hundred Yen, three hundred and fifty Hong Kong yuan, eighty thousand Columbian pesos, a yarmulke with *Benjamin Kahn's*

Bar Mitzvah, April 19th, 1994, printed on the inside, nineteen assorted mint candies, two cigar cutters, fifteen business cards (eight his, seven others'), four ball-point pens, five laminated name tags, and six condoms (all different varieties, none with packaging in English).

I put all of those things into a plastic grocery bag, except the currency, which went with the pesos into the front right pocket of my jeans. I brought the bag to my room and stored it in my closet.

I closed the closet door and turned to leave my bedroom, but I had an overwhelming attraction to my bed. A night in a DeVille can do that to a person. I mindlessly undressed to my birthday suit and slipped between the sheets.

It was cozy there, but I also felt awful about everything, from stealing Mom's crystal to that film reel bonking down onto my head. I started to cry a little, and I found myself thinking about the 8mm movies.

In fact, I knew about those films. I had been clued into their existence on only one occasion. It was the day the *Chicago Herald* ran a feature article about Dad, "Manufacturing in Sri Lanka." I remember Mom made pork tenderloin the night it came out. I was nine. Dad acted like it was no big deal, but I could tell he was proud. At one point while we were eating, Dad knocked his wine onto his plate of food. Instead of cleaning it up, he used his fork to mix it all into stew, which Mom didn't think was as hilarious as Dad and I did.

It was after dinner that Dad produced the movies. He fumbled and tinkered with the projector for over an hour, but he never got it to work, and we never viewed the footage. For me, after that night, those films disappeared entirely.

I thought about Dad that night with the article and the movies. I wasn't sure what it meant, that Dad, with evidence of his successes there in print, became at once a jollier parent, an infant at the table, a worse husband, and somehow more connected to his past. If in that moment a therapist had handed Dad a brick of clay and instructed him to mold it into whatever shape came to mind, I wonder what he would have created. A lion? A Rolls Royce? An Oscar? He probably would have said the brick was fine as it was, or if he was feeling playful, maybe he'd have given the brick a few thumb presses, creating a small pocket to store some of the gruel he'd mixed up earlier.

I thought about Dad and those movies, yes, but my mind was also simultaneously occupied by a different matter, Dad's condoms. That latex was gutting me good.

I supposed each condom was one from a dozen, and that they were purchased for a single reason, hookers, and what remained, the leftovers in Dad's closet, were each in fact a souvenir from a certain occasion—keepsakes from his many adventures.

I figured Mom most likely knew about the condoms, too, and that made my heart sink a little deeper.

Lying naked in bed, my chest began to throb, and it hurt, badly. I remember that. I also remember feeling how wet with sweat my pillow got, even though I didn't know why. I don't remember closing my eyes at any point, but I must have. I must have, because the next thing I knew, I was roused from what felt like the sleep of the dead. I heard the front door close. I heard a set of keys drop on a table. I heard a set of footsteps coming up the stairs.

I didn't move. Mom hit the top of the stairs, and then it was quiet. Had I left evidence in plain view? I was sure I had, something as obvious as an unflushed dump, no doubt. I heard more soft footsteps in the hallway, which was followed by silence. It sounded like she'd stopped just outside my door.

I made a plan. As soon as Mom twisted the doorknob, I

would jump out of bed and scream like a lunatic while I pulled on some clothes. I might even throw pillows at her, if she didn't get the point right away, a soft, horizontal avalanche of pillows, followed by bedding and finally dirty laundry. I didn't want to, but my mind was unable to work through alternatives.

I listened, but I heard nothing. I imagined Mom was on the other side of the door, also preparing for a tête-à-tête, and possibly collecting pillows herself.

Then I heard something, faint but unmistakable. It was running water, from the other side of the house. Mom was in the shower.

I quickly got dressed and scurried out the front door.

Chapter 7

That night I took the DeVille out for a short excursion. I had
an objective, but it was entirely generic, like I wanted soup, but
the soup can label I pictured was black and white and just said
Soup. I wanted to somehow get myself tuned in to the world of
8mm movie projectors. I remembered there used to be a camera
shop in the middle of the business district, so I headed in that
direction.

I didn't get more than a hundred feet before I became
aware that driving at night was much more difficult than I
remembered. I hadn't driven any distance in the dark in two
years, and I was alarmed by how little I could see. It felt like the
car was draped in black velvet, and only the brightest lights were
penetrating its opacity.

Driving mostly blind felt dangerous, and it was. I was engaged
in an unquestionably perilous activity, but there was an element
of unreality—how can this be?—which was, I suppose, why I
didn't immediately swing the car around and head back home.

When I reached the first busy street, I turned right onto it,
and as I did, the front end of the car jumped the curb. "Whoa,"
I said. I accelerated gently.

My fists were tight on the wheel, and I had my face pulled
up close to the windshield. I continued infraction-free for about
a quarter of a mile, but there was a funky merge that somehow
resulted in my turning onto a one-way street. That rattled me
good, so I turned left into an alley. A car was coming at me from

the other end of the alley, though, and suddenly, inexplicably, I couldn't remember which side to drive on. I picked and swerved to the left, and that activated a radical sound and light show from the approaching car—a bit on the excessive side, if you ask me.

There was a White Hen Pantry at the end of the alley, and I turned in for safety. In pulling into a parking space, I scraped the underside of the bumper against a cement barrier—I heard it happening, felt the friction, but even moving very slowly, I was unable to bring myself to stop partway through.

Driving shouldn't have been so grueling, so hair-raising. I've always been a confident driver, but it felt like one of my first times behind the wheel.

A little bell jingled when I stepped inside the White Hen Pantry. Thankfully, there was a pinch of comfort to be found. I moseyed through the aisles, taking note of life's essentials stocked there: ten flavors of Now and Laters, batteries, corn nuts, washer fluid, Chicago Cubs beer coozies, Doritos, ultra-hot-pink snack cakes. And even though I wasn't exactly hungry, something funny came over me when I saw the self-serve nacho station just beyond the freezers. I became voracious.

I selected a medium-sized tub of chips, and I strategized. The only limitation on the amount of cheese sauce and meat sauce available to a customer is determined by the size of the tub—all-you-can-eat hideousness for $2.49, and like a true patriot, I alternated pumping the two available sludge varieties from the dispenser until my tub could accommodate no more. I would need a spoon.

The cashier, a man in his fifties, gave me a look that married equal parts pity and disgust, but I didn't care. I wanted to be back in the car, pronto, to commence inhalation. But I got distracted by the swimsuit issue. It was propped up next to the register—I wanted.

Desire can balloon in both scope and intensity. I reached to snag a copy and set it there alongside my nachos, but the rack of smut behind the counter also caught my eye.

"That'll be all?" the cashier said.

It was a time for action, which my current state accommodated. "I'll take a *Penthouse Letters,* too," I said, figuring it had the least bark of the bunch, which seemed appropriate on account of the pity and disgust already displayed.

The cashier sighed and stepped toward the porn. He scanned the shelves as if looking for a black bowling ball among a wall of black bowling balls.

"There," I said, pointing, but that did no good. Then, further decisiveness. "I'll just take a *Hustler,*" I said, *Hustler* being front and center. "On the top rack," I added. My face flushed, and it occurred to me that if I was too ashamed to buy porn, I probably shouldn't buy porn—but this thought didn't much influence me.

"You want a *Hustler?*" He stopped and looked at me. "And you want a *Penthouse Letters?*"

Just then the bells jingled. A woman about Mom's age came in. I hoped to hell she had business in the back freezer, or that she was a super nachos kind of lady in for a quick fix, but, of course, she came right to the counter. She looked familiar.

"Excuse me," she said. "Do you have fire-starter logs?"

The cashier turned to her slowly and said, "I'm with a customer. Just a moment, please," which I would have ordinarily considered a heroic, master-of-his-castle type gesture, but not at that moment. Like smoke rising in a movie to reveal some gruesome battlefield carnage, this woman's identity was taking shape in my mind. I'd definitely been inside her home at some point, yes, I was confident I'd sat on her couch at least once in my life, and maybe even peed in one of her toilets.

"So you want both?" the cashier said to me, now in a less

bothered and more professional manner. It made me think his prior confusion had actually been a kind of punishment, his way of beating me on the head a few times with a rolled-up newspaper.

"No, neither," I said. Ridiculous and pathetic. "Or, actually, yes, give me both."

I could sense the woman losing interest in fire-starter logs and transferring her attention to my transaction. I glanced at her face—gears were most certainly turning there, too. She was no doubt also on the verge of understanding that I had been in her home for a birthday party or some such gathering years earlier.

The cashier rang me up, and I looked at the counter, then at my wallet, then at the plastic bag and tub of nachos in my hands, then at the door, then at the blemished front wheel well of the DeVille, then at the DeVille door handle, and then I finally blinked and took a breath, but only once I was back inside the safety of the car. I put the keys in the ignition, but I didn't start the engine. I waited for the woman to come out of the White Hen Pantry, and when she did, she was kind of leering in my direction as she hoofed it across the lot. She was not heavier a fire-starter log, which felt just to me somehow.

She got into her car, but instead of immediately driving away, she did a full circle of the parking lot, a maneuver whose only logical explanation was corroborated by the barn owl eyes scanning the dark for a glimpse of the jackpot: me, actively engaged with one of my treats.

It wasn't until I was parked in Mom's neighborhood and waiting for sleep in the DeVille that I realized who that woman was. Lynn Baker, my third-grade confirmation teacher. She had three kids, one in my grade, the others one grade up and down— must have been a long three years for Mrs. Baker.

Mrs. Baker was a card-carrying member in the Mothers Circuit. I feared the Mothers Circuit, particularly the mothers of my peers and the mothers who were friends with Mom or had been at one point. They were hard to differentiate, because they were all connected somehow and engaged in an empty-nest competition to rustle up information on my generation. They sought dirt between cocktails at book club. They were judge and jury at garden socials. *Oh, just look at those violas and sweet alyssum—and did you see so-'n'-so in the blotter?*

My only hope was that she hadn't recognized me, which was unlikely but possible. I attempted to will that idea into truth, but I could feel myself sinking deeper into the DeVille's bucket seat. I wasn't able to muster up much in the area of positivity at that moment. My pile of what needed sorting seemed to be growing exponentially.

The last feeling I had before falling asleep was deep regret. I wished I'd bought one of the crappy convenience store bouquets for Mom instead of the nachos and porn.

CHAPTER 8

In my dream I was in a bumper car at the top of Machu Picchu. I was steering with one hand and had a filled-to-the-brim daiquiri in the other. I was super thirsty, but every time I stuck my lips out at the giant straw, some jerk would ram me from the side or behind, and it was all I could do to keep from dumping the whole daiquiri on my lap. I had a boner, too, which added another undesirable element to my bumper car situation.

When I awoke, I had a boner in real life, which accounted for that part of the dream, I suppose; and, not that I believe every element of dreams can or should be looped back to reality, but it so happened that the DeVille was rocking back and forth, the whole car, bump, bump, bump. I had no daiquiri, but I did have serious cotton mouth. And then someone was banging on the driver's side window, *bang, bang, bang.*

I was in the driver's seat, reclined all the way. Over the course of the night, I'd released significant heat and moisture into the cockpit of the DeVille, resulting in windows that were fogged opaque from the inside. I didn't move, hoping that would suggest to the banger that the car was without occupant. But the knuckles or whatever came again, bang, bang, bang. I looked in the rearview to check my presentability: a low one on the one-to-ten scale. I tried to comb my hair flat with my fingers, with little success. Bang, bang, bang. Sigh. I turned the keys in the ignition and activated the little motor in my seat to push myself upright. I took a breath and rolled my window down about an inch and peeked out.

I had figured it was the fuzz, or maybe I was blocking a street cleaning machine. But no. Mom, which shouldn't have surprised me, but it did. She immediately had her face against the little crack.

"Good morning," she said.

I considered closing the window, but she'd also stuck her fingers into the crack.

"Sleep okay?" she said. Mom was extra smiley, which simultaneously made me annoyed and relieved.

"This thing is roomy," I said enthusiastically. "I slept fine."

Mom frowned. "I brought coffee," she said, and she held a mug up to the window. "Coffee?"

I was surprised at how malleable I was. I turned off the car and stepped out. Just like that.

Mom was wearing a cobalt tracksuit, and she had a new confidence about her, which is maybe why I got out of the car without much resistance. She showed no signs of stress. I tried to remember her ever looking so relaxed and at peace, but nothing came to mind. She leaned back against the hood of the car. "Sit down," she said, patting the area next to her.

I was apparently without the energy to do anything else. I sat, and Mom handed me the coffee.

"I'm not here to apologize," she said.

My heart sank a little. I looked at her, and though I had a lot to say, shitloads, actually, I found my mouth doing this sort of largemouth-bass-pucker type thing, my lips silently chewing at this little pocket of air.

Mom looked at me funny but also put an arm around me. "I'm here to bring you home," she said, and she kissed me on the side of the head.

I looked at her, still offering her my strange, fishy kisses, and

I nodded my head. That was it, nothing else discussed, not for the moment. And maybe that was progress—a gnat's breakfast portion of progress, but still. We left the car where it was and walked back home together.

CHAPTER 9

I'd been back from China for a week, and prominent among my accomplishments was that I was having some success settling back into my childhood bedroom. I spent hours at a time in the confines of those four eggshell walls. At first I intimated to Mom that I was battling a stomach virus via frequent pretend visits to the bathroom, but I don't know if she even noticed. Next I hung a *Journaling in Progress* sign on my door, a direct response to a journal Mom bought me and slid under the door, which I suspect was à la guru's prescription. But I wasn't journaling. That was a lie, too. I was mostly sleeping.

I slept and had simple thoughts—mostly kept my eyes shut—for several days, but when I could sleep no more, intense boredom started to grow in that room. From my bed I scanned the room's contents repeatedly, attempting and failing to reimagine the yearbooks and posters without their tiredness.

To admit to some lethargy would be an injustice to all slothful creatures. The only thing I exercised was my brain, but even at that, in my horizontal, half-wakened state, the way my mind was functioning had me feeling like I was on my back, not much different than a hockey puck, and some larger creature was gently tapping me into various bays and inlets on a frozen lake, each location on the ice representing a different, twisted memory that I would have rather not revisited.

So it was a dark kind of lake.

I thought of the night I did drugs at Club Hawaii Hawaii

in Pingnan. I never understood the redundancy in the name—double the leis or something—that is, had there been anything Hawaiian about the place, which there wasn't.

I had a serious drunk on, and it was early afternoon. Ten or so Americans had come out to Pingnan to see what it was about, including three hot blondes from Ohio, which isn't an exceptionally notable part of the story, except that they are a fine representation of an increase in audience. At one point I headed to the bathroom, and as I urinated, I heard a commotion in one of the stalls. I bent down to look under, and I saw a lot of feet. I knocked and heard shushing. I yanked hard on the stall door, and it snapped opened. That little space was packed with teenagers. Not that they invited me, but I forced my way in and pulled the door shut.

With me, we were eight people crammed into that squatter stall. I didn't know what we were doing there, but I was up for an adventure. Some giggly guy offered me white powder on his upside-down pinky nail, which was approximately one inch long. I snorted, said my thank-yous, and left. It was a forty-second transaction.

I don't know what I snorted, but it got me majorly fried—probably horse tranquilizer. I went straight to the dance floor, which was empty. I climbed up onto a tall speaker and proceeded to idiot-dance my face off. The Americans all laughed at me.

The kids in the stall probably went to Pingnan, where I taught. A few might even have been my students. I was too loaded to know.

I thought about Hank the Canadian and when he told me he might have killed a man. He was shit-faced when it happened. *Shifazzed,* Hank pronounced it. Hank was also shifazzed when he told me the story.

Hank was weekending in Hong Kong and met some women

from Buenos Aires. Hank said he was extremely shifazzed, used *shifazzed* even when talking about maybe killing someone. He said he barely remembered it at all, but a man tried to rob them. Hank beat up the robber. He couldn't remember very well, he kept saying, but he thought he remembered the girls trying to stop him, but he could hardly remember. He remembered a good part of actually getting shifazzed, and he kind of remembered being on top of the guy and swinging both fists, and that there may have been a body not moving. He said he woke up in the morning covered with blood. He didn't remember parting ways with the girls, and he never saw or heard from them again.

I don't think Hank remembered telling me the story. He was too shifazzed, as per usual. The morning after he told me, we woke up at the party and Hank started drinking again. It was 9:00 a.m. First Hank offered me a beer. Then, in all seriousness, Hank asked me if I'd ever checked out the Bible. He said that there was some cool stuff in there.

I relived these memories, not exactly by choice, and after enough time, I got fidgety. I needed something to do with my hands. I had that journal from Mom, and since it was one of the only new object in my room, I took it in my hands—the attraction to it was that simple. It was a composition notebook, the Holstein variety. I spent my first two intimate hours with the notebook attacking it with a black pen, filling in each of the white spots on its front cover; the next two hours, same pursuit on its back cover. Next I opened the thing and scribbled in stories like Hank maybe killing someone and my adventure at the club doing drugs, etc., etc.

The problem with really spilling into a journal was that it became precious and forbidden, and I became paranoid about privacy—none should have access to the unfiltered goods, not like that.

Plus, something about the journal entries was making me feel sick. To me, the person who lived those things seemed lead-hearted and completely uninspired. Reading my journal did not make me feel good.

On top of that, all that digging at certain memories brought out others from the back of the cupboard, where I'd rightly stashed them. In the end, there were too many to exorcise all of them into my journal, so the bad bits and pieces of my life surfaced and collected in my mind, and ultimately floated on top like dirty tidal foam.

After three days of journal use, I took to hiding it when not at it with a pen, like sealing it in a baggie in the tank of the toilet when I showered, or putting it in the pillowcase of the pillow I lodged between my thighs as I slept.

That became my routine, constantly writing in my journal and obsessing over its security. I'd get paranoid and wouldn't leave my room for hours at a time. Then I'd hide my journal and attempt some normal activity, like making a sandwich. But, as I smeared mayo on a slice of bread, for instance, I'd suddenly worry Mom was looking for my journal—which was, admittedly, a completely unfounded and irrational fear—and I'd frantically stop whatever pursuit in progress; i.e., drop the sandwich, hustle upstairs to retrieve my journal, and hole back up in my room. I was, admittedly, turning a bit crazy.

CHAPTER 10

I managed seven days of this escapism. I didn't talk to Dino, and I'd barely spoken to Mom since she'd gotten me from the DeVille. Mom became less tolerant of this by day four, and by day six, she was knocking on my door every few hours. She'd knock, then enter without my consent, at which point I'd pull the top sheet over my bare chest and soulfully shake my journal in the air—the equalizer, as if it substantiated all.

I think that period of mindlessness was something I required. It felt compulsory. But after those seven days, I got good and sick of myself. I'd hit the human threshold for how long one can lounge sideways on an unmade bed in one's underpants.

Mom made a sound, a pleasant "Uhhm?"—like the second tone in Mandarin, the rising tone—when I walked into the kitchen. She must have been surprised to see me after my tenure in the lair, to see me apparently ready for social interaction, my hair wet, my clean-shaven cheeks still rosy from the steam of the shower. I had my backpack with me, packed with treasures: poncho, flashlight, porn, the 8mm film, crystal, and my journal.

"Good morning," I said, and I gave her a kiss on the cheek. I wanted her to ask, who is this new and enhanced son?

"Good morning to you. Did you get a good night's sleep?"

"Nope," I said as I opened the refrigerator. "Just time to get up." I was starving, but on a cursory scan, everything said *flax* or had tiny green colonies expanding where the plastic wrap was loose.

I watched Mom look down at my backpack and grimace. "How about I make you some breakfast?" she suggested.

"Sure," I said, "that'd be great."

Mom hopped up from where she'd been reading a book at the island and began rummaging through the pantry and refrigerator. "How about pancakes?"

"Perfect."

With Mom's back to me, I moved toward the hardcover tome Mom had been reading. I leaned on the island and peered diagonally so that Mom wouldn't see me checking it out. The calligraphic type read *Balance: Cosmos and You.*

"What're you reading?" I said.

"A very interesting section on the balance of the universe. Proportions. Harmony. Did you study any philosophy in China?"

"What, like feng shui? Tai chi?" I said. I wet my finger and began flipping through the pages.

"Don't lose my place. Please."

"I won't." I looked down. "Page sixty-nine."

Mom made a noise, not a Mandarin second tone, but a Cantonese second tone, low mid to high rising. "Ehhrruuhh." It was an odd moment and an unlikable sound. I considered myself fortunate to have otherwise avoided Mom's creation of that noise.

"What?" Up and about as I was that morning, it felt like a sixty-nine joke from Mom could really set me off course.

Mom twisted around and pointed the unidentifiably old box of pancake mix at me, and as each syllable parted her lips, she compressed the cardboard slightly so that tiny puffs of pancake mix coughed out from its ripped corner. "Did you just say page sixty-nine?"

It was alarming. "Mom, don't."

"Sixty-nine. I don't believe it. Don't you see the significance? It's staring you in the face." Mom came over, reached toward my backpack. "Do you have a pen in here?" She started at the zipper.

I flailed, twisted the backpack away from her in a swift, violent motion. I crouched into an attack position, placed my body between Mom and the backpack, and yelled, "Get out of there!" I didn't mean to react so strongly, but that bag was verboten.

Mom closed her eyes and put her chin to her chest, started into some heavy breathing.

"I'm sorry," I said. "It's private."

In sync with a deep breath, Mom moved her arms—sleeves lightly dusted in pancake mix—into an elegant ballerina's second position. I didn't remember Mom ever dancing. She kept her eyes closed, took two more deep breaths, and said, "Everett," exhale, "this is an excellent display of the chaos that resides," inhale, "in an unbalanced environment." Exhale, "We were warned, but didn't react." Inhale. "And so here we are."

"What are you talking about?"

Her arms were still in second position, and her eyelids remained on display. "Yin and yang. Don't you see? It's not a mistake. There are no mistakes. We have to seek out life's indicators. And you know what?"

"No."

Mom opened her eyes, and her face shifted. She looked happy, even. "The two of us? We must have some powerful energy. This is big."

Jesus. "I get it," I said. "Page sixty-nine, because it looks like a yin-yang."

She nodded, kept nodding. She dipped and raised her chin with such dramatic flare that I had a third-grade-bully impulse to start tearing pages from her book.

"This is crazy," I said. "And stop nodding your head like you know something you don't. Sixty-nine is a sexual position, Mom, not a sign about chaos."

Still nodding, "Know what else?" she said. "Dad's birthday is June ninth."

"What the hell does that have to do with anything?"

"Everything is interrelated. Everything."

"You're living on Pluto, Mom. This is bonkers."

"Pluto isn't a planet. Very controversial, actually."

Ay! "No, this conversation."

"What you don't get, you choose not to get. You don't allow yourself to see the full spectrum. You're missing all the peripherals."

"At least I don't invent things."

"Neither do I," Mom said. She was calm; had, despite my own blown fuses, asserted rationality, however absurd it was, throughout the entire conversation. A small part of me was impressed by this fortitude and resolve, but I felt I was approaching Mom as a stranger, as an unknown; this was not Mom as I knew her. She had sprouted foreign right before my eyes. Bits of light danced in front of me warp-speed-style, like I'd been clubbed in the head.

Mom and I sometimes fought when I was growing up. My defense was usually trailer-hitched to a rightly deserved reprimand, but our shouting always ended with Mom in tears. I learned Mom's screws and how to turn them, which I wasn't proud of, but that's how it would go down in the heat of the moment. Dad was the more effective disciplinarian. Taking a few minutes to wag his finger at me impeded on his downtime, though, so even when I was very young, Dad enforced swiftly with loud shouting, which would scare us stupid, both Mom and me. I think that's why, by the time I was in high school, Mom had stopped telling Dad about the majority of my indiscretions.

So this was a new kind of brawl for Mom and me, and there was no screw-turning to be had.

I twisted away from Mom and toward the door. Okay, I said to myself as I left the kitchen, backpack hugged to my chest, in part to keep my heart from popping through my ribs and dancing a jig there on the floor. Okay, again, as I grabbed my wallet from the hall table drawer and walked out the front door. "I get it!" I shouted at the street.

This wasn't my first time walking down our street crying, but it'd been many years. I hadn't felt especially connected to Mom in a long time, true, but I always felt I could count on her. Mom was a rock, and that never changed, so the argument that had just transpired had my body crumbling in on itself. I watched, through an alien lens, as the walls of its varied elements collapsed onto me from all directions.

I was mashed up inside and out, not to mention that sobbing on the sidewalk had me paranoid about encountering a member of the Mothers Circuit. I kicked it up to a canter—the most hideous of my gaits—and attempted to rationalize the previous ten minutes.

It was a typical parent-child relationship, I thought, but in the inverse. Radiant with foundationless confidence, Mom was the teenager selling violent, drug-fueled, drunken orgies as the rite of passage for any well-adjusted individual, and I was the parent; not buying, thank you.

Yes, good, a scenario, I thought, and I followed with attempts at common sense. This was a type of relationship that occurs in nature. Stop. Breathe. Naturally occurring. I tried to wrap my head around only that.

But, of course, it wasn't that simple, and I was inconsolable. I blamed China for changing me into the person I'd become. Okay, who I really blamed was myself for who I was in

China—and for who I was, period. I got too comfortable in China, *tai shu fu* (a surprisingly handy phrase). Over two years I grew into a hollow entity that moonlighted as a near-celebrity.

My teaching gig was laughable at fourteen hours of classroom teaching per week. I had no office hours, no office or professional space of my own; at most I sometimes appropriated other teachers' desks for twenty-minute blocks when I was too lazy to go back to my apartment between periods. There was no set curriculum for my English classes, which meant fourteen slightly varied monkey dances per week, a luxurious sixty minutes of inanity for my students every seven days.

My classes were often canceled and replaced with silent study hall. Dino's twice as often.

I didn't act responsibly for those two years, and I wasn't required to put my heart or mind into anything I did in China, though I spent my first six months in Pingnan trying to do exactly that. Eventually I gave up. The people around me weren't willing or able to accept my efforts. There was never reciprocation.

It wasn't entirely embittering. I adjusted. And even when I left for good, when Vice-Principal Pu told me repeatedly that I'd always be welcome to teach at Pingnan, which was decent of him, it never felt like more than a one-night stand, so to speak, like I was never really on anyone's radar, even when I was the main attraction. A one-night stand, one class period at a time, one school visit at a time, one drunken escapade at a time. It was alien, that unaccountability, and I maintained it by being my moderately competent, mildly amiable, mostly unmemorable self.

I don't doubt that several hundred young adults in Guangdong Province still remember crossing paths with a certain *gwei lao* (white devil—me), and they may even know my face for a number of years to come. But when I consider the twenty-four months I lived in China and all the men and women I tried to know but never did? The people I occasionally got beers with—I'm not sure we graduated beyond boozing buddies.

And Mom? The house?

I didn't want to continue as—and I hadn't realized I'd always been—an outsider and a stranger, no matter where I was. And I had a terrible feeling I'd remain that way indefinitely. Worst of all, I could blame no one but myself.

The crisis was real, and the crisis was me.

CHAPTER 11

Maybe because of transference or what have you, the ultra-sour conflict with Mom bumped Dad's 8mm movie reel to top priority. I'd spent most of the day and into the night walking the streets thinking about it. I did manage a little shuteye once I was brave enough to reenter the house, but as soon as I was awake in the morning, I grabbed my backpack, slipped into the DeVille, and headed out in search of a solution.

I needed to watch that film, but even so, I couldn't claim my forward movement had much focus. I'd spot a camera store or an antique shop, but when I did, I could activate myself only insofar as to locate a parking space and to park. I never got out of the car. I didn't even unbuckle. I'd sit there and perform a perfunctory one- to two-minute observation, and each time, one shop after another, I'd solidly determine there was nothing of value to be found there, which was stupid—of the exceptionally stupid variety—especially since I was aware of my self-sabotage for the duration of that morning's efforts. But I was unable to modify my behavior. That was just how I was motoring that morning.

I think my reclusiveness was in part a reaction to a new fear—a fear born from the fundamental dysfunctions of recent events—that I no longer knew how to behave around other people. I worried that I no longer had the ability to anticipate or predict the behavior of others, which was a debilitating tonic to sip on, not to mention an exhausting prospect. I was not psyched that this was how I would now be pushing forward through the calendar.

After driving aimlessly for over an hour, I found myself steering, practically absentmindedly, and oddly unexpectedly, toward Tucky's dojo, the location of which I'd found on the internet. In no corner of my mind did I expect to find a warehouse of 8mm projectors there; it was more like some kind of magnetism pulled me to that place.

If pressed about it, I suppose I was ready to begin familiarizing myself with the beast.

Tucky's center of operations was a converted barbershop that sat between a florist and an electronics repair center. The dojo still had a barber's pole out front, which admittedly appealed to me. I wondered if the barber's pole was a reflection of Tucky's eccentricities, or if he was just lazy or broke.

The dojo appeared more or less dormant—except for the endless twisting of the barber's pole—and my mind began to wander. The barber's pole reminded me of when I first arrived in China, of my interim lodging before I was shipped to Pingnan.

I wet my bed my first night in that hotel, my first night in China. I wasn't drunk or sick, just whacked out of my mind from travel. I didn't know what to do when I woke up all soggy, but, to be sure, it would have served me well if I'd been able to trade in a few of my heart thumps for a dose of calm or levelheadedness.

I stuffed the soiled linens in a shopping bag and headed down to the lobby to figure out my next move. Once there, I spent approximately ten minutes circling a giant plastic ficus tree near the front door. I was building up the courage to hand the receptionist my bag of wet sheets, and I was very nearly mentally prepared to do so when the elevator opened, and the program director, whom I'd met the night before, stepped out.

I hid behind the ficus, but that didn't vanish me the way

I'd hoped. I scanned for a better place to lie low and spotted a barber's pole in a hallway just off the lobby. I scurried over and ducked into the barbershop.

There were probably ten people inside, and they each, whether in a chair or behind one, ceased their activities in order to look me over. A man with blondish-orange spiked hair, the kind with frosted tips, gestured for me to sit down in his empty chair. I didn't. Instead I placed my bag on the floor near a wastebasket and said, "My friend will pick this up in five minutes."

Eager to be of service, the frosted-tips guy nodded to me. "My friend. Pick up. Five minutes," I said again. "Thank you." I turned and walked out of the salon, then double-timed it out the hotel's front doors.

I spent the next four hours in an open-air market near the hotel, and yes, I cultivated and embraced an appropriate degree of regret, shame, and humiliation in myself—not to mention that under my jeans, I was still wearing the boxer shorts I'd slept in. It's not as if when I wet the bed, I automatically knew the day's events would ultimately instigate a swift penance.

No one ever confronted me about the wet sheets, and when I finally returned to my room, my bed was made with fresh linens. The staff was probably just as afraid to broach the topic as I was.

Activity at Tucky's dojo snapped me back to the present. A man exited the front door. There was the ponytail. It was the same dude from before, except this time he was in sweatpants, and his little man-boobs were nestled tight in a navy thermal top.

Tucky locked the dojo and took off down the street, and with his first stride, he was immediately speed walking. It was the wholly intolerable kind of speed walking, his arms pumping in front of his chest like some kind of ridiculous North Korean military cadet, except Tucky was no soldier, and he wasn't marching in Kim Il Sung Square—Tucky was just some hippie dipshit super walking past a flower shop.

I knew I would have to confront Tucky at some point, but today wasn't the day.

He went halfway up the block and stopped abruptly next to a beat-up Toyota Corolla. He fished keys out of his pocket, walked around to the driver's side door, and got in. From that point on, Tucky moved at a snail's pace. He clicked his seat belt, fiddled with the radio for a long minute, I suppose until he found some tolerable tunes. There were no other cars around, but he checked each mirror, his blind spot, put on his turn signal and shimmied the Corolla out from its parallel parking spot. Tucky cruised down the street at about twenty miles per hour, and I watched until the Corolla was out of sight.

I turned on the DeVille and pulled into the street myself, and as I did, a new destination came to mind, as well as an odd sensation—I was driving the car and had been all morning, but it didn't exactly feel like I was at the wheel. In any case, I now knew where to find an 8mm projector, and it had nothing to do with Tucky. In fact, the projector I was thinking of was the only functional projector I'd ever seen, and it was in a safe place, a place I knew well, even if it'd been many years since I'd visited.

Chapter 12

Sound the trumpets, an alumnus returns!

Something like that. Especially since I had my childhood backpack with me as I ascended the front steps of my former grade school.

Had I been pressed to describe the school in great detail while I was sitting in front of Tucky's dojo ten minutes earlier, I would have had a tough go of it, but stepping inside, I was amazed by how exactly the same everything was—the railings and linoleum, the moldings and little lockers—how it all felt like I had entered a giant time capsule. Probably most of the school was unchanged from when it was first erected in the 1950s. The building itself was outdated. Nothing was broken, exactly. It was more that the style was no longer very desirable. Not that a first-grader gives a crap about that kind of thing.

There was a sign front and center in the hallway: STOP! Visitors Must Sign In and Obtain a Visitor's Pass. That sign was not a contemporary of my backpack. I'd planned to be transparent during my visit, but the sign's directive tickled my disobedient side. I remembered, though, that I had a *Hustler* and *Penthouse Letters* in my backpack, and that perverts haven't been tolerated in schools during any era, so I stepped into the front office to announce myself.

The receptionist looked old enough that she may well have worked there when I was a kid. I explained that I'd once roamed these halls and was fresh back in town. Then I carefully unzipped a corner of my backpack, reached in, and pulled out the 8mm film.

"I found this among my father's things. He recently passed away." The receptionist produced an assortment of sympathetic noises. "I'm trying to find a projector so that I can take a look at it, but so far I haven't had any luck. Do you think there might be a projector here somewhere that I could use for a few minutes?"

She was nodding her head before I'd even finished. She asked me to log in on a visitor's sheet, and she gave me a name tag.

"You'll want to see Amanda in the library. Do you remember where it is?" she said.

I laughed nervously, "Ha ha ha," and said, "Of course, I remember. Thanks very much." But I had absolutely no idea. I just wanted out of that office, pronto, on account of the vulnerabilities I'd just offered up on a platter.

I walked out of the office and turned right. As I passed each classroom, I mostly heard the voices of teachers, and through the little rectangular peek-hole windows I saw students at their desks. On my right, I passed the room where I'd spent first and second grade—those were the kinds of scraps that'd stuck with me, generalities and big-picture stuff, not many specifics.

I walked to the end of the hallway and went up the stairs. I remembered the banisters, strangely. They were covered in a thick coat of glossy royal-blue paint. There was one height for kids and another for adults, and in the middle of the stairway was a space. It was clear from the top of the building to the bottom, such that someone could drop an egg all the way down, or, if they so desired, and they pulled their body in tight as if preparing to luge, anybody, small or big, could shoot down through that space, whoosh, to splat on the cement basement floor. I've never understood why stairwells are designed with this capacity.

The third- and fourth-grade classrooms were on the second floor, and I had stronger memories of this area—but I still had no idea where the library was. I passed by a row of lockers, and while I doubted it was *the* locker, one in particular stuck out to me. Not that I had any powerful memories associated with my grade-school locker, but it was one of my first private domains, even if it was only mine temporarily. That seemed more significant than anything else, for some reason, my cardinal stamp of ownership.

I made my way back down to the basement, where the kindergarten classes were. I recognized the room I'd been in when I was that age, and when I peeked in, there were children scattered throughout the room taking naps on their little mats.

I finally found the library. It was located directly across from the office where I'd gotten my name tag. What a schmuck; realizing that made me doubt any business I had in the building. It felt like what I was doing was wrong—I probably was very much in the wrong, peering in at those innocent kids—my heart agreed, and it did its insanity thing for a fast ten seconds—but I opened the door to the library anyway, and I walked in.

It was more dollhouse-sized than I remembered, but so was the rest of the school. There weren't any children present, thankfully. The library's only occupant was a woman about my age. She was sitting behind a desk typing, and when she looked up to see who'd come in and for what, I recognized her.

It was Amanda Marlowe, Sissy Marlowe's sister, younger than Sissy and me by two years. Sissy had been my dream girl for most of two decades, and because of that I hardly ever spoke to her. If anything I knew Amanda much better than I knew Sissy, which was strange since Sissy and I were in almost every class together, knee-high to college. Amanda started hanging around at keg parties my senior year, and maybe because of my inability to formulate sentences in Sissy's presence, I took a liking to the younger, more down-to-earth version.

"Everett?" Amanda said.

I felt myself smiling. "Hi, Amanda," I said. "It's good to see you."

She got up and gave me a hug.

"I heard you were in town," she said. "Are you here for the substitute teacher job?"

"What?" I said. "No, not that."

"You should totally apply."

I must've had a dumb look on my face, but I did register the idea.

We were quiet for a moment, and then she said, "I'm so sorry to hear about your dad." The way she said it, the generosity and sincerity—I didn't get that very often. And even though I knew there was really only one way she could have known about my homecoming—the gorgefest at the White Hen Pantry—I wasn't flooded with anxiety, not like I would have expected. Amanda didn't seem fazed by it, either, and maybe that was why. Standing there post-hug, I felt calmer and more at ease than I'd been in a very long time. I even felt a little warm. Maybe a lot warm, actually. I might even go as far as to say that a part of me knew immediately that this was a girl I could love, that I could marry, which was corny as hell, but it coursed through my body like I'd been tasered.

We chitchatted, and I found myself guardedly flirting, like I'd better take this one seriously from the get-go, which was another feeling I hadn't had in a long time. But then light, either from the lamp on her desk or from the sun outside, hit her ring finger just so—and, of course, why wouldn't someone as totally beyond decent as Amanda not be hitched already? My euphoria slipped away, and the space it'd bullied for itself was very quickly recolonized by more familiar feelings. I got a little choked up, which I hate to admit, but at least I had an excuse for my behavior. I plainly explained the nature of my visit and asked if she could help. Amanda was very sweet and went immediately to get the projector, and me, I walked over to the windows and looked at a class having recess outside.

The last time I saw Sissy Marlowe, we were at a party the summer between my sophomore and junior year of college. Sissy, I was always gaga for her, and for whatever reason, maybe pity, maybe in reaction to something more sinister in her life—like she'd severely wronged someone, or someone had dished something nasty her way she needed to recover from—Sissy made a decision to give me, and only me, her complete and undivided attention.

I wasn't smooth or suave, not at all, but that didn't seem to matter. She laughed at my bad jokes, she kept touching my arm, she told me about her life at college, and so on. And then she took my hand and led me into the house and up to one of the guest bedrooms.

She turned off the lights and kissed me ferociously. I'd never been kissed like that, so feverishly and passionately. I could barely keep up. She threw me on the bed, peeled her tank top off, and stuck her chest in my face. Next she magically unbuttoned our shorts and took down our underpants at once and used my thing like a marker to doodle on her sex, which was an act birthed in another galaxy. She did that for maybe three minutes, three incomprehensible minutes—doves, firecrackers, flutes, pinwheels, all present at once. I was seeing the road signs to nirvana, but suddenly it stopped. She hopped off me and had her clothes back on like she was a firefighter and the firehouse alarm had just sounded. I was still flying around the room on my magic carpet, and Sissy and her beautiful canvas had already left the room, all without a word. My poor marker and I were left by our lonesome, wondering what in the world could have possibly gone wrong. I haven't seen Sissy Marlowe since that night, and I'm not sure that I want to. But I'm not sure that I don't want to, either.

I walked over to Amanda and watched her ready the projector. She fed the film around a series of spools and rods—it took an amazing number of steps to load the machine.

"Ready?" she said. I nodded.

I thought maybe Amanda would give me some privacy for the viewing, but she plopped down in a chair next to the projector. The machine clicked to life, and I saw Amanda's nose wiggle slightly, like she was avoiding a sneeze or else attempting to produce, genie-like, a tub of buttered popcorn and a Coke.

The movie came on. It was grainy and shaky, and because of either its age or the lighting on the day it was shot, there was a sepia shading to the scene. Clearly it was not a lost Werner Herzog masterpiece, but both Amanda and I were captivated.

The footage was of a picnic on a small lake beach somewhere. There were card tables set up, and several generations were represented in the dozen or so people there. I guessed it was the 1950s. The men were mostly in white T-shirts and dark slacks, the women in sundresses. The camera operator started the film from a short distance away, a panoramic shot, then approached the gathering to get close-up shots of everyone's faces. They were kind faces, happy on that sunny day at the beach. I didn't recognize anyone.

Four older men were playing cards at one of the tables. They were all drinking beer, and two of them were smoking cigarettes. One of the men hammed it up for the camera with some eyebrow exercises. Next the lens swung toward the lake and filmed two young boys and a young girl running from the water and at the camera operator. They had goofy expressions and were waving their arms like tentacled sea creatures.

The camera captured two women who were fussing over a

picnic spread, getting things together for lunch or dinner. They were both shy. One of them grimaced and walked out of the frame. The camera stayed with the other one who remained, and although she was sheepish, she tolerated the attention, and on some level, I think even appreciated it. I guessed it was the camera operator's wife, based on some flirtations.

The camera advanced a few feet, and there was a shot of a cooler. A hairy arm reached down, lifted the lid, and retrieved a cold one. Then the film went dark.

Next was about two minutes of film inside a bowling alley, same sepia shading. I recognized some of the people from the earlier scene. The adults weren't dressed as casually as they'd been lakeside. There was a lot of polyester. Again, the camera captured a close up of each face. Generally speaking, people looked less happy than they had at the lake. I guessed that the lot of them had been drinking for several hours.

A boy maybe ten years old stepped up to bowl, and all eyes were on him. He looked familiar. The camera got in close. It appeared that the camera operator asked the young bowler a question, to which the boy rolled his eyes in response. The camera zoomed out. The boy steadied himself, concentrated, and let it rip: the ball went directly into the gutter. The film captured a devastated expression on the boy's face. It was painful to see. And again the film went dark.

Fin.

I think that boy may have been my dad.

CHAPTER 13

There's an unavoidable reality for people who put their lives on hold for years at a time to live abroad: when they get back, they have to pick up where they left off, which usually means restarting from the same murky area on the time line that they'd, through grand gesture, tried to sidestep, only this time around they're a little older and a bit less patient with the system they're reentering.

A lot of people skip town because they don't have answers; often that's how they're shipped home, too. I was no different. I was full of fear and indecision when I left for China, and those things didn't magically disappear because of a temporary relocation. If anything, in strange ways, I incubated those things, did the same with some of their sibling and cousin emotions, too. I kept them warm in China and gave them sustenance, but more, I provided cozy little nooks inside myself where they were able to develop and grow, and, importantly, I respected their privacy and hardly ever disturbed them.

It'd been three days since my blowup with Mom. I'd been avoiding her ever since, kept a low profile around the house. I quietly urinated in the seated position and only flushed when necessary. On my hands and knees, I peeked around corners to ensure safe passage. I procured sleeves of crackers and ate them in the basement at odd hours. I tiptoed from carpet to carpet like a cat burglar—all I needed was a black bandanna with scissored eyeholes. But mostly I kept myself out of the house, and once I'd seen the 8mm movie, I drove around with no destination in mind and let thoughts bob around in my head—Mom, Dad, Tucky, Dino, China.

I was lost in those bobbing thoughts when I pulled into the parking lot of the Mega Supermart on Devon in Chicago. I needed to pee on account of the five coffees I'd consumed, plus I hoped a bottle of water would help level out my shakes. Thirdly, urinal use appealed to my sense of manliness in light of my recent seated-urination practice.

Despite the enormity of Mega Supermart, I couldn't find a single serving of agua in the entire place, but I continued wandering anyway. Wide-eyed, I patrolled two aisles, then I hit the bathroom and squeezed out a few ounces of unhealthy-looking, dark-yellow urine. I did the whole store like that, two aisles to urinal, two aisles to urinal, until I ran out of new territory. It was oddly satisfying.

The next morning I did the same thing at a Mariano's, and in the afternoon I hit a Kmart, and soon I was spending all of my time in these stores. It felt right to explore the Jewels and Dominicks, the Home Depots and Targets. I was reacquiring American culture and quickly developed a rhythm. It was lock-wheeled shopping carts and me aimlessly trolling the aisles, and it began to feel like my cart and I had transformed into something else, the two of us nighttime drunken drift-fishing on Lake Michigan, sometimes in true darkness with just a single spotlight cast down on the cart and me and the aisles to our sides.

I learned that the human body, after enough hours, can nearly become one with a shopping cart. Snipers talk about similar relationships with their rifles, jockeys, their horses. An extension of the self. I occasionally put something in the cart—some chicken thighs or an economy-sized box of garbage bags, once even a giant shrink-wrapped rectangle of two dozen toilet paper rolls—but I didn't buy them. I would either place them back on the shelves or ditch the cart outside the restrooms.

What seemed important about those excursions was the cart—the shopping cart as my prop, my crutch, my hands on its smooth plastic handle, and me slinking gradually by the hour, the curvature of my spine bending ever toward the steel baby seat/purse caddy as if my T3 through T10 vertebrae had a negative charge and were attracted to the positive charge of the stainless steel cart.

I picked stores that were outside a forty-minute radius from home to maintain anonymity and facelessness, a successful endeavor until day five, when I saw my high-school physics teacher at a Whole Foods in Des Plaines. It was a Sunday. He came out of the men's room, slowly wiping his hands on his slacks, and walked directly to my shopping cart. I'd abandoned it near the bathrooms a few minutes earlier and was observing it from a distance, as I liked to do. Nonchalantly, Mr. Lundenberger reached into my cart, flipped through the few layers of its contents, pulled out two packages of eel maki, and dropped them into his basket.

He was so casual, like his movements wouldn't have been at all different if he were at home ironing in his underpants. He took a step away from the cart, but then he stopped. His face scrunched toward his nose. His head jerked one way, then the other. He released his basket, and it fell to the ground. With the same hand, he grabbed the air in front of him. His head jerked again, his face re-scrunched. He grabbed at the air, six grabs, and after the sixth, he opened his hand close to his face and nodded in satisfaction. He stepped back to my cart and reached in it briefly, I think to wipe his hand. Then he picked up his basket and headed to the checkout.

Strange. And it was unmistakably Mr. Lundenberger, our

mediocre physics teacher and graduate of the University of Rochester. Mr. Lundenberger would launch into untenable stories about undergraduate boozing and free loving whenever his lesson plans were too sedative, which was often. "Back in Rochester, it was springfest my senior year. Or was it junior year ..."

Against my better judgment, I had applied to the University of Rochester, and it was one of the stops Mom and I made on our East Coast college tour. In Rochester we stayed with an old friend of Mom's, Mrs. Webber. Apparently they hadn't seen each other since Mom and Dad's wedding, but they were immediately giggling and touching each other's arms with "I know" and "Can you believe it?" In my life I'd never seen Mom so happy, and Mom good was good for the team. Plus, Mrs. Webber had a daughter who was two years younger than me, a bubbly, totally bodacious counterpart. That was also good for the team.

The four of us sat drinking wine for several hours. It was the first time Mom offered me alcohol, if that helps indicate endorphin levels. Mostly Mom and Mrs. Webber swapped stories while the daughter and I half-listened and stared at each other across the table. It was one big sloppy ball of happiness.

We kids got sent to bed around midnight. I was in a guest bedroom on the first floor, and from there I could hear Mom and Mrs. Webber as they continued talking in the kitchen. Mrs. Webber was recently divorced, and she spilled uninterrupted for about an hour. The content wasn't very interesting to me at the time—besides, I was busy plotting how to get upstairs to my new ladyfriend.

But my fantasies were interrupted. I heard Mom's voice and found myself listening.

Mom brought out the dirt. Nothing about me, but Dad. I didn't hear all of it. Mom increasingly whispered. There were frustrations. There was unhappiness. Mom cried and laughed. Mom said she was jealous of Mrs. Webber's freedom. That I heard. Maybe it was a gift that I didn't have access to it all, but even so, I got the gist.

It was the first and only time I heard Mom talk like that. I knew Mom and Dad weren't happy, generally speaking, but I never knew the extent. It had a slow, grinding quality to it. My heart raced through the night and skipped beats every few minutes. It's strange how scared I became that Mom and Dad were on the brink of divorce. Maybe they had been, I don't know. Even with Dad the way he was, I never pictured us without him, though if they'd asked my advice on divorce more recently, I might have prescribed it. Moot point.

Sleep never came for me that night at the Webbers', and I was groggy and cranky in the car the next morning and near tears every ten minutes. Mom may have known why, but we didn't discuss it. She was likely nursing a wicked hangover, so she may not have been able to think about anything else. The closest we got to saying anything was later that afternoon, when Mom told me I looked tired. She asked if their talking had kept me up the night before. I lied.

I trailed Mr. Lundenberger out of the Whole Foods, my thoughts returning to the eel maki. What had compelled Mr. Lundenberger? Did it make his life endurable? Was the act somehow portentous? Maybe a nibble at the rush of shoplifting? Was it the kind of thing I'd be doing if I'd taken a job like his instead of going to China?

I was deep in thought about these things as I came up on a shopping cart. Instinctively and without compromising my stride, my hands went to the ready position in front of my chest, and I began pushing it. I looked down and saw the cart was full of bagged groceries, and a glance to my side revealed a woman busily attending to a double stroller. I pushed onward.

It was a beautiful sequence, grasping the handle and slumping forward over the purse caddy, my legs automatically accommodating the additional torque required to bring the speed of the cart to that of my forward motion. It occurred to me that I could push carts fifteen, maybe twenty hours a week, if it paid well enough. I wondered what the remuneration might be for such an occupation. Probably minimum wage, unless cart pushers required a team leader, which they likely did, because what self-respecting brigade wouldn't need a lieutenant? That's where my mind shifted as I hoofed it across the lot, what I contemplated in that beautiful moment, sun hot on my face, as I imagined afternoons with the cart gatherers, our finger-pistol shoot-outs and synchronized end-of-shift fist-pumps, right up until the point when something solid made contact with my neck, which caused my legs to flip up toward the sky and my head, in an opposite motion, to slam down against the parking lot asphalt.

It took several minutes to explain—"I just returned from abroad ... don't think I've ever seen so many T-bone steaks in my life ... God, dizzying ..."—and the mother understood my state to the extent that she apologized for leaving her cart unattended, and no, she would not be pressing charges, which was decent of her. The shopping-cart gatherer who'd clotheslined me (no doubt the commanding officer of the parking lot crew, if such a position does exist) wasn't as accommodating and insisted that I have a discussion with the assistant manager to determine whether or not the police should be involved.

The assistant manager was about my age, and he seemed more sympathetic than the shopping cart gatherer, either because he secretly appreciated the natural beauty of me with cart, or else he couldn't imagine it at all. He didn't call the cops.

On a parting note, I asked the assistant manager if he'd ever consider a conversation regarding the sale of an additional line of dried mushrooms in his store.

"Are they yours?" he said.

"They are, direct from China. And they are delicious."

"I think I'd better pass," he said. "And if it's not obvious, we'd prefer that you do your shopping elsewhere from now on."

"No problem," I said. "Your loss," I added as I left that Whole Foods for good.

CHAPTER 14

My insides were spumy as I drove home, burping and contracting like I'd chugged a bucket of truck-stop hand soap. Plus my aching head. I don't know the exact recipe for a concussion, or how it's supposed to taste, but concussion or not, the clothesline had effected moderate to severe trauma, about a six-and-a-half on the ten-point scale of zero to death.

When I stepped into the house, I heard Mom in the kitchen. I intended to maintain my below-the-radar status and inch my way up the creaky stairs to my confines. I'd made it up three steps when the phone rang. I froze, my left foot airborne an inch above the fourth step.

"It's for you," Mom said. Foiled. And more significantly, Mom had found a way to break our silence. It nearly had me slobbering and snot-bubbling. I suppose there was a long list of influences that contributed to my brittleness at that moment, but I didn't have the stamina to deal with it, not in my weakened state, so I lugged myself upstairs to use the phone in Mom's bedroom. But the phone wasn't there. The cordless and its base had been unplugged and removed. I tried Dad's office, but the phone was gone there, too. Something was fishy.

I edged back downstairs at the pace of a tortoise and with the approximate confidence of a recently abused kitten.

Mom, in black slacks and a black sweater, was waiting for me in the kitchen, holding the phone in her upturned hand and looking pretty satisfied. I reached for it, but her fingers tightened around it. Her strength surprised me.

"Only if you promise to talk to me when you're done," she said.

I nodded my head, and she released her grip. It was an impressively patient trap, considering I hadn't received a phone call in a week. I wondered how long Mom had been camped out in her tree stand.

Mom left the kitchen, and I took a few deep breaths, like I'd seen Mom do, attempting some centering. "Hello?"

"You hanging in there?" It was Dino, and he sounded a bit concerned.

"Barely," I said. "The freaking shopping cart guy at Whole Foods clotheslined me today for almost no reason."

"Clotheslined? Like, wrestling? Could have a lawsuit on your hands."

"I didn't think about that."

"I want to hear all about it. That's the perfect story to tell on a drive up to Oshkosh." Dino's delivery irritated me. It felt rehearsed, as though it could have been segued by absolutely anything I said: someone just threw a Molotov cocktail at my car; I'm holding in my fingers a gold filling that isn't mine, which I found in my mashed potatoes at the Homade Country Buffet; this very minute a hamster is licking my testicles in a surprisingly satisfying way. Score, says Dino, perfect road trip material. I want to hear all about it!

"Now's not a great time," I said.

"*Carpe diem,* Everett."

He didn't win any points with this, either. "My mom's kind of lost it. I've got to try and reel her back in."

"The country air will do you good. You can sort through it all with some distance."

I began to imagine my conversation with Mom. The idea of blowing town did have its allure. "Can we go tonight?"

"Tomorrow morning," Dino said, as if reaffirming plans hatched months ago.

"I talked to the manager of Whole Foods about the mushrooms. No dice."

"Before or after he clotheslined you?"

"Different guy."

"In the car," he said.

I went to my room and spent a few minutes tossing around on my bed in a tortured state before finding Mom. So far it'd been a pretty bad day. Further review of recent events precipitated additional squirming on my mattress, but when I arrived at my interaction with Mom from five minutes earlier, I found a bit of optimism. The Mom who'd handed me the phone was familiar. In fact, I concluded that it had to have been the Mom from the past. She was protective, concerned, loving, and even a little sly.

I admit that my head injury may have had something to do with it, but it didn't seem far-fetched to think that I might have been doing Mom some good. Like maybe my presence was in fact a kind of kryptonite to the crystals and all, and I was slowly draining their powers. And if that was the case, we might have been nearing the point when Mom could appreciate her wackiness and apologize, and I would for mine, and we'd huddle up, spit out ideas for a game plan. I slowly stretched my limbs and could nearly touch all four edges of the bed. The idea gained momentum in my mind. It was a positive development.

I felt the clothesline bump on the back of my head. It was bigger than Mom's crystal, though just as hard. That bulge on my skull, it made me think of a hit-and-run accident we saw coming home from church one Sunday morning. I was around eight years old. A van sideswiped a cyclist, who flipped off the road headfirst into a giant oakleaf hydrangea. The van was driving toward us, so we had an unobstructed view. Dad slammed on the brakes. We watched the van accelerate, then disappear down a side street. Dad didn't hesitate. He spun the car to the opposite curb and leaped out. Mom and I were stuck frozen. Next thing, the cyclist was sitting in the backseat with me, blood dripping from cuts and scrapes all over his body. It was horrifying. Not just the gore, but blood was getting all over the interior of Dad's car. Dad didn't seem to notice, which I suppose was in part what horrified me the most. Even apple juice was off-limits in Dad's car. Buckled up, the whole backseat area felt like my responsibility somehow, and I had no plan for how to contain the stain.

We took the cyclist to the hospital and even waited around for several hours until he was discharged. No major injuries. The cyclist thanked Dad profusely. He even put his giant bandaged hand on top of my head and ruffled my hair. "You've got a special dad," he said to me. "But I'm sure you know that."

I again traced the contusion on my head with my fingers. Exhausted, despite any new outlook, I rolled off the bed and onto my knees. I wobbled myself upright and made my way downstairs to the kitchen. I put the phone back in its cradle and sat down at the table across from Mom. She was holding a steaming cup of tea with both hands like it was a power source. She looked at that tea for a long minute before she brought her eyes to meet mine.

"How can I help you?" she said.

"What?"

"How can I help you? Help you in your life. I'm your mother, and while I won't say I understand what you're going through, I love you and care about you, and I want to help."

"I don't understand what you're going through, either," I said.

"Now we're getting somewhere."

"We're nowhere." Other than losing the crazy, I didn't know

how Mom could help me. If I had to identify an area in need of help, it'd be big and contain absolutely everything. Or nothing. I didn't know. I couldn't contribute properly to the exercise.

"I'm happy to share with you whatever you want to know. I think some of the things I've learned might help you."

"That's what I'm talking about. I don't want to learn what you're learning. I want my old mom back." My heart rate increased in response to further appreciation of my pathetic state.

"I'm still here, just evolving. You, too, are evolving. If we were sitting at this table ten years ago, having this conversation, it would be different. We wouldn't be, is what I'm saying. It was so opposite and different. Now I've got the rest of my life to live. You, too."

Those ideas of Mom's came out garbled, but I got the gist, and I was glad that at the very least they didn't sound regurgitated. "It was different because of Dad," I said in my singsong voice.

Mom thought. "Maybe that's part of it, but not everything."

"Dad wouldn't have put up with the incense."

"He wouldn't have," she said. "And that makes me sad. Sad for me and sad for you, sad for Dad."

"Was it really that bad? I mean, is all this worth it?" It felt like I was losing focus.

"I refuse to let another day go by," Mom said. "I'm finding new ways to better myself. That's precious. It's also why I want to help you. How can I help? What do you want? Start there."

"Help yourself," I said.

"I am," she said. "But I have help to give."

"Help Tucky."

"Help each other?"

"Help," I said.

"Don't get upset, but I've got major déjà vu right now. I

really think you might benefit from some of the tools Tucky can help you build. The writing is on the wall."

"What wall? And I don't want to hear that name, Tucky."

"We're getting nowhere," Mom said.

I opened my mouth to speak, but nothing came out. The clock on the microwave blinked 00:00, as it'd done since I got home, its state probably since electrical current first passed from the socket into its capacitor fifteen years earlier. I swallowed, said, "I'm going to Oshkosh in the morning."

I got up and went to my room where I tried to force the mess I had in the forefront of my mind into rarely accessed areas of gray matter. I crawled under my comforter and attempted some centering. I felt horribly unbalanced, and when I closed my eyes I got the spins, but it wasn't run-of-the-mill dizziness. I wasn't an upturned turtle getting flicked around in circles. It was more like I was in a bad tailspin, my entire body whirling every which way as gravity pulled me through the air toward some dense surface.

I found myself repeatedly imagining getting up from my bed and walking to the stairs, for no other reason than I felt compelled toward the height available there. From the top of the stairs, I'd step down to the landing, where I was further drawn to the distance to the ground at that spot. Then, and I can't say why I kept doing this, but I'd practically collapse into the banister, and instead of that barricade containing me, my waist would connect with the smooth wooden handrail and create a sort of hinge, my head would swivel down as my legs sprang up, and the mass of me would very elegantly flip-flop right over it—and I'd enter into a free fall.

I tried to deviate from my stairway-tumbling, but it was nearly impossible to distract myself, and when my mind was finally able to transport itself to a new location, it landed me at the granddaddy of my acrophobic activators, my trip to the foothills of the Himalayas in Yunnan Province.

I was alone on that trip, and the guidebook had said it was a beginner's trail. Sure, it was incredibly beautiful there, but it was guaranteed death with one wrong move or a slip somewhere.

The worst was a five-foot-wide cement path with no guardrail and a thousand-foot drop on one side and a cliff straight up on the other. I crawled for two hundred yards, hyperventilating and sobbing, grabbing at clumps of weeds in cement cracks as I inched my way along, all the time swearing death to *Lonely Planet.* At the end, I lay splayed on rocks, petrified, until two happy Danes came bouncing along the trail from the direction I was headed. I begged them to tell me if it got worse. They promised it got better. They lied. There were three more expanses of death trail, which combined for over seven hundred yards of death trail.

It's as if I've got a magnetism toward these ledges, and I can't trust myself to not approach them, to not heave myself over. I've never been suicidal. I don't want to die. That's what makes the compulsion so horrible. It unfolds in my mind, and I can see my little feet running to the edge and jumping—or in Yunnan, clumsily logrolling the five feet across the path until gravity sucked me past the rim—and there's instant panic and regret. What have I done?

My trip to Yunnan wasn't just cliffs. After the last death-trail portion, the path opened up to a plateau where a farmer was working his field. Somehow I explained that I needed down from that place. He understood me, even though the words barely came out. I offered him a fistful of sweaty money, but he didn't take it. We walked together for over an hour until we got to a small village, which was splendid and wonderful, except that we hadn't yet lost much altitude, and it was starting to get dark.

We went to a certain house, and my guide faced me and

pantomimed driving—I haven't often found myself in that situation, when elements that are completely out of my hands seem to be gelling in my favor.

Half an hour later, I was sitting shotgun in a two-ton dump truck. The driver had two speeds—at rest and full bore. I think he drove like that because he loved that truck, loved driving it fast. It was almost dark, and soon we were on a road just like the death trail, same cliff and no barricade, only the road was a bit wider than the trail. We whipped around the corners. The driver knew the roads, obviously, but still. He laughed at my whimpers but didn't slow down. Eventually I just closed my eyes and waited it out.

He dropped me off in another small village at a guesthouse run by his brother. They offered to make me food, to get me tea, but I declined and went straight to my room. I fell onto the bed and into a coma, slept in my clothes with my shoes still tied.

In the morning they drew me a map showing me how to get to a bus station. There was a small river I had to ferry across, but otherwise, they said, I wouldn't have any problems.

When I finally set out, I was substantially calmer than I'd been the night before, and I was able to appreciate how beautiful the area was. I'd spent the night in a small valley—mountains towering all around, immense and humbling like I couldn't imagine.

Two hours later I hit the river. There was an old man sitting in front of a one-room house. He didn't speak Mandarin, and obviously I knew jack shit of his dialect, but somehow we understood each other. I asked about the ferryman, and he pointed to my watch and said it'd be two hours.

He indicated for me to sit and poured two bowls of moonshine. I tried to give him some money, but he wouldn't take it. We drank for four hours until the ferryman arrived.

A few times we communicated, but mostly we sat in silence listening to the river, the leaves blowing, the birds. It was a Confucian kind of afternoon, like maybe I ought to have rattled out a few bad poems, but anyway.

When the ferryman got there, instead of our heading out, he sank down onto the ground next to the old man and started drinking with us. I didn't get across the river until it was dark again, but when we got to the other side, the ferryman walked me to a guesthouse a half hour away. We had no flashlights, and we were truly ripped, but it was a clearheaded drunk, almost like drugs. I've never been drunk like that, before or since.

When I woke up the next morning, it was to the squeal of a pig being slaughtered. First there were yelps and shrieks, and that was followed by the buzz of an electric saw. I got out of bed. Apparently I'd slept naked. I pulled on clothes and went outside to watch the butchering, but by the time I got there, I mostly saw silhouettes retreating, like a man with a hindquarter over his shoulder, etc. The only thing left at the spot was the pig's head, and I stood and watched a small boy with a handheld blowtorch char its face.

Chapter 15

As he said he would, Dino picked me up at 9:00 a.m. sharp, which I thought bode well for the enterprise. He was driving his dad's Ford Escort, which Dino inherited after Parkinson's also took cars from his dad. The Escort had a turning knob on the steering wheel and an ancient CB radio in a homemade caddy that fit into in the emergency brake console.

I got in and Dino put up his hand for a high-five. I complied. Apparently we were a couple of dorks, but I didn't mind. I had some new energy, which allowed for something like a high-five. I felt good. The good came into me just after I left the house, almost like I'd passed through a force field somewhere near the front stoop and popped out refreshed on the other side.

"What's with the kiddie backpack?" Dino said.

I replied with a noise. "Eh." Which meant *it's not worth pursuing*.

We were silent as we made our way on the interstate. It was a cool and damp morning. A major thunderhead had come through the night before, and a few of its low-hanging sister clouds hadn't yet left the area. I wondered if Dino would ask about my clothesline incident the day before. In my mind it was a kind of test.

"Fine worm-hunting weather," I said, "but lousy picnic forecast."

"What? Oh, right. You hunt?"

"Yeah, I put on my orange vest and hunt worms. Family

tradition." It was something Dad used to say, but I didn't share that with Dino.

I reached between us and started turning knobs on the CB radio. The white ink hash marks on its dials were worn away. When I found the power knob, an antiquated, scratchy sound came out of it. I wondered whether it sounded that way out of the package, or if tweeters lose their cheep in old age.

"This thing work?" I said.

"My dad made us listen to it on road trips."

We weren't picking up any communiqués, so I cranked knobs at random. Doing so, I inadvertently turned the volume up full blast. The noise was horrible. I tried to find the volume again, but couldn't, so I started cranking knobs, maybe a little harder than I should have. When I located the volume, I turned it too hard in the wrong direction, and it broke off in my hand. I eyed it peripherally, so that Dino wouldn't see. It was busted clean off. "*Zhao ni ma,*" I said softly.

I held the knob up and said over the noise of the CB, "Sorry, didn't mean to break it."

"Fuck, man, that's my dad's." Dino reached for the cigarette lighter and pulled out the CB cord. The car went silent. I felt bad, even if I simultaneously appreciated hearing Dino drop the F-bomb, like old times.

"Maybe we can glue it. I think we might be able to glue it." I doubted we could glue it.

Dino took the knob and dropped it in the ashtray. I was afraid to touch the CB again, or anything else in the car, so I put my hands in my lap. It occurred to me that we probably ought to have been discussing sales strategies, mushroom-transport options, etc., but my clumsiness seemed to have popped Dino into a different dimension. We continued north on the interstate like we were in two separate little bubbles.

Maybe Dino and I weren't really that different. In China,

we basically got along with anyone and everyone, and even with each other a good deal of the time. We managed pleasant exteriors even though we were both so damn unhappy—and we both had it, that deep-down existential sadness that was too dark to think about, never mind speak out loud. On top of that, we had for years been devising ways to skirt around our issues, especially Dino. He was ahead in the game on that one. But that was our shared dream, that ditching out of the States promised a successful escape, or at least a respite, which was of course by then certifiable horseshit, but anyway.

About an hour north of Milwaukee, Dino broke the dead air. "My dad isn't very well," he said. I'd been close to speaking myself, but for me, it was because I needed to pee soon. "We're getting ready for the end."

"My mom went through something like that." I hadn't, which Dino knew full well. I had little to offer.

"My parents went to church every Sunday for my whole life. Now it's the only time my dad leaves the house. Every Sunday."

"Do you go?"

Dino nodded.

"It's not against the Xuan Gong?"

"Nothing like that."

"Body and blood of Christ?"

"No."

"You get funny looks?"

Dino laughed. "It's ridiculous. Actually, no, the priests don't, but the collection dude did once. And this old lady who always sits in the front row, like I'll be punished, like it's supposed to make me feel guilty."

"And so because you don't want to go to church, it's okay to go. I mean with the Xuan Gong stuff."

"How can I explain it?" Dino wasn't agitated. He seemed to genuinely want to help me understand, which was irritating in an unexpected way.

"It doesn't matter," I said. "I'm just fucking with you."

"Why?"

"Just a joke."

"I don't do that."

"You did do that." I said it slowly, for effect.

"I shouldn't have. I'm sorry."

"No big deal. You can still do it."

"I don't want to."

That was how the conversation ended. I supposed it was progress, albeit an awkward, purely surface kind of progress.

We continued north past Fond du Lac to Oshkosh. From Chicago, the trip took a little over three hours. Oshkosh is big and flat. It rests between Lake Butte des Morts and Lake Winnebago, and only Winnebago has size and depth enough for whitecaps.

"You've got directions to this guy's house, right? What's his name again?"

"I know where we're going."

"His name?"

"Ron. But we're going to Kuang Fa An's."

"What's the plan?"

"That's what we're going to discuss. Ron said just to get there, and it's a done deal."

"What's a done deal?"

"Everything."

That was reassuring.

Chapter 16

Mr. Kuang lived in one of few five-story buildings in Oshkosh. There was a bike rack out back, plastic tubs of empty beer cans lined the hallways, and I smelled skunky weed when we passed one of the doors.

Mr. Kuang came to the door, and he was a teenage Mr. Kuang, twenty at the most. He was wearing blue jeans and a long-sleeved Green Bay Packers t-shirt. He invited us in and offered us a seat on a lumpy futon.

"I've got diet pop, water, I could make some tea, I guess," our host said as he hovered in front of the refrigerator. "Or," he said as he sniffed a carton of OJ, "yeah, diet pop, water, or I can boil some water." He had a deep Wisconsin accent. Big time.

"I'll take some water," I said. "Thanks." I was hungry, too, but I didn't want to be rude.

"Nothing for me," Dino said.

He quickly washed two plastic cups from the sink, filled one from the tap, and emptied what remained in a two-liter bottle into the other. He handed me my drink, tossed a video-game controller off the Papasan chair and tilted it away from the television/video game console and toward us, and sat down.

Dino's left leg was bouncing up and down like a maniac's. Not exactly the streamlined business model he'd anticipated, but I wasn't thrown off. I liked being in a new place, meeting this guy. Why not? It got me out of the house, anyway. Dino was much more heavily invested in it—as per how he rolls—so

I could see how this setup might have disappointed him. Me, I was taking it all in stride.

"So," I said, "Mr. Kuang, Ron's your brother? Is he here?"

"You can call me Jeff," he said.

"Your brother?" Dino said.

"He's not exactly my brother," Jeff said. "He's more like a cousin."

"Your cousin or like a cousin?" Dino said.

"More like a godfather. It's a coincidence that we have the same last name."

"Are you a student?" I said. Jeff impressed me. For a young guy, he was dealing with two strangers in his home very well, not to mention Dino's crazy leg. Dino was hopped up like there was a jury foreman in the room clearing her throat before she read Dino's death-sentence verdict.

"Yeah, I'm studying sociology at UW–Oshkosh, even though I'll probably go to optometry school. The family business. Anyway, I was trying to graduate early, but it's looking like that's not going to happen. I've still got some freaking electives, plus my advisor is a total fart."

"Congratulations," I said.

"I'm thinking sign language. You know, for the language requirement. And I've got to redo my lab science, so, you know, that too."

Dino was visibly steamed. He said, "Mr. Kuang, what's the deal for the mushroom sales? Does Ron have a plan?"

"You can call him Jeff," I said. Dino perked up, slightly too militant a movement for my tastes. It reminded me of Mom popping into better posture when she remembered to better it.

Jeff shrugged. "My parents changed it to Jeff when we got here. They don't call me Jeff, but you know, everyone else does. Just easier."

"When did your family move?"

"I was a baby, twenty-two years ago."

"Have you been to China?" Dino said.

"Sure, lots of times. I'm going back in a week, which is why, you know, your question, the answer to your question is, the plan: I'm going to bring the mushrooms back with me. Ron thinks we need someone down in Chicago to make sales. I mean, people around here don't care about mushrooms. There are a few Asian groceries, one in Fond du Lac, two in Green Bay, another in Sheboygan, but you know, they won't pay for the premium."

"So you're on board with this?" I said.

"Why not? It's the premium."

"Can somebody just sell the premium?" I said. "What about FDA approval or something? I don't know."

"My buddy, Vic," Jeff said, "he sells venison jerky all over, like gas stations and whatnot, and he doesn't have FDA anything. Like, barbeque, red-hot, whatever you want, he sells it."

"Around here is one thing, but what about selling the premium in Chicago?" I said. "People may look a little closer there. And what about Ron?"

Dino turned to me. "Jeff's right," he said, a little like he was possessed. "If Vic can sell his venison jerky, we can sell mushrooms. It's not a problem. Nothing we'd get thrown in the clink for, anyway."

Jeff took a nervous swig of his diet pop, perhaps imagining what his first few hours behind bars would be like, but he shook it off. Jeff was all right in my book. "Nah, they couldn't do that," Jeff said. "Plus, Ron's got connections in the police department."

That's when Ron showed up. He entered the apartment without knocking. "Look at these fucking guys," Ron said when he saw us. "I wasn't sure you assholes would actually show up. But here you are."

The room had been vitamin-D deficient, and Ron brought the sunlight. My body soaked in his good vibe. I got giddy, couldn't contain myself and started laughing, and so did Jeff, but Dino was more reserved. Maybe he remembered drinking with a different, more civilized Ron in Guangzhou. But for me, Ron was just as I remembered, battered Packers cap on his head, ridiculously foul-mouthed and wholly enthusiastic.

We had met Ron walking near the Pearl River in downtown Guangzhou. He came up to Dino and me and in a pretty thick accent and said he was "real fucking glad to speak some English with some regular fuckers." He was in his fifties, a retired Wisconsin state trooper, shot in the line of duty, hip injury, and was living on his pension. No shoulders, he looked kind of fragile. He had glasses and was wearing the same beat-up Packers cap. It was his first trip back to China in fifteen years. His wife had just left him, and his daughter was a freshman in college. That loneliness was heavy, and he either didn't try to hide it, or he couldn't.

What a foul-mouthed dude. King of the high-fives, too, which Dino loved, that dipshit. All pronouns for Ron were either "asshole" or "fucker." And he was all about "titties" and "buttercup asses." He kept saying that, "buttercup asses." And he emphasized ideas with his hands, like two-handed breast-honking and butt-caressing. He took us "assholes" to a bar he knew had lots of "major mclons." Though when we got there, no melons were to be found, major or otherwise. It was practically empty, except for some bleached-blond karaoke dude in leather pants who kept dedicating Beatles songs to us. But it was all right. We laughed a lot. Ron talked about somehow capitalizing on his dual citizenship. I remember that. Apparently that'd been the moment of birth for the mushroom scheme, or at least when it was sexed into existence. Dino and I eventually left the bar, but Ron stuck around. He said he had faith that the tits would arrive, but I suspected he just didn't want to go back to his hotel, back to being alone again.

Back in Jeff's apartment, I could still see some of that desperation in Ron's eyes, same as I saw in Guangzhou, but he was otherwise full-throttle, and just having Ron there with us made it feel like the project was getting some traction.

"It's not fucking brain surgery, for Christ's sake," Ron said. "Even a handful of assholes like us can pull it off."

We made a good plan. When Jeff got back from China with the first batch of mushrooms, Dino and I would return to Oshkosh to package them, and we'd transport them south to Chicago for sales. I dug the excitement of entrepreneurism. With no middleman, it would all be profit. And if we were successful, there would be a lot of cash. I only had six hundred dollars left of my teaching bonus, but at that moment, I was willing to put it all into the business. I'd even hit up Mom for extra dough, if need be. I found myself believing in the project, that its variables made sense. True, it was smuggling, even if a mild variety, but once we got established we could find a way to import the product lawfully, find legal representation, incorporate, order the company windbreakers, etc.

Dino had the fever, too. We rolled down the windows when we got in the car. Our combined electricity needed to be tempered by at least fresh air.

"Let's eat," I said. "My treat. I'm fucking starving."

"Actually, we've got one more stop before we head home."

"Whachoo talkin' 'bout, Willis?" I thought he was kidding.

"I've got one more quick stop to make while we're up here. Visit a friend. Did I forget to tell you?"

Dino so easily ruined things. And worse, he projects this fake-obliviousness while he's doing it, which is infuriating. At the same time, though, I wanted to maintain my good mood, if I could.

"It's cool," I said. It felt right to stay upbeat. I did file Dino's indiscretion in my mind, but I moved on from it.

"She'll fix us up with a meal," Dino said.

"She? Give me the nod, I'll disappear."

"It's not like that. Mei's a friend."

"Does she have a roomie?" I thought of middle-school make-out parties, round-robin boobie inspections. That was my mood—the improbable now possible.

"No, I met her in San Francisco a few months ago."

"Sounds romantic. No sparks? All the way to Oshkosh to see her, that's not nothing."

"Just a friend."

"Chinese?"

"Half Chinese, half Mongolian."

"Interesting. But no friends?"

"No friends." Dino didn't leave even a possibility.

I looked at the woods to my right. I stuck my arm out the window, all the way out, practically to my shoulder, which felt slightly unsafe, even if it wasn't. Dino shot me a glance, as if to say, What the hell are you doing? I pointed my fingers and pulled my thumb in tight, and I worm-wave danced my arm in the sixty-mph wind. I hadn't done it in many years, and I can report that it still provided pleasure.

CHAPTER 17

Mei was attractive, had a thin face with a flat nose, and she somehow appeared fragile despite her big shoulders. She lived on Lake Butte des Morts in a one-room summer cottage that looked like it'd recently been winterized. A roll and a half of pink insulation was unraveling underneath an eave near the front door, and inside, insulation-face was still visible between ceiling joists. There was a small dining table with four chairs, a two-coil electric range, sink, and mini-fridge. The focal point of the room was a large picture window that faced the lake and had a desk underneath. The desk itself was made of two sawhorses and a wooden door. The house was undecorated, very neat and clean if not spartan, all except the door-desktop on the sawhorses, which was, in comparison to the rest of the house, post-apocalyptic.

Dino introduced me to Mei, and she immediately began fixing us tea.

"Maybe you have something to eat for Everett?" Dino said.

Mei winced, probably in embarrassment.

"That's okay," I said. "I'm not actually that hungry."

Mei opened and closed cabinet doors, but each one was as bare as the others. They were so empty that I began to doubt human life was being sustained in those confines. Truthfully, I was starving, and I began imagining that Mei and her house were actually a front for a subterranean tiki bar that was only accessible via a secret passageway hidden in her floor. Twist a table leg, tilt a book, and the entrance appears. As I watched Mei search for edibles, that clandestine tiki bar continued to take shape in my mind.

The clientele was almost exclusively female, and more specifically, attractive women who enjoyed giving back rubs to strangers, which was kind and generous of them. Inside there was wall-to-wall ruby shag carpeting, and it was decorated with Deco sconces and a disco ball. They served deliciously cold twenty-five-cent drafts at this place, and on arrival, management gifted each patron a piping hot plate of buffalo wings.

But in reality, Mei's house was absolutely another man's Shangri-la, and Mei most certainly lived there full-time, as evidenced by her chaotic door-desktop. Its messiness was in the genus of Dino's room in China, and the way it contrasted with its surroundings was evocative of Mom's altar.

"We'll stop on the way home, or, actually, never mind. I'm not even hungry," I said.

Mei didn't put up a fight. She didn't mention food again. I searched my pockets for sustenance but found nothing—I would have wrestled any beast just to suck on a stick of Juicy Fruit.

Dino and I sat down at the table, and when Mei approached us, I could see that her cardigan and slacks fit very loosely. She was thinner than I'd initially thought, thin without the clothes to accommodate the thin. It might have been a recent transformation, or if it wasn't, she hadn't had either the cash or the inclination to build a new wardrobe.

Mei carefully poured me a cup of tea, then for Dino, and as she poured her own, my stomach announced its emptiness, the loud and sustained noise of an immense cauldron bubbling off the last of its contents. Dino pleaded to me with his eyes, but what exactly did he want me to do?

"So," I said, "You and Dino met in San Francisco? Were you there on business?"

Mei gave Dino a questioning look, and he smiled back at her.

"We met at a Xuan Gong gathering there," Dino said.

"Oh," I said. "There are meetings like that?"

"In fact, Mei administers a lot of the Xuan Gong activity here in the Midwest."

"Are there a lot in Wisconsin?"

"Several thousand," Mei said.

"Huh," I said. "That's a small army." I could see on Mei's face that she didn't like the word army, but oh well.

"Plus tens of millions in China." Dino said. "Millions more around the world."

"And you have meetings?"

"Meetings, instructions, educate the public, match new practitioners with mentors, that kind of thing."

I glanced back over at Mei's desk and noticed that there were cardboard boxes underneath and on either side of it. There were piles of books, and there were stacks of DVDs in packaging like the one Dino had given me, which I still hadn't watched.

I was in a main artery of the Midwest's Xuan Gong activity. Jeff's pad was much more my style, and I brainstormed some decorating we might do at Jeff's to make it feel a little more professional. A wall calendar, for starters, maybe a dry-erase board to track inventory, a 3-in-1 printer, plus a stockpile of hot wings in the freezer, which would hurt no one.

Dino and Mei began whispering to each other, even though I was just as near to both of them as they were to each other. Merci beaucoup, hint taken. I got up from the table and took my tea over to Mei's desk. Mei eyed me, but neither of them made any efforts in my direction. I watched them back. Mei began to nod her head emphatically, apparently in agreement to whatever diarrhea Dino was carrying on about. I turned and looked out at the lake, and I found myself thinking about a fight I had with Dino when we were in Pingnan.

It had to do with these icicles Dino made in our apartment. He taped pieces of string to the roof of the freezer and sprayed them with water a few times a day. It took a month. Sometimes I'd open the freezer and look at them, and every time I did, standing there with my face practically inside the freezer, cold pouring out around my head like I was in some horror movie cemetery, I would stand for several minutes and fill with dark thoughts. I contemplated sabotage, of course, but more than that, I would practice embracing a hatred I had growing in me, as I simultaneously tempered it. I was practically meditative at those times, and I never touched the icicles.

Eventually the icicles grew too big for the freezer. Dino took one out and walked around campus showing it off to the students, which I'm sure was his plan from the get-go. I watched from the balcony of our apartment. Students packed around Dino and wanted to touch the icicle, but he wouldn't let them. Dino looked very pleased with himself.

At one point, Dino started taking long licks of his icicle, which turned my stomach something fierce. He also held it out for the students to lick, which was too much for me. I kept hoping V. P. Pu would show up—no, not for a lick—but to bear witness and take appropriate action.

Some teachers investigated, including Mr. Dragon. Dino held the icicle up for a physics teacher, Yi Lao Shi, to take a lick, but she declined. But when Dino held it up for Mr. Dragon. Mr. Dragon made wide eyes and lapped at it like a dog, which got the crowd roaring.

Dino didn't like Mr. Dragon stealing the spotlight. He tried to pull the icicle away, but Mr. Dragon followed the icicle headfirst and kept tonguing it. The students screamed with laughter, but Dino got steamed.

Mr. Dragon grabbed Dino's wrist and forcibly steadied the icicle. Dino got this scared look on his face. Mr. Dragon lowered his mouth onto the icicle and took a big bite, crunch, and that was the end of the icicle game. Dino came back to the apartment and went straight to his room, slamming the door behind him.

That night, Dino, Xiao Mu, Edwards, Mr. Dragon and I went drinking at the restaurant across from the school gate. Dino was a total sourpuss. He got wasted and kept looking at Mr. Dragon like he wanted blood.

Everyone saw him doing it. He was acting like a total crybaby, all because of that stupid icicle. Mr. Dragon made special efforts to be friendly with Dino, but nothing worked. We all tried with little success. Dino ruined the night.

I yelled at Dino when we got home. Dino said it had nothing to do with the icicle, but that Mr. Dragon was an asshole, and that next time he saw Mr. Dragon, he was going to tell him exactly that.

I started toward the kitchen. Dino knew, and he lunged across the apartment to stop me. There was still one icicle left. I opened the freezer door, but Dino whacked it shut. I hip-checked him and got the freezer open, and I got a hand on the last icicle just as Dino rammed me into the countertop. I held the icicle above my head and pushed Dino away with my free hand.

We got tangled up and fell hard onto the floor. Our knees and elbows pummeled each other's bodies. I took the body blows, opted for offense instead of defense. I got my arm free from his and banged the back of Dino's head a few times with the icicle. That pissed him off good. I'm sure it hurt like hell, too. He grabbed a handful of my chest-fat and twisted. I hammered the icicle against his forehead five or six times, and I threw it against the wall. It shattered into pieces. We rolled off each other without a word and headed to our rooms to sleep it off.

Back in Mei's cottage, I had some fury in me after rehashing that battle with Dino in my mind. I considered walking over and poking Dino in the chest with two of my fingers, poking him hard and telling him very simply to go fuck himself, but I instead turned toward the picture window and took a few deep breaths. That calmed me a bit.

It was still overcast, and the gray template made it look colder outside than it actually was. Trees weren't bare, but that far north, leaves were already layering on the ground. Small ripples shook across the dark lake, and I saw a solitary loon floating near the water's edge. The loon was looking straight ahead, its body moving in unison with the tiny waves. It turned its head clockwise ten degrees, bobbed a little longer, and dove, disappearing into the water.

"It must be deep there," I said.

"What?" Mei said.

"There's a loon," I said, pointing.

Mei didn't look up. "That's Luo Lan." I watched for the loon to resurface. Mei said, "Jun Hua probably isn't far. Another loon." She looked up and smiled. I imagined my face reciprocating, but I'm not sure it did.

Back out the window I scanned for several minutes more, but no loons. I looked down at the mess on Mei's desk. Miniature books, as though fortifying the cabin's wall, were piled underneath the window, hundreds of books the size of a deck of cards, with the pyramid-like emblem of the Xuan Gong on the covers. There were papers, books, DVDs, a computer, etc. but most of all there were index cards, three columns of index cards stacked nine inches high at one edge of the desk. From what I could see, each of those cards had contact info on them, some in Chinese characters, some in pinyin, some in English. I wondered why Mei wouldn't just use her computer instead of all those index cards. Then I noticed that one of the cardboard boxes to the left of the desk was entirely full of loose index cards, also written on, hundreds if not thousands of index cards. I fought an urge to run my hands through them like packaging peanuts.

"So, guys," I said, gesturing with my tea cup, "What's the difference between Xuan Dafa and Xuan Gong? Do they mean the same thing?"

"Essentially, yes," Dino said. He looked to Mei for corroboration, and she nodded, smiled wryly. "We can talk about it on the way home," he said. His tone was a little too spirited for my palate, but anyway.

Dino and Mei leaned in toward each other, and this time they spoke at such a soft level that I couldn't understand a single word even when I tried. I started helping myself to a few of the pamphlets, made myself a nice swag bag of materials. Either Mei and Dino didn't notice or they didn't care. I sort of turned my back to them, obscuring my actions while I took an index card and wrote my name down on it. I supplied all of the pertinent contact information, and I stuck it into the middle of a giant stack of index cards. I did the same with thing five times and slid them into different piles. Vanished. I have no clue why I did that. Maybe it was because of how they were excluding me, if that isn't too simple an explanation.

I looked back out the window and pretended to be deep in thought myself as I searched for the loon.

I noticed a small charcoal grill a few feet from the house, and I imagined a half dozen chicken wings sizzling on its hot grid. But when I looked closer, where its briquettes should have been, there was ash, yes, but it was ash from paper, and there were white paper corners that'd burned into triangles of various sizes. Apparently that was Mei's incinerator, for the index cards and whatever else of the paper trail.

Movement on the lake caught my attention. I spotted two this time, both loons about a hundred yards from shore, just their heads visible on the water, but only for a moment. One disappeared. Dip. And the other, dip. I waited for them to resurface, but they never did.

I launched into questions as soon as Dino and I were back on the road. "Why were you guys whispering? What's so secret? You know, Mei burns those freaking index cards."

"Sorry about that. Mei likes to talk Xuan Gong in a very personal way."

"I suppose that's a personal way."

"She just doesn't know you yet, but I can tell she likes you. I mean as a friend."

"She did absolutely nothing to indicate she likes me. Nothing."

"Mei's father is in a prison in Gansu Province, has been going on five years, because the government accused him of being a Xuan Gong practitioner."

"But he is, right? A Xuan Gong."

"Yes, but what does that matter? It's an egregious human rights violation. His wife hasn't been able to visit him in five years. Mei hasn't seen him in eight years, not since she left to study in Madison."

"Why would anyone's destination be Wisconsin? What about New York or San Fran?"

"Try and understand; we're talking basic human rights. A family torn apart."

"That's not it at all. Just if it were me, that's where I'd go, where there's a community in place, not Wisconsin."

"She has community, she is community."

"I guess we went to China where there was no community, but we weren't going for the long haul."

"They accused him of stealing from the school where he taught."

"I'd probably go to Hong Kong or Kunming. Long haul."

"What's he going to steal?"

"Have you even met him?"

"I don't have to meet him. People who practice Xuan Gong don't steal."

"But how do you know he's a good Xuan Gong? There must be bad ones out there. Bad Christians, bad Muslims, bad Jews. No bad Gongers? A little side business with chalk from the supply closet?"

"You just met Mei. Does she seem like the daughter of a criminal? Their lives are ruined because of a cruel, propagandizing dictatorship. Have some heart."

"The whole thing," I said. "I don't know."

"I've got some books for you, to see if what we're doing makes sense."

I didn't answer Dino. That seemed more civil than telling him where to put his books.

We drove the next twenty minutes in silence, cruise-controlled on a county highway and stuck behind a tractor-trailer. Then, two cars ahead of the truck, a medium-sized blob zoomed across the highway, from left to right, about five feet in the air. It was almost dark, so I doubted I'd actually seen anything, but a few seconds later, another blob flew across the highway at the same spot, also left to right, just in front of the car ahead of the tractor-trailer. I looked ahead to the right and saw they were turkeys. Four of them who'd made the flight successfully were now moseying into the woods, making their way, one after the other, as if each of them hadn't just stared death in the face.

And again, this time in front of the tractor trailer, a giant turkey flew across the road. "Hey," I shouted. "Do you see those fucking turkeys?"

I don't know why I didn't expect another, but I didn't, not really, and then there it was, barely airborne, flapping its way across the road just a few feet ahead of us, and closing. It was a giant subject, big enough to quite possibly crash through the windshield if we hit it right. Dino didn't react at all. We weren't slowing, and it was upon us. I watched as it flew past Dino's side of the car, not more than a foot from the windshield. Its tiny right eye was approaching mine—too tiny an eye for me to register the fear within, though I'm sure it was there and in abundance. The turkey was close enough to tickle with the wipers, but I remained hopeful. Until, thud, and for an instant a gnarly turkey foot was tight against the edge of the windshield, then gone.

We'd only grazed it, but who knows what kind of damage that can inflict. The car was fine. I brought my face down toward the side mirror and watched the turkey flailing in the air behind us. It fell to the ground, shook around a bit—was getting smaller since Dino still hadn't decreased our speed any—but just as it was almost too small to view, it appeared to get up and, I think, waddle into the woods after its friends.

Chapter 18

I woke up early the next morning with the help of an alarm clock. I only slapped the snooze four times. I heard no tunes, and I smelled no witch's brew, so I slipped downstairs. Having slept until at least ten practically every day since returning, I'd forgotten how the house was in the early morning. It felt unoccupied, vacant, like even I wasn't among its inhabitants.

Maybe it's the light of early morning, the way the sun bursts through the eastern-facing windows, how it spotlights certain floor and wall spaces that are otherwise lost to shadows. The unfamiliarity is hospitable—even inviting, somehow.

I started by making coffee, and I turned on the tube. It was tuned to PBS, and as I listened to java getting tinkled into the pot, I watched a few minutes of yoga. The instructor was on some tropical island and perched on a cooled magma terrace with surf pounding in the background. All of the movements were explained thoughtfully and precisely. There was substantial encouragement, and there was purity there, too, an earnestness, even if it was postcard-ideal, maybe in spite of it.

The yoga affected in me a determination to improve. I looked at the kitchen floor's ceramic tiles in momentary consideration—but I didn't downward-dog it. I'd already accomplished quite a bit just being awake at that hour. Maybe yoga on another day, I thought.

I took the milk out of the fridge and decided to supplement yoga with other exercise. So with the milk jug, I did five reps with the right, five with the left. Biceps, I always start with the vanity muscles. I unscrewed the cap and into the coffee it went. I promised myself five more reps on each arm when I put it back. I went to the front door and got the newspaper.

I intended a sit-down with Mom that day, which was why I was up. I was tired of it all. Maybe on the car ride home from Oshkosh I'd stumbled on a new perspective, a reappraisal of relationships or some such. I didn't know exactly, but what was nagging at me felt new and felt born in the family-relationship hemisphere. Mom wanted to help, but she also needed my help. Maybe we could help each other, especially if I initiated anti-brat patrol, vigilantly on the lookout for infractions carried out by yours truly.

It was my fourth cup of coffee, and I'd made it through to the Culture section when Mom came down. It was just before seven. She looked relaxed and even vibrant.

"Namaste," she said, bowing, her hands pressed together in front of her. She pointed to the television where the credits were rolling on the yoga show. Mom swimmer-shook her arms, which fluttered the sleeves of her robe.

"Considering it," I said.

"I practice three days a week, on the suggestion of you-know-who."

"Tucky."

"Yes, Tucky. I want you to meet him—you know, meet him meet him. Anyway, glad you're up." Mom ruffled my hair with her fingers. Like I said, the house was accepting at that hour.

"Just wanted to get a move on things today, like it's been enough time sitting around."

"I know."

"Plus we're full steam with the mushrooms, but we need to think about the house. At least I do, which means you sort of do too."

"Let me get caffeinated before we plan out my life."

"We're not planning your life, just some kind of plan for the house."

"Plan my life," Mom said again. Then, suddenly Mom muted the TV, grabbed a calendar, a pad of paper, her journal, a box of highlighters, and sat down. "So?" she said, looking up at me.

At first I thought Mom might have been mocking me, but she wasn't. I'd raised myself out of bed that morning with very good intentions, but Mom there with her collection of office tools, carefully arranging her six neon highlighters on the table, was completely unnerving. Sure, I'd initiated it, but I hadn't actually mapped out anything in my head. It was more than I could handle. Just deciding to talk to Mom had taken so much energy already. "I was sort of thinking we'd start with the broad brushstrokes," I said.

"Okay, brush away."

"How can I help?" I said.

"Let's make an outline so that we can brush in the middles."

"Forget brushing," I said.

"How can I help you?" Mom said, sort of trying to get all serious.

"I want to help you," I said.

"The realtor is coming today."

"I can help with that."

"What will you brush?"

"Her hair," I said.

"We'll brush it together."

And we began—both of us, as if choreographed—pulling phantom brushes through the sultry locks of the invisible heads stationed in front of us, which for me marked the end of our discussion.

"Hey," I said, "I think I read something about this." I pointed to the television. Yoga had been replaced with the morning news. On screen there was an egret in its nest, the nest built on a corner of bare iron girders of a would-be structure. Truth was I had no clue about the story. The image on the screen could have been anything. I tossed out a Hail Mary. "This is in Australia," I said. "Development destroying the natural habitat."

Mom embraced my interest. I think she wanted to be supportive, even if she may have been as eager to wash her hands of the master-plan-powwow as I was. She went to the television and turned up the volume, stood next to it with a hand on her hip. "It's in Oklahoma," she said, "but same sad story." She watched intently, and I did the same, one, possibly both of us, feigning genuine interest in that singular tragedy.

It was as if neither of us had planned to do anything else while we were together in the kitchen that morning; however, there's something to be said about healthy interaction as forward movement, and maybe that was headway enough. A baby step, yes, and it wasn't yet eight in the morning.

Janice Sugarbottom, founder of Sugarbottom Real Estate, Inc., arrived at eleven on the nose. "Good morning," Janice said as I opened the front door. "Everett, well, look at you. Wow, how are you? I heard from a little birdie that you were in town. I hope I'm not late. Am I late?"

She was exactly on time, which she knew. I'd seen her creeping around the side of the house and into the backyard five minutes earlier. While she was back there, she checked her wrist every twenty seconds, even as she cranked our garden hose back into its long abandoned reel. And the little birdie comment, I immediately connected the dots—super nachos and/or *Hustler* via Mrs. Baker to so-and-so to Janice Sugarbottom. But that didn't faze me, not like I would have thought. I was more fatalistic about it than anything else.

Maybe I'd matured somehow, though I doubted it.

"Nope, right on time." I said. "How are you, Mrs. Sugarbottom?"

"Janice."

"Janice."

Janice's appearance seemed built on calculated proportions. She was Mom's age, but something about her suggested an availability of youthfulness. She wore light lipstick and light eyeliner, but enough lipstick and enough eyeliner. Her stylist was some kind of genius. Janice's chestnut hair had just the right number of silver streaks; the chestnut said *I'm spry!* and the streaks whispered *Don't think I haven't logged my time in the trenches.* Plus the joke of her name, Sugarbottom—though, I have to admit it did look fairly delicious that morning, as if her navy pantsuit was 60/40 wool/Lycra.

Janice Sugarbottom was something special. True, Janice was one of the mothers I feared, a real champion among the Chatty Kathys in the circuit, but the business aspect of the visit helped curb my fears somewhat. We knew the Sugarbottoms from years back. At certain times in my life, the name Sugarbottom was uttered in our kitchen with some frequency. Mom and Janice were on the PTA together, Janice as Chairwoman, Mom as part-time alternate board secretary. I went to school with Janice's kids, Dennis Sugarbottom, who was a year ahead of me, and Cindy Sugarbottom, who was a grade below me, even though we'd been in kindergarten together.

Janice walked into the foyer and then into the dining room. She made loud clicking noises with her tongue as she peeked behind the art on the walls. She folded over a corner of the foyer rug, inspecting the floor underneath, but the way she peripherally eyed the underside of the rug itself, and I suppose the artwork too, it seemed like she might have been more interested in conducting a quiet, ad hoc appraisal of house contents.

"Well," she said when she'd seen enough of the entryway. Next Janice went to the kitchen, and I followed. "Little Denny is doing fine. He lives in New York with his lawyer fiancée." She swung open the refrigerator and stood looking for a long time, longer than anyone needed just to check that the thing kept cold. She was having trouble shutting the crisper drawer when Mom came into the kitchen.

Mom was styling, white pants, black top with a paisley silk scarf around her neck. "Don't you look fabulous," Janice said. She walked over and gave Mom a hug. "I am so sorry about Douglas." Janice shifted from a hug to her hands on Mom's shoulders, tipped her torso back for proper effect. "Are you okay? Is there anything I can do?"

Mom patted one of Janice's hands. "What would be great is if we can get this house sold quickly and for a lot of money." Ho-ho! Maybe Mom still had a few tricks up her sleeve. It was great to see her in action like that. She looked her best, plus there were zero signs of her patchouli-kooky. It occurred to me then, and felt like one of the most tormenting things about Mom, that apparently she could be normal when she wanted to be, and so why didn't she maintain that normalcy indefinitely?

"That's exactly what we're going to do. Right, Everett?" Janice let go of Mom and came toward me. I was down on the floor trying to slip that damn crisper drawer back into place, and I nearly had it. "You're so lucky to have this guy around to help. My kids are all over the country. I was just telling Everett that Dennis is engaged, lives on the upper west side of Manhattan. And Cindy is with Teach for America in New Mexico."

"That's wonderful, send them our best," Mom said.

"I surely will." Janice spoke loudly, so loud that I could see Mom tense up a little every time Janice said anything.

"So," Mom said, "What's first?"

"Yes. First things first. I need to do an inspection of the

house. But don't worry, I didn't bring my white gloves. There's work to be done, always is. We'll start a list. There's an art to getting houses ready for the market. We'll start that process today. I'll also connect you with my packing crew. They're real life-savers, and work for cheap, but don't ask me for their immigration papers, if you know what I mean. Anyway, after we're done here today, we'll go and see a few condos that I think you're absolutely going to love."

I got the crisper drawer back in and hopped up off the floor. "We're going to look at condos today?" I said.

"You bet we are. As long as everyone is up for it?" Janice looked over at Mom.

"I'm up for it," Mom said. "I'm sure seeing new places will help this whole process along."

"You bet it will. It's exciting. You get to move somewhere new. I'm very excited for you."

Janice exuded enthusiasm, and I noted its effects. Along with that and other lessons from Janice, I figured those things could be appropriated and implemented within the mushroom sales team.

"Ah-ha," Janice said. She picked up a notepad and pen from the pile of planning supplies Mom had gathered earlier and we hadn't used. She handed them to me, saying, "You don't mind playing secretary, do you? I really think best when I can talk with my hands."

With that we were off. *Clean out refrigerator; ditch microwave; re-grout tiles in first-floor half-bath; paint walls in dining room; paint trim in front of house; vacuum footprints off stairs; get kitty pee-pee stains off hardwood in foyer or find nice runner.*

Our family has never owned any animals.

We headed upstairs next, which for Mom and me was clearly the most unsettling area of the house, though I suspected the basement would put up a good fight, too. Upstairs were bedrooms and Dad's office. We started in Dad's office.

"Somebody's been busy in here," Janice said. It didn't look like anybody had been busy in there. If anything, it looked like Dad had been working at his desk all morning and would be back from the bathroom any minute. *Empty office and make it a bedroom; new sheets for bed; buy air mattress.* I started to leave the room, but Janice stopped and opened the closet door. "Nice big closet. That's a great selling point." My heart sank.

We moved onto my room next. The sinking feeling worsened, and my heart tightened. The entire project had become terrifying. "My room is the same as Dad's office, only it's pretty dirty. I think we can just put down the same instructions for there, too. Probably no need to even go in."

Janice laughed. I couldn't tell whether it was a my-room-is-a-sty-too chuckle, or a you-poor-thing-now-be-a-good-boy-and-turn-your-head-and-cough type deal. Either way, she charged into my room without hesitation. It wasn't dirty undies on the floor that worried me, though they were plentiful. It was the undeniable focus of the room, my two oversized duffle bags from China, sitting where they'd sat since I plopped them down the day of my return. Spilling out of them were crumpled clothes, books, a ridiculous number of scrolls (three versions of the four seasons, plus others), kitchen utensils, and plastic bags in many colors. Those bags were tight with randomness; I'd filled each of them full by plowing the accumulation on tabletops and other surfaces with my forearm. All that crap was exploded from the duffle bags. Interestingly, there were clearly defined piles—like bomb craters in the inverse—of nearly identical circumference and density, about six feet each in diameter and overlapping for about three square feet. It was shame and embarrassment in the shape of a Venn diagram.

"I didn't realize you'd just gotten home," Janice said.

"He's had so much to do helping me," Mom said, "that

I've barely left him any time to himself." I smiled my thanks to Mom.

Janice stepped over a corner of explosion to check out the closet, which was in about the same shape I'd left Dad's after ransacking it. "Hmm. Nice closet size in here, too."

I desperately wanted all humans out of my room, but I was also worried about moving on, in particular to Mom's room, to Dad's closet.

"Probably we've seen enough," Mom said.

Remove everything but bed and dresser; fresh sheets for the bed.

Mom's room was next, which was, as always, in pristine shape, save for the altar. Janice eyed that secretary desktop long and hard, and Mom watched her with a catlike twinkle in her pupils that indicated a readiness to maul. Neither of them acknowledged the desk, and rightfully so, but I did fear for Mom, for both of us—the unrelenting wrath of the moms.

Janice poked her head into the bathroom. *Scrub shower doors, maybe replace; fresh towels.*

I began to walk out, felt that if I believed deep down and hard enough that we'd seen enough of closets for one day, that it'd be contagious, but Janice's thoroughness was too far imbedded. Janice opened Dad's closet door.

"Wow," Janice said.

I had my eyes closed, mostly in an effort to exonerate myself, at least for the moment, but when I opened them and looked into the closet, everything was in perfect order. All the ties, suit jackets, shoe horns, wingtips, etc. were again where they ought to have been. I walked over to Mom and put my arm around her shoulder. She put hers around mine, then kissed me on the temple.

Mom was back. I almost felt like crying.

We declined on the trip to see condos that afternoon. Mom said it'd been too ambitious to think we could do both things in one day, on the first day. Janice conceded. "I did clear my afternoon and set up several appointments," Janice said, "but don't think about that another second."

That night I dreamed I was a stowaway on an old schooner. I was hiding in a little nook in the forecastle when the ship hit something—a rock, an iceberg, maybe—and salt water started pouring into my tiny space. The forecastle was filling up fast, but when I tried to get out, the latch I'd entered from was locked from the outside, and when I looked through the keyhole, there were a handful of sailors on the other side laughing at me.

Sometimes it feels like significant points on the timeline of my life are demarcated by a brain-warping dream. The night before I left for China, for instance, I dreamed that I died. In the dream I was a grunt—rucksack and fatigues—roughing it knee-deep in a bog surrounded by a dense rainforest when three dark figures high in the canopy used automatic weapons to make mincemeat of my torso. Gasping in a puddle, I didn't just feel death coming, but I existed for a moment after my death where everything went black. There wasn't just an absence of light, but that space was devoid of all, blank, somehow nonexistent.

Or just after the first time I had sex with a stranger without a condom, I woke up in the morning, still very drunk, to a nightmare where a fist-sized hairy spider had squeezed out of my left nostril and was scampering over and around my body at twice the speed of my reflexes.

Chapter 19

Early afternoon the next day, Janice dropped off the notes I'd taken, typed up and printed on her letterhead, Janice's smiling face and silver-streaked hair in the top left corner of each page. She also gifted me a pair of coveralls. "Here you go," she said, "for the dirty work." They were bright blue, like a European airport baggage handler's.

Janice's not-so-subtle urging aside, I liked the idea of a no-hassle, one-piece uniform. When Janice was gone, I held the coveralls up for closer inspection. They were snazzy but, I thought, too small, and the legs definitely too long—something one of my super-thin Chinese colleagues would have looked good in had any been six foot seven. Yes, maybe an über-thin Vice Principal Pu in the blue coveralls skulking around the tarmac at Dusseldorf International, shirtless in the heat with a cigarette hanging from his mouth.

I kicked off my shoes and pants and stepped into the coveralls. I got my feet through, but when I tried to pull them up, the waist was so small that I couldn't get them past my thighs. The tag said *Grande*. Maybe they were a European cut.

I tossed the coveralls onto the China pile on my floor. Then I went to Dad's office, still in my underwear, to check email.

There was a note from Jeff saying he was back from China with ten kilos of premium, which made me giddy. I picked up the phone and called Dino to find out when we'd make the run up to Oshkosh.

"I know," he said, "But I can't go this week. I've got meetings."

"Xuan Gong?" I said.

"Since you ask, yes."

"And that's why you can't go to Oshkosh?"

"Couldn't you borrow your dad's car? It doesn't really take more than one of us to go up there."

"Maybe. But, hey?"

"Believe me, I've been making contacts all over the place. Get the premium down here and it's sold. Seriously."

Fuck it. "Fine, I'll go. But you'll take over once they're down here, right?"

"Exactly."

The tone of Dino's voice, the ease with which he dismissed the mushroom project, and the Xuan Gong now trumping all—those things somehow congealed in me and took the shape of two giant bells that for a fast few seconds banged against each other where my heart should have been.

It seemed to indicate a potential for major unraveling, but at the same time, there wasn't actually much to unravel. Plus I had faith in Jeff, and some in myself. We could oust Dino if he kept it up. I emailed Jeff and told him I'd shoot up there in two days.

There were three other emails too, all completely unexpected. The first: *Hello Teacher Everett, Do the Macho Man Randy Savage really lives near you? You stop lying bad boy. Welcome back China. Your friend, Winnie the Pooh.*

I typed the following response: *Dear Winnie the Pooh, Yes, of course Macho Man lives near me. We had power shakes for breakfast together this morning, and later tonight he's going to teach me how to DDT on his dog. Yours, Teacher Everett.*

The second email was from Mei and it contained a list of Midwest Xuan Gong meeting times and places. *Please join us for a meditation session, friend.* I doubted she knew it was me, that I was the Everett she'd added to her mailing list, but maybe she did. I filed the email away in my mind and clicked back to the inbox. It was an intriguing idea: Everett at a Xuan Gong meeting.

The third email was from Peter Green. I don't even know how he got my email address. In high school, there'd been a short run where Peter and I connected. We were acquaintances but both got cut from sophomore soccer tryouts the same day, and he gave me a ride home. Later that same week, we both took jobs lifeguarding at the YMCA's indoor pool, and even though we didn't see much of each other outside of work, we passed a lot of hours together in that chlorinated heat, loafing around in our tank tops.

Apparently Peter was back living at home too, and he'd heard from his mother via another mother that I was back in town.

Dude, if you're back in the mix, he wrote, *come meet me up at Paddy's tomorrow night. The band is killer, and it'll be good to catch up. I'll be there by eight.*

I wrote Peter and said I'd be there.

The idea of normal human interaction was magic. Yes, magic, but anxiety about my weight surfaced. I didn't know what clothes to wear. Obviously, not the coveralls. I knew the pants, the jeans I wore every day, but I needed a shirt. Back in the day, Paddy's got a pretty crunchy crowd most nights, and other times it was hardcore yuppie. But what the hell did I know? I hadn't been there in years.

Still in my underwear, I dug through the China pile on my floor for a shirt. I tried on a few, but they were all too tight to even bother with a mirror. Jesus, could I actually have been getting fatter? The idea of further distention was suffocating. Nothing fit, and even my go-to wardrobe, what I'd been wearing since getting home, felt like spandex. I tried my navy XXL *I climbed the Great Wall of China* t-shirt, which I'd never worn before, and the fabric clung to my belly and lifted my man-boobs like a sports bra.

Next I headed to Dad's closet. There was plenty available in there, but Dad never shopped with an excursion to Paddy's in mind. There were a few button-downs that could work. I took a blue plaid one off its hanger and tried it on. It was too big, but workable in a jam. I put it on the bed and tried a khaki version. It was also too big and probably too safari. Or was it too safari? Not bad, but definitely safari.

I was observing myself sideways in the mirror in boxer shorts and the safari shirt—with a handful of extra safari fabric bunched in the back so that the shape of my belly was visible—when I heard a noise. It was Mom. When I turned, she was standing at the threshold knocking on the door frame. I was mortified. Mom smiled at me. Maybe she was remembering something from my childhood. Her smile wasn't sinister. She looked almost nostalgic.

"Nothing fits anymore," I said. "I'm too fat."

Mom came over and rubbed my back. "We can find something in here," she said.

I felt ashamed. "Do you remember Peter Green?" I said. "Guy I used to lifeguard with in high school?" Mom nodded, yes, which I didn't buy, but so what. "He asked me to go see a band tomorrow night at Paddy's." I played casual, but I was bubbling.

"That's wonderful," Mom said. She seemed relieved and possibly as jazzed as I was. "So you need something to wear to the bar." Mom approached Dad's closet with purpose. "Not that shirt you've got on," she said. Her face was deep in hanging fabric.

I didn't take the safari shirt off. Mom didn't need a gift-glimpse of my softness.

"Try this on," Mom said, handing me a collared navy knit shirt with a sailboat embroidered on the breast. I took it and stepped into the bathroom. "Oh, please," Mom said, "You can put it on in front of me."

I didn't respond and stayed in the bathroom, but I didn't shut the door. I offered that to Mom. The scene reminded me of shopping when I was growing up. Mom would make me try on clothes in the aisles as we shopped. "Nobody cares," she'd say. Even at a young age, Mom dismissed my reluctance to bare myself in public, which felt like an attack on my burgeoning masculinity. So I'd relent, stripping to nipples or tighty-whities, for instance, in the ladies' shoes section at T.J.Maxx.

The navy sailboat shirt fit decently enough, but I hardly had it on and Mom was handing me a dozen others to try, literally a dozen, which was exasperating. I've never enjoyed shopping that way, and I tensed up remembering how, on the occasions that Mom afforded me the luxury of a fitting room, she would inevitably search me out by shouting my name at the row of stalls. She'd shout until I could take the embarrassment no longer and I identified myself. Then she'd heave piles of clothing over the top of my door and hang around talking to me loudly until I'd tried on every last garment.

It was of course my fault. I'd asked for help that afternoon, so I couldn't exactly be mad, but in less than two minutes I'd hit my limit. "This shirt is fine," I said, meaning the navy sailboat one I was wearing. It was a size too big, and the lower half was stretched enormous, but I didn't care.

"I'm not sure it fits well," Mom said, and she began piling shirts on my chest, one on top of the other, checking their color. "This one is cute," she said about a bright white linen button down. "Very sharp."

I took the shirts from my chest, headed to Dad's closet and laid them neatly on top of the shoe layer. "Thanks, Mom,"

I said. "I'm all set." Mom looked confused, standing there clutching several layers of shirts to herself. "Thanks again," I said as I left. I went straight to my bedroom, closed the door, and got under my comforter.

I'm not sure why it was such an intolerable moment with Mom, but it was. Mom and I hadn't always operated via expedited transactions like that, like we had since I'd been back.

Maybe with Mom steady on the road back to regular, I was in turn regressing. I considered going back out to apologize, but I had no fuel in me. The tank was empty, and I couldn't even move.

CHAPTER 20

The moment I clicked my eyes open the next morning, I was ready for business. I must've hit my sleep cycle just right, which was an exceptional transaction for me and would have been altogether celebratory except that it felt married to a new itch I had in me, and it itched bad, like an emergency-dirty-spatula-down-the-shirt-collar kind of itch. The Xuan Gong. I wasn't exactly sure why it'd arrived, but there it was.

Maybe while I'd slept, I'd had the opportunity to more fully absorb Dino's behavior from the day before, and that'd refreshed my spite for him, cold shower-style, but I think there was more at work than just that. I rolled myself off the mattress and put on a shirt. I bypassed my morning urination even and went straight to the computer to open up yesterday's email from Mei. My plan was to hit a Gonger meeting and gather some intel.

As I proceeded with these four minutes of activity, I noted methodical competence in myself, which was unfamiliar. It felt like the day's movements since blinking awake had been conceived of, mapped out and signed into action in their entirety during the previous night's sleep, which wasn't a comforting sensation, necessarily, but it wasn't balance-wrecking to recognize, either.

I scanned through the meeting times and locations in Mei's email. First and foremost, I needed a Dino-free environment, so the western suburbs were out of the question, as was everything in the Loop or Chinatown. There was a meeting that day at noon at a giant shopping mall in a northern suburb, *near the food court.* That looked as promising as the others. Why not a little *qigong* exercise at the mall? Plus, if Dino or Mei came crawling out of a dressing room and into the meeting, I could act like my wandering into their meditation room was a wild coincidence—"Excuse me, please, can anyone point me to Yankee Candle?"

I'd been to that mall before, but it'd changed names, and I suppose owners, since I'd last visited, not that anything was different. Same manicured hedges and an obnoxious parking lot, and the music piping through the place wasn't any worse than I remembered. I made my way to the food court and noted the variety of popcorn shops and sunglasses boutiques along the way.

In truth, I wasn't certain what I hoped to gain from the experience. I think mostly I wanted to understand, even if only in the large-scale, global sense of it. Maybe I was more open to the possibilities than I'd like to admit, too, but at the same time, I wasn't exactly seeking, either.

One of the Gongers had taped a handwritten sign near the pretzel kiosk that pointed the way, which was helpful. It was at the end of a hallway, the one with the bathrooms, inconspicuously slipped in next to a janitor's closet.

I peeked inside before I entered—the coast was clear, no familiar faces, so I stepped in. It was a large room, empty of furniture, a carpeted, windowless space, relatively hidden real estate for the mall. I suspected it was used for employee training seminars or something along those lines when not occupied by the Xuan Gong.

There were about forty people gathered, a number that surprised me, but also provided some relief. That many people meant I could attempt some blending in.

A quarter or so of them were Asian, and the rest were mostly white. No one appeared to be under thirty or so, except for me, and other than a woman who looked like she was about four hundred, most others capped off at maybe sixty-five.

They were a friendly bunch—if anything, too friendly. Nearly everyone I passed stuck their arm out for a handshake. I got a "welcome" every five seconds, which was unsteadying. People were spread out and facing the same wall, like in an aerobics class. I made my way through the gauntlet to the back row.

I was very obviously the new guy in a tightly knit group, and people kept looking over and smiling. Those who hadn't had the opportunity to speak it to me mouthed "welcome" across the room, which, again, was kind and all, but I didn't want the attention. Some women in the front of the room were doing stretches, and so that's what I did, too, a few deep knee bends to assert my dedication to craft and practice, i.e. don't hassle me, I'm local.

An Asian man in his late forties came in through the door wearing a loose-fitting black silk number, almost like he was there for karate class, except he had no belt indicating his sparring level.

On his entrance, the entire room seemed to gasp and hold its breath. The teacher took his position at the front of the class. He nonverbally greeted everyone with slow sweeps of his arms across his body. Then, and still without any verbal command, the room transitioned into a kind of tai chi exercise sequence. I mostly watched, which was fine by me, but there was a woman with a buzz cut in the row in front of me who kept turning her body in my direction, putting herself on display, instructing me, smiling between close-eyed moments of meditation. To appease her, in hopes of getting her to stop doing that, I started doing my own thing. I pointed my arm at the ceiling a few times. Next I took to slow-chopping several invisible two-by-fours I imagined floating in front of me.

I sufficiently amused myself in that room as the sands poured through the hourglass. I chopped invisible cinderblocks, a watermelon, even a piñata, but I wouldn't say halving those invisible objects with my slow hand-chops felt like I was engaged in a transcendental experience. And yet, as I observed the activity in that room, I concluded that what was all around me was essentially innocuous.

Plus, I appreciated the way I was able to fake it as a Gonger, my dancing and board-breaking, etc. I thought I put on a convincing face. It reminded me of a musical I was in during high school—not that I had much of a role, forgettable chorus dancer #23 or what have you. Back then I was in the last row too, lip-synching to a hammed-up version of Eddie Murphy's "Party All the Time" with the lyrics changed to reflect our collective aspirations for the Chicago Cubs. "Next year Cubbies win all the time, win all the time, wi-i-in a-ll the ti-ime."

Amazingly, I began to remember some of the choreography from that performance, and so instead of chopping, I started slow-swinging my invisible baseball bat through the air and snagging fly balls at the ivy wall. I even started humming the song too, but just the chorus, over and over, which was all I could remember. The buzz cut lady turned toward me at one point, probably when my humming had too far entered her orb, but I played it off like it was part of my meditation process.

I'll admit that I was near, or might even have crossed over, to the point of enjoying myself—"Party All the Time" can do that to you, if you let it—but I got yanked out of my little happy place and plopped back into reality, which was standing in the back row of a Xuan Gong meeting taking place in the shopping mall food court's auxiliary space. The teacher began to speak.

"We will now begin group meditation. I'd like you to concentrate on your chi energy. Please close your eyes and feel the chi inside you. Relax and breathe. Chi is very powerful, and so I encourage you to let your exploration take its course." He paused for a moment, then said, "Let it happen."

I assumed people would slink down into lotus position, that there might be some fingertip-tapping or whatnot, but something else happened. People's bodies started to slither, others began to shake. Arms jiggled and heads bounced, some in a rhythm and others in unpredictable ways. One guy near the front started doing super-fast squats.

I giggled but held back the avalanche of laughter. I'd never seen anything like it. Closest thing was in college when we experimented with hallucinogens on a camping trip.

"Feel the chi rising," the teacher said. "It wants to come out. You should let it."

Maybe two minutes of this exercise had elapsed, but that was all it took for the whole place to explode its cuckoo. I'm not sure what kind of expression I had on my face, but it was enough for the teacher to check me peripherally every ten seconds. He wasn't admonishing me exactly—I wouldn't say that. He instead looked proud of himself, to be at the helm of this activity—like he wanted me to recognize his authority and defer to it somehow.

It felt like what the teacher did next was for my benefit, to further evidence his powers. "Chi will make you yell," he said. "Chi will make you jump. This is natural, let it happen."

This, amazingly, bumped the group up even another notch. We were a bus that'd been teetering on the edge of a cliff, and that was the nudge that sent us sailing off into oblivion. It was like a poltergeist, people hopping around, waving their arms, shouting and singing in tongues. It was too much for me, even as a spectator. "Whoa," I said.

I quickly made my way around the edge of the room toward the door. I looked over at the teacher one last time before I left.

He was watching me, smiling. I don't think he wanted me to stay, not exactly, it was more like he thought I'd be back, which was maddening, even if I'd put those words in his mouth. I wouldn't be back. I had an impulse to make that crystal clear to everyone in earshot, but I didn't. I instead swung open the door and hightailed it to the food court.

Chapter 21

Me in the blue sailboat shirt strolled into Paddy's at 8:16 PM. I was casually late by design, even though I'd sat in the Paddy's parking lot in order to achieve it. Walking inside, Paddy's was smaller than I remembered, and much skuzzier, but, that said, Paddy's was never famous for its décor, which was someone's approximation of Medieval revival, if I had to guess. So, no, it wasn't a particularly glamorous spot. Paddy's survived over the years because the staff never nitpicked about serving minors, a point greatly appreciated by the student bodies of several local high schools.

There was a handful of customers sitting at the bar, but I didn't see Peter. The hard rock cover band was tuning up in the back, so I headed to the end of the bar, near the band, where I could survey the entire place. I ordered a beer, then watched a very heavy, very short goth chick come out of the bathroom. Maybe five foot two, early twenties, she had shoulder-length black hair, black lipstick, black nail polish, and plug earrings the size of quarters in her droopy lobes. She wore platform flip-flops, a black skirt, and a striped tank top that revealed a lot of cleavage.

Not really my type, but there was something striking and beautiful about her exactly as she was. Her face was perfect, and maybe that was it, but it seemed like something more. I tried but couldn't imagine her any other way—blonde, twenty pounds lighter, without the discs in her ears. It felt like anything at all different on her would have been ruinous, even covering up her dainty little toes, which was ridiculous, but that was the kind of impression she made on me. She just was right—maybe the kind of beautiful that can't be wrong.

She came out of the bathroom and walked directly toward me. I braced myself. She intimidated me, so confident and out there. On some uncontrollable plane in my mind, I thought her weight should have bothered me, even though it didn't. Super-sizing usually flaws perfection, at least it does on me, which is to say, my extra weight hasn't aided my general cause any. For instance, this woman would surely have been more interested in a slenderer version of what I offered.

The girl leaned in next to me, picked up a bottle of beer there to my left, and took a swig, but she didn't make eye contact with me. I sideways-glanced and saw a birth-control patch stuck to her upper right arm. It had center-stage placement and was bold like a prison tattoo. She took more beer, and, as the band started into its first song, she slipped out of her flip-flops and kicked them practically underneath my barstool, which felt intimate. She shutter-stepped onto the dance floor, and alone out there, began moving seductively with her eyes closed. She quickly found her groove, free-styling on ten square feet of dance floor.

I wondered if we were compatible, or even if we might complement one another. She started to sweat. I thought maybe she was dancing for me. I looked down at her flip-flops. Maybe I wasn't supposed to safeguard them. Maybe they were instead an invitation: by orienting my flip-flops three feet directly below your buttocks, I hereby cordially request your company on the dance floor for a boogie-down.

I couldn't take my eyes off the girl; nobody in the bar could. It also had to do with that birth-control patch, which wasn't so much attractive or a turn-on as it was a curiosity. It produced a mix of pity and intrigue, and possibly some reflection. What was she saying with that thing? What wasn't she saying with that thing?

I wondered if I presented the world with an equivalent of that birth-control patch.

I thought of my drug-induced afternoon at Club Hawaii-Hawaii in Pingnan, when I snorted white stuff off a teenager's pinky and idiot-danced on top of a giant woofer. A display like mine probably dosed introspection to some onlookers. If it had, I hoped it inspired self-assurance and a pleasure in knowing they were not me.

The goth chick continued to dance, and during the third song, a young, very slim dude with heavily gelled hair—in a gray suit, his yellow tie loosened just so—snuck up behind the girl and wrapped his arms around her at the neck. She jumped in surprise, then turned toward the guy, lit up, and fell into him adoringly. They kissed on the mouth. And they grooved, just the two of them on the dance floor. It was a warm moment, which made everyone in the bar either doe-eyed or thirsty. Me, lonelier. I looked to the band for distraction, but they were in on it too. I watched the guitarist, a dude in cut-off jean shorts, raise his eyebrows to the drummer and point to the dancing couple with his chin. The drummer shook his head, which wiggled his pony tail, and he wagged his long tongue, Kiss-style, which was a little over the top, but anyway.

I fought it, but got a little gooey, even sort of piney. I don't witness love like that very often. It was beautiful and sacred, even if the gelled-hair guy actually looked like an a-hole. I scanned the bar again and got this creepy feeling like I was the only one in there who didn't know love, which was maybe ridiculous, but hey. I felt singled out, and I quietly awarded myself the medal of most alone, which paired nicely with my blue ribbon for whiniest.

I don't know about love. Mom was the sole being on the planet who'd ever articulated love for me, which I contemplated briefly. Then I gifted myself another trophy, this one for the most pathetic admission of the evening.

Maybe I'd felt love. I tried to think of a time of even one or two brief volleys at the ping-pong table of love, but nothing came to mind. There was always the problem of reciprocation—requisite and completely out of my hands. Yes, a caveat that ended my musing session flatly. I drained my beer.

The more time that passed without Peter showing up, the easier it got to convince myself that I'd never expected anything different. It was my fault. I was the one who'd ditched everything by leaving two years earlier, and that gave my friendlessness a kind of karmic justness.

I stayed at Paddy's until the set break, about an hour, then headed home. Peter never materialized, which was disappointing, yes, but I as I drove home, I accepted it as punishment, and I attempted, with mild success, to occupy my mind with other things.

I tried a little empathy on for size. Good for them, I thought, meaning the gel guy and birth-control-patch girl. At least someone would be getting some that night. I hoped they'd screw through the wee hours. That was my tiny gesture, a wish for the greater good of the planet.

Chapter 22

The next morning I left for Oshkosh at six, which was early enough that I had almost no chance of encountering Mom. I wasn't interested in discussing Paddy's, and I didn't feel like lying, either. Everything attached to the Paddy's excursion was embarrassing. I left a note on the kitchen table telling Mom where I went and tiptoed out to the car.

Janice Sugarbottom's workers were coming to the house for the first time later that day. A better version of me would have stuck around, but I didn't. Driving north, I felt low. I attempted brainlessness in an effort to dodge the guilt, but the guilt kept creeping in like fast-growing, invasive ivy throughout my body. I promised myself I'd call Mom from Oshkosh to see how everything was going, and to apologize. It was a long ride.

Had anyone walked into Jeff's apartment as we sliced open slightly-imperfect plush doggy dolls and extracted plastic baggies of mushrooms from their insides, they would have thought we were up to much worse than we actually were. With each of the doggy dolls, Jeff's grandmother had broken a seam, tugged out the batting, replaced it with premium, and sewed them back to their slightly imperfect states.

"We should smuggle drugs," Jeff said.

I'd had the same thought. It was too easy. "What did your grandmother think?"

"She giggled the whole time, like it was so funny that we

couldn't just bring them over. She described secret agents sniffing the dogs, then mushrooms pouring out of stuffed animals like doggy-doo."

"Has your grandmother ever been here?"

"No, never. She's almost eighty, so it's hard now, you know. Dad wants her to move here, but, you know, she's his mom. Plus she has heart disease. We see her as much as we can, take turns, at least one of us every month."

"What about other family?"

"They're mostly super-shady, and a lot went south for work. She's got friends, and they help, but I'm not sure what we're going to do once she starts to go downhill. That's what my dad says. But she's strong. She sewed up these stupid dogs."

We emptied the bags of mushrooms onto the table. At one point, after I went to the bathroom, when I reentered the living room, the pungent smell of the mushroom really hit me: earthy, spicy, robust.

Some of the mushrooms were drier than others, so we next separated the dried from the semi-dried. "Must've picked these just before you left," I said.

"They didn't think I was serious, I mean about buying, so when I actually, you know, put money in their hands, I think some of them even cleared out their own kitchens."

"What'd you pay?"

"Hundred bucks, which is, like, way more than enough, even split a lot of ways. It's poor there, peasants and stuff. It's the pine woods, kind of like the UP, you know, Michigan, in that part of China."

We divvied the mushrooms into small piles. It reminded me of college when I occasionally helped my freshman roommate break up one-pound bricks of rag weed. We weren't nearly as efficient in college—bong rips every ten minutes lent little to our productivity.

Our last step was weighing out the mushrooms that were dry enough into eight-ounce portions and putting them into 12-inch-square plastic bags that we sealed clean with the blade of a cleaver we heated by candle flame.

When we'd finished bagging the mushrooms that were ready for sale, there were fifty-three, and I put them in the trunk of my car. There was another equally large portion of mushrooms that would continue drying. Jeff took a large screen out of his window, and with the mushrooms scattered on it, balanced it on two exposed rafters in his bedroom.

Chapter 23

Dino wrote Jeff, Ron, and me an email three days after Jeff and I unpacked the first shipment.

> *Hi guys,*
>
> *It occurs to me that we're going to need more mushrooms in a hurry. I've gone ahead and used my frequent-flyer miles to book a ticket for this Friday. It's a red-eye, but that I was able to get a ticket with miles is a small miracle.*
>
> *Jeff, can you please alert your family that I'll be heading that way? I'm going to spend a few days in Beijing, a stipulation of my ticket, and then I'll be off to Yunan on November 4th. I guess I'll be needing some help getting there, too. Is there a phone number? Some directions, maybe?*
>
> *Glad the business is moving along, gents.*
>
> *Here's to the future,*
>
> *Dino*

Three minutes later Jeff wrote us all back:

> *Hi Dino, Hi Everett,*
>
> *Okay, Dino, since you've already got your ticket, we should go forward with the plan, but we still have all of the mushrooms from before. Have we made any sales? I'm going to arrange for my cousin (real cousin, ha-ha) to meet you where the bus lets off in the middle of town (there is no bus stop, just where the bus stops), and there's only two buses a day, no problem. Full directions, names and phone numbers of my grandmother, friends and relatives are in*

the attachment.

I'll call my relatives and tell them to get hunting. We're going to have a lot of mushrooms!

Cheers,

Jeff

And one to just me:

Everett,

It's a little strange that he already wants to go and get more. Have we sold any? I guess it's not a big deal, because he's using his frequent-flyer miles, but still. It's not like plush puppy dogs grow on trees! (ha-ha)

Cheers,

Jeff

To which I replied:

Jeff,

Don't worry too much about Dino. He gets a little overanxious when it comes to things like this. At least he's not spending our money to do it, at least not yet. I say we let him go ahead and get more mushrooms, and we'll reassess once we've sold some of these things.

Talk to you soon,

Everett

And this:

Dino,

What the hell? You don't think this is something worth discussing? We don't need more mushrooms. We need to sell the mushrooms we have.

Sold any?

Got this in return:

Everett, relax. Everything is on track. Lots of irons in the fire! We need more product. Why waste all our time trying to sell what we don't have?

Dino

Then, before I had a chance to reply, I got this:

Also, Everett, I'm a little leery of showing up there without an official invitation. Probably mushroom smuggling isn't a good one for the customs forms. Could you write to Vice Principal Pu and see if he'd extend me an invitation from Pingnan? I'm not going down south, but maybe I could visit a school in Beijing or something. I'd ask myself, but you know as well as I do that he liked you more. What do you think?

Thanks,

Dino

True, V. P. Pu and Dino never really hit it off, but I loathed using what currency I had with V. P. Pu. I did, however, have faith in the premium, and V. P. Pu's stock would rise if he managed to arrange a school visit for Dino in Beijing. Probably it'd fly. I copied Dino on the email.

Dear Vice Principal Pu,

My warmest wishes to you, your school, and your family. I trust Pingnan Middle School had a wonderful National Day celebration last month? I missed being there this year after being part of such impressive displays the last two years. Please be sure to extend my warmest wishes to Principal Xi and everyone at Pingnan Middle School. I hold them all very dear to me.

One of the reasons I am writing today is that my fellow teacher Dino is fortunate enough to be returning to China in a few weeks. I am very jealous. He won't be traveling to the south, unfortunately, but he will be in Beijing. Although I haven't yet discussed this with Dino, I thought I might see if you had any colleagues in Beijing who might be interested in having an American visitor at their school? I've been working on developing some great lesson plans with Dino since getting home, and I'm sure he would make quite an impression in an English Corner discussion, for example, or in an advanced English class, perhaps simply to answer questions about his wonderful experiences at Pingnan Middle School.

Do you think this is something you'd like to do? If so, please let me know as soon as possible so that I might help facilitate the meeting.

Again, my warmest wishes to you. And thank you again for making my stay at Pingnan Middle School so wonderful.

All very best wishes,

Everett

The next day I got a reply from Vice Principal Pu:

Dear Everett,

Thank you for your kindly words about Pingnan Middle School. The students of Pingnan Middle School must miss you very much.

Dino can be welcomed at Dingpan Middle School in Beijing on November 14. A car will waiting for him at his hotel at 7 o'clock thirty. Which is the hotel?

Also, when will you come back to China?

Regards,

Vice Principal Pu

I forwarded to Dino with a line at the top:

which is the hotel?

Dino back:

Thanks, pal, that really makes life easy. I'll be at the Xin Chi Guan Er at the West Railroad Station.

From Vice Principal Pu:

Dear Everett,

Yes, but such a hotel? Perhaps he will relocate once he has seen those shabby conditions.

You didn't answer when will you come to China?

Regards,
Vice Principal Pu
Final email:
Dear Vice Principal Pu,

Thank you for your help. You are indeed a powerful and well-connected man. That is something I have long admired about you.

As for when I will come to China, just as soon as I can find the time. As you can imagine, life in the United States is very crazy and there is not often time to do what one would like. But I love China, and I loved being a teacher at Pingnan Middle School. I very much look forward to returning to China as soon as I can.

Sincerely,
Everett

Chapter 24

Janice Sugarbottom came over for another walk through of the house. Mom and I trailed her, and I again had secretarial duties. Janice's crew had been busy, and we were making headway. Productivity: large areas packed into boxes and scoured; mounds of trash bags built in corners and rebuilt in the alley; a covert asbestos removal mission in the basement.

"Fluffer. Everett, write down fluffer, whole house," Janice said.

Fluffer, whole house.

"What's a fluffer?" Mom said.

"It's someone with a great eye for decorating who can come in and work magic using what's already here."

"I see."

"That's a good thing, dear. That means we're getting close. Calling in the fluffers is a very good stage to be at. We're not quite there, but we're close. Those girls, I have a few girls I use, they're so good at it that they'll make you wish you weren't moving. But not really."

Suddenly, Janice must've caught one of her crew doing something unsugarbottomly on the other side of the room. She muttered under her breath, and as if a circuit breaker flipped, Janice turned from us and wildly goose-stepped at the now wide-eyed worker. I cringed in collective fear with the worker, but also in reaction to the way she moved, which made her backside much less delicious-looking.

I asked Mom if she knew where the term *fluffer* came from. She laughed and said, "I'm not a total prude."

Yes, Mom still had some juice in her.

As for the business, things had sort of been on hold while Dino was in China, which is to say, the mushrooms I'd bagged with Jeff remained undisturbed in the trunk of the DeVille. If pressed, I could have argued it was in quiet protest, that I didn't think it was fair for me to take sole responsibility for sales, but the truth was I didn't have any idea where to start. I feared placing even a fingertip on the premium.

So I did very little, on any front, other than a few odd jobs for Mom, until I heard from one of the business partners. I got word from Dino first. He called me three days after he got back from China. I could tell by the sound of his voice that something was wrong. "Did you get the mushrooms? What happened?" I said.

"I got the mushrooms. No problem. Beautiful part of the country. I could live there."

"What's going on?" But I knew as soon as I said it.

"My dad's not well."

"Shit," I said.

"Doctors say any day now. My mom didn't tell me when I was on my trip. I called them once, from Beijing, but not after that. I didn't even know."

"So forget the Xuan Gong and spend some time with him," I said, and I immediately wished I hadn't, even if it was true. I didn't have to face the last moments with Dad, and Dino's situation filled me with a new gratitude for that, and a new sadness, among other things.

"Whatever," Dino said. "He doesn't even know who I am."

I didn't expect to hear something so cold blooded, but that was the reality of the situation. "Sorry," I said.

"Maybe you could come and see him?" Dino said. "And we can unload the puppies."

The proposition caught me off guard. In part it felt like he was capitalizing on the moment, which rubbed me the wrong way. If I'd had more time, I might have produced an excuse, but I also knew firsthand the humiliation of aloneness. It didn't need to be me that visited. He just needed someone, and there was no one else to ask, not really. "Sure," I said. "Tonight?"

"Tonight would be great," he said. "Come by around seven?"

After I hung up the phone, I remembered that I did have an excuse not to go. I promised Mom that I would mop and paint the crawlspace behind the water heater and boiler that night, a horrible Janice-assignment I'd put off since our first walk through. Visiting a dying man seemed righteous reason enough to put it off for another day, though, or to try and wrangle one of Janice's workers to the job. I'd already muscled through *clean and paint under the basement stairs,* which was a similar area to the crawlspace. Both were untouched since construction of the house eighty years earlier.

It wasn't just about avoiding the work. True, there was no archaeological thrill to be found in those spaces, no pottery or hand tools to uncover. But more, something in those confines made my heart pound like crazy. The rot there undermined afterlife. They were like catacombs where an absence of life decayed somehow, a pure nothingness in its hereafter, quiet in the darkness. A forgotten resting place turned aggressively inhospitable, where one whisk of the broom turned the air dank and poisonous with long-undisturbed plague bacteria.

Chapter 25

The first and only time I met Dino's parents was in China. When they arrived, I was two months in, and Dino had eight months under his belt.

Dino's dad was in a wheelchair at that point, but if you'd asked me then how long he still had, I would have said a lifetime. It was difficult to think of him in China and to now imagine him at death's door. The proposition promised to deliver an ache, with more on the way. I could practically feel that ache approaching; its inevitability was clear—that heart-thump moved as surely toward me as a dump truck sinking to the ocean floor.

The China trip was the last time Dino's dad got on an airplane. It was also the last time he left Cook County. In some ways it was the beginning of the end for Dino's dad. I doubt he ever recovered from the stress of it because of the sad way the sick process the wear of travel. Stresses advance into their bodies through holes the size of hula hoops. They collect and fester there waiting to be forced out of the system, except that in the sick they exit through chutes the size of drinking straws.

Dino's parents stayed across the border in Hong Kong most of their trip. At least there, handicapped accessibility seemed to have entered the general consciousness. Almost nothing in mainland China accommodated a wheelchair, and the few wheelchairs I saw looked homemade, converted from a bicycle and a small wagon, with crank-arms at chest level driving the front wheel. Those vehicles were efficient enough to achieve slow progress among the cars and motorcycles on Pingnan's busy streets.

Principal Xi, a man obsessed with the quantifiable, was proud to host Dino's parents on campus—add two additional American guests to the tally, please—so he charged his best man, Vice Principal Pu, to ensure a smooth visit.

V. P. Pu arranged for the school's driver to take Dino and me into Hong Kong early in the morning to retrieve Dino's parents. His mom and dad were waiting in front of the hotel when we arrived, and within two minutes, the direness of their situation was obvious. Just getting his dad into the van was a procedure. Dino bent down and put his dad's arms around his neck. Next he slid his own hands around his dad's torso. Dino gently lifted his dad into the front seat of the van and positioned his legs beneath him.

They had some trouble with the seatbelt. The driver kept insisting that seatbelts weren't necessary, but Dino was patient and tugged the belt across his dad's chest a quarter of an inch at a time until it clicked.

There was a closeness between Dino and his dad that my dad and I never achieved. At that time, while Dino's family and I hightailed it from Hong Kong to Pingnan, my dad's cancer hadn't yet shown itself. Sitting in that van, I couldn't imagine going through the same motions with my dad. I never had to, of course, because I never got home to see him while he was sick, but I remember wondering if my dad would have had the same courage if he'd been in a wheelchair, and if I would have had the same resolve as Dino. I didn't know, but I doubted it, which is unfortunate.

We arrived at Pingnan at lunchtime, and several hundred students, all in their navy blue pants and white shirt uniforms, were gathered near the main gate waiting for us, as was a thirty foot red banner: *Welcome Pingnan Middle School to Dino Mom and Dad.*

"Oh, my," Dino's mom said. The students gathered around the van. They waved and peeked through the windows at us like we were bona fide rock stars. Dino's mom was ear to ear, we all were, but it occurred to me that we still had to get Dino's dad out of the van and into his wheelchair.

I was nervous for them. Our campus had gawkers. The school gawked regularly—the whole town too, if not everyone I encountered in China. It seemed entirely acceptable to stare at something while trying to understand it. Or to stare at it if it was amusing, or gross, or different, etc. In fact, I never encountered a situation when it wasn't okay to gawk. At times, practically everything I did felt like a spectacle. *Ah, good for you. You noticed my pale skin. Can you believe how pasty I am? Look a little closer and you'll see that sweat has completely soaked my shirt. I know, right? What's up with that? Now look down, down, take it in. Ha! I'm soaked through my slacks, too! Amazing! Now check out what's in my hand. It's a bag of groceries. And, yes, that is a bottle of Coca-Cola in there. Typical, right? I probably brush my teeth with that stuff! But seriously, my groceries, you might be interested in knowing that I have some poultry inside with the Coke. I selected, purchased, and had killed that chicken all by myself at the market down the street. You missed it? Too bad. Now, that was something you don't see everyday.*

So, a young white man carrying a grown white man down from a van and plopping him into a wheeled chair in the middle of Pingnan was a potential regional headline, and the students didn't disappoint. They were visibly shocked and didn't hide it, but what struck me was Dino's calmness, and how his parents took their cues from Dino. Dino helped his dad out of one seat and into the other, as simple as that, and with the same care and patience that'd impressed me outside the hotel in Hong Kong.

There at the front gate, students gifted Dino's family everything from greeting cards and drawings to used DVDs and tiny plastic figurines. I stepped out from the spotlight to watch from a distance. Only then did I hear John Denver's "Thank God I'm a Country Boy" playing over the school-wide PA system, another subtle gesture from V. P. Pu.

Students tugged my shirtsleeves and asked about the wheelchair. They didn't seem afraid, just curious. That also impressed me, but I wasn't comfortable giving any response. I had no idea what to say, so I just kept repeating, "It's okay, it's okay." And as I watched student after student take pictures with Dino's family, I wondered what it might be like to have to explain an illness to strangers for a quarter of a lifetime.

John Denver clicked off mid-song, and V. P. Pu came on over the loudspeaker. "Students," he said, "line up to sing the school song now."

Our massive entourage slowly made our way across the main courtyard to the six story classroom building, which was flanked by the cafeteria on one side and the teachers' dorm where Dino and I lived on the other. Vice Principal Pu hurried toward us from the administration building. When he arrived, breathless, the students got quiet and fell into line. They were often lovely, obedient students, and they were especially so that day. V. P. Pu shook hands with Dino's parents. Next he took a pen out of his breast pocket, to use as a baton, and conducted the school song. Even the jocks sang.

Next, Dino led his parents into one of the classrooms for a more intimate encounter with some of the kids. Students at Pingnan Middle School were divided into classes first by grade level and then by rank, rank determined by test scores alone, so that the smartest students were in class one, second brightest in class two, and so on. Vice Principal Pu insisted that Dino and his parents meet with the highest grade of class one, which made some sense because of their English proficiency, except that class one met on the top floor of the walkup building. So the lowest class, class eight, the athletes and flunkies, got ousted from their ground floor room for the visit. They weren't even allowed to look in through the windows.

I was jealous but also happy for Dino. I hung around outside the classroom to listen. Simultaneously, Vice Principal Pu—still reeling with pride and enthusiasm, and trying so hard to create the perfect environment for his guests—put the John Denver album back on the PA system.

"This is my mother, Leonora, and this is my father, Angelo," Dino began. "Those are Italian names, Italian, I-tal-ian. Like Dino is I-tal-ian."

"Do you know where Italy is?" Dino's dad said.

Dino said, "Europe. Eu-rope. But we live in America now, in Chicago. *Zhi jia ge.* Chi-ca-go."

The students watched in quiet amazement.

"You can see that my father is in a wheelchair. A wheelchair. A chair that you sit in, and a wheel like on a bicycle.

"He has something called Parkinson's Disease. Do you know what that is?

"It's a disease when the body doesn't have enough dopamine. Dopamine helps the brain talk to the body. Dopamine. *Duo ba an.* Parkinson's. *Ba jin sen shi zheng.* Do you know this?"

"Ahhh," exhaled the students.

"You can see that he is okay. I am very happy to see my parents. I like to hug them. See?"

I left Dino and his parents for their moment with the students and headed back to our apartment to try and clean up a bit. I was glad Vice Principal Pu was still cranking John Denver as I dragged a sponge across the surfaces of our kitchen.

That night we all went out to dinner with the high-ranking, non-English speaking school administrators, which was the highest honor the school could bestow on a guest, even if everyone diverted back to their native tongues after two minutes of failed communication. We ate at the swanky restaurant across the street from the school's front gate.

I'd never been inside before, but I'd eyed that restaurant since day one. I often walked out of my way so that I could pass by its zoo out front, one of the most expansive and exotic in Pingnan. It was good marketing, that street-side assortment of culinary offerings—ducks, snakes, lizards, peacocks, etc. I once tossed a piece of gum at the nose of an alligator in a cage there, to see if it was actually alive, and it hissed at me.

After dinner I didn't return to Hong Kong with Dino and his parents. I said my goodbyes, but I didn't go to bed. I wasn't as tired as my fake yawns indicated. Instead I flagged down a motorcycle taxi and negotiated for a twenty-minute ride. It didn't really matter where we went. "Away from the lights, and home," I said.

It'd rained during dinner, so it was unusually cool that night as we set out on the motorcycle. Cool and high humidity, yes, but what struck me most was how increasingly thick the air got as we rode. It was dense with nutrients, with growth, life, decay and compost. I breathed it all in. And as my driver and I zipped past the periphery of new construction and into the darkness, I remember feeling emotionally light, and unfamiliarly carefree. I wasn't processing, and I had no anxiety. I just was, and that was good. Happy, too, I suppose, but it was more than that.

CHAPTER 26

Dino's house was west of the city. I'd never been there before, but Dino said I couldn't miss it, that there was a giant Italian flag above the garage.

The house was very much in an enclave there. The driveway opened to a cul-de-sac at the end of a one-block, tree-shaded street. That small street was only accessible via a busy county highway that was for miles without greenery, lined on both sides with parking lots and early-era strip malls. Chairman Mao would have been proud of the nature conquered there.

Dino's mom answered the door. She hugged me, and stepping inside, I saw Dino's dad on the other side of the room in front of the television. His torso was strapped upright to his wheelchair, and his head was slumped to the left, earlobe to clavicle.

"Everett's here," Dino's mom said. "He's come to see you."

I walked over and put my arm around Dino's dad. I rubbed his shoulders and back. His bones were hard and sharp on my fingers, and it smelled like he'd gone to the bathroom. I felt myself frowning.

"You've got a wonderful son," I told him. "He was a great roommate in China, and he's a terrific business partner. That son of yours is really aces," I said, *aces* sounding wholly contrived as it came out my mouth. I'd never once used aces like that.

There was no visible response from Dino's dad. Dino's mom told me to sit down while she made coffee.

"Is Dino here?" I said.

"He rushed off last minute to a meeting, something about those mushrooms, I think." She pointed to a garbage bag full of premium next to the front door.

Dino was at some Xuan Gong crap, no question about it. That made me nauseous, plus the way everything in the room was hitting all of my senses. The excursion was already exhausting.

"He said he'd be right back, so probably any minute."

Dino's mom put a cup of coffee, a dish of sugar and some milk in front of me, then walked over to the television. She changed the channel to a reality show featuring teen models in bikinis. They were carving a dugout canoe in a jungle. "You don't mind, do you? It's trash, but he's hooked," she said, pointing her thumb at her husband.

Dino's dad still hadn't moved, at least not that I'd seen. He may or may not have been watching that tele-junk. It didn't matter. Anything to keep the routines intact, I supposed.

Feeling clueless on protocol, I sat quietly with my coffee and watched the bikini girls slap at mosquitoes and slowly scrape the hull from a centuries-old hardwood tree trunk.

I thought of the last time I saw my dad, when he and Mom brought me to the airport on my way to China. Conversation was casual in the car. Mom was anxious, and Dad used the ride as a last minute opportunity to offer advice. "A man wearing a necktie demands respect," I remember him saying, in particular because when he said it, he twisted away from the steering wheel to point at the backseat, where I sat in a t-shirt.

I'm not sure what I would have said to Dad if I'd known it was our final goodbye. Standing curbside at the airport with my luggage ready to roll, Mom hugged and kissed me, and even cried a little, which almost had me in tears, but not quite. Dad wasn't as emotional, but he did have a gift. Dad reached into a plastic bag and produced a brown fedora with a peacock feather in its band. It was an odd present, especially since no one in our house ever wore hats. Even stranger, Dad placed it on my head, gently, which felt intimate, even if my shoulders collapsed in humiliation the moment Dad's fingers dropped the thing loose. I had no idea what seed could have planted the fedora idea in Dad. I didn't even know how to interpret it. "Business casual," he said. That made Dad smile, looking at me with his gift on my head. Maybe Dad was proud, like with that hat I was finally an adult—a fedora marking my passage to adulthood.

The very last with Dad was a firm handshake. "Good luck, Everett," he said. "It'll be an adventure."

I turned around, and heading into the airport, I was focused on only one thing, how long before I could remove the hat. Other than that, I don't remember what I felt walking away. Probably it was a mixture of relief and sadness, and disappointment somehow.

Dino didn't return home before I left his parents that night, which was at the end of the TV show (incidentally, the ladies didn't finish the canoe—no prizes awarded). I said goodbyes, heaved the bag of premium over my shoulder, Santa-style, and went out to the car.

I turned the key in the ignition and leaned back against the headrest, closed my eyes. I listened to the motor and found myself imagining each piston and connecting rod as they bounced furiously in their cylinders. I heard its chorus and listened more closely, concentrating to a point where I felt I was confidently identifying single spark-plug bursts. Then, for no particular reason, I found myself struggling to remember what I'd just said to Dino's dad, what I said as I left. I couldn't remember. They were probably last words, and already I'd forgotten. I tried to listen to the engine again, but it sounded vague, was less interesting. I turned on the radio.

Whatever parting words I offered Dino's dad, they were, I'm sure, unremarkable.

CHAPTER 27

Dino's dad died three days later. Jeff came down from Oshkosh for the funeral service and sat with Mom and me near the back of the church. To our right was a large stained-glass window, an abstract piece constructed of parallelograms of different shades of red, yellow, and blue. I studied the window. Constant wind outside bent and shook the trees that separated the glass from the bright sun, giving motion to its colors and texture. Shapes and shadows flickered, then vanished on the shiny canvas like it was burning.

The church was nearly full—all praise the dutiful Catholics. From what I could tell, Dino was sturdy throughout the process, maintained an elbow for his mom to clutch, though I, at least, could tell by his facial expressions, even from the back of the church, how far he'd already removed himself, that his eyes gestured little more than mild, surface gratitude to those around him.

A cousin of Dino's gave the eulogy, which was mostly devoid of substance. Lots of *Praise be the Lord, Save our souls*, etc. Dino should have given the eulogy, but I didn't give the eulogy at my dad's service either, so who was I to criticize.

Dad was buried in a family plot outside Jackson, Tennessee. His service had been held outdoors on the cemetery's dew-wet grass. It was a clear September morning, picturesque even, except that throughout the service there were buzz saws ripping in the distance, and a mulching, chomping machine transitioning something substantial into a mound of wood chips and tanbark.

There was no wake, no open casket, just Mom, me, a half dozen blood relatives—none of whom I ever knew existed—a gravedigger, and a priest. If we'd had the service in Chicago, maybe parishioners from our church would have shown up. But our small version was simple, which I liked, and I wasn't embarrassed by its size, even if I maybe should have been.

I didn't know much about that small town in Tennessee, little more than its geographic coordinates, but Dad returning to his birthplace somehow felt appropriate, buried there with his family.

Sitting at Dino's dad's funeral, watching the stained glass that looked like it was on fire, I understood something new about my dad, that he'd pulled off a grand illusion: he vanished his Tennessee childhood. A lot of energy must have gone into burying that part of his history, but I didn't know why he did it. I didn't know if it was shame or something more. I even once heard Dad tell a stranger at a wedding that he was born in Denver. That illusion must have been a horrible vulnerability. I wondered if it woke him up at night.

For me, Dad's past was unspoken, and thus nonexistent. I didn't speculate about it much, and what questions I did have, I understood them to be off limits. Growing up I simply accepted that I had one set of grandparents, Mom's side. I never met Dad's parents. Maybe once Dad told me his dad was a tire salesman, but I may have invented that. Dad's dad died before I was born, and I have no memory of Dad's mom, though there's photographic evidence we crossed paths when I was a baby. Dad was an only child, like me, like Mom, so no aunts, no uncles or cousins.

The relatives at Dad's funeral were decent, if only because they were generous enough to attend. I regretted not making more of an effort to connect with them. We barely got past handshakes, which was a mistake. I hope I can correct that in the future. Maybe one day there'll be a funeral where I can at least repay the favor.

Probably my attitude was shaped by Dad, gross hubris passed on down the line like hemophilia or diabetes. But in fact, our relatives didn't wear straw hats or holey overalls. They didn't camp out in the parking lot either, tuning banjos and long-sipping on coffee cans of moonshine. But even if they had.

There was one undeniable difference between them and me, I discovered, and that was the way we spoke. My relatives' accents were batter-thick. Before then I'd never heard anything like it, at least not up close. It was startling, the drawl and its pacing, the idiosyncrasies, etc. And more than anything, hearing it gave me an appreciation for the decimation of Dad's version. Dad's speech didn't have even traces of drawl. If anything, there were certain words he pronounced strangely, like tarp, orchestra, snowball, and wiener, plus a few others I can't remember. I used to keep a list in my mind that I'd add to whenever a new word came out of Dad funny, but I forgot most of that list because I feared writing it down might allow for its discovery. Dad didn't pronounce those words Southern-style or Midwest-style, just they came out of his mouth upside down and sideways somehow.

I was self-conscious about my weight at Dad's funeral, even though I was surrounded by strangers. None of my suit buttons buttoned, and I had to super-suck just to fit the last belt hole. That may have contributed to my diffidence.

I also remember being sad, but I didn't cry much, which also made me standoffish. Maybe if I'd been surrounded by sobbing and wailing it would have been different. I'd say I negotiated most of Dad's funeral with significant detachment, but that changed at a point.

The gravity hit me unexpectedly. I was the front left

pallbearer working in tandem with four relatives and the gravedigger when it arrived. Dad was just about to be lowered into the ground. It nearly crumbled me.

What happened was that I finally saw Dad in the casket. Not literally, but in my mind it was as if I was looking through the mahogany and velvet with x-ray vision. I watched his lifeless body, thinned and weakened during his final months, his only animation the result of us clumsy pallbearers. And more than that, I became lodged in the moment. I tried to remember Dad laughing, Dad healthy, Dad shouting, anything other than Dad in that box, but I was unable to navigate inside my mind. I couldn't locate those memories. It was as if an impenetrable wall blocked my access to all Dad-related long term memory. The end result was the forced processing of Dad's death with Dad in the present—no dialogue, just a one-man show starring yours truly. I suppose that was loss, maybe the definition of mourning, my attempt at reconciliation without discourse.

Not surprisingly, I wasn't able to explore my feelings very far the day of Dad's funeral. Thinking about that day gets me much sadder than when I lived it. I guess that's regret.

That fiery stained-glass window—it wasn't menacing, exactly, but it did have ethereal qualities. I stared at the bright sun through the glass. When I tilted my head just so, it was framed perfectly by a small red patch of the mosaic, and its heat became strong on my face. I couldn't tell if its rays were being filtered or magnified, whether or not its lens was illuminating my face bright red. My eyes began to water from its intensity.

Dad cried once. It was the only time I ever saw him sniffling and red-faced. Mom, Dad, me, we all cried that day. It was my brother Michael's funeral, another small service, even though that one was in Chicago. Probably intimate by design.

I was only three years old, so it's tough to pull up particulars. I remember purple throughout the chapel. Maybe it was Lent. I remember sheer purple fabric covering the large crucifix behind the altar. Also there was a white-haired woman with a guitar who sang the hymns. She sang alone, sang to us in the pews.

I don't think of Michael very often, just once in a while something reminds me of him, a tiny casket, purple organza. Nothing encountered frequently in life.

After Michael's funeral, Michael disappeared. I suppose that was another grand illusion, but I don't think Dad should take complete credit for that. If my parents talked about him, if Michael wasn't actually evaporated from our lives, I wasn't included in the conversation, at least not that I remember. I just have that single memory of Michael via that photo when he's lying on the floor in his baby-fat birthday suit, a red, raw incision—and the dozens of staples keeping it closed—running the length of his chest. That was my brother.

A few times I've imagined what it would be like to have someone to charge through all of this business with, but it's a loose idea, and I never find myself pursuing it very far.

I'm not sure what Dino felt during his dad's funeral. Maybe he was overcome by emotions, desperate for human touch, but I doubted it. Xuan Gong practitioners believe in reincarnation, which would've meant Dino's dad's primordial spirit was at that point already working on building qigong energy as another being. Maybe Dino was thinking breathing-healing and healing-breathing as he watched the train of the faithful shuffle up the aisle for communion.

The day redlined me. My heart felt deflated and soft, wrinkled like a dying balloon. I watched the altar boy in white Nikes fidget, then yawn, and I took that as a sign, permission from the altar boy to shut my eyes and will the storm I had in my cerebral-upstairs to nothingness.

Chapter 28

After the funeral, Mom insisted Jeff spend the night with us, which was a relief. Jeff was there as a buffer. Last thing I needed was Mom poking around looking for a way to broach something substantive with me. And not just that, but my radar was back on high alert for anything of the half-baked variety, in a bad way. I feared that the past twelve hours had been like a stick jabbing and tapping at the nest of *Looney Tunes* Mom had inside her, getting everything all worked up to a frenzy. That had me on the defensive, like all I needed was a single reference to the cosmos and I'd be dreaming of stuffing Mom headfirst down the garbage disposal.

But as it was, all three of us were quiet and distant in our own ways. We ordered a pizza and ate together drinking beer and watching the news. Then we headed to separate corners for early sleep.

I was out cold for nine hours, which would have ordinarily been a welcome change from my normal tortured-state nighttime routine, except that I knew better. It was an unhealthy coma, not more than one heartbeat a minute, a kind of hypothermic shutdown of functions because of the freely flowing information that'd resurfaced in my mind. There was a lot, most not good, and none of it was filed away. Those heavy, random snapshots blew around wildly; they knocked into each other and bounced off the vaulted ceiling of my skull as if I housed an epic sandstorm—I contained it, but barely.

In the morning, I managed to drag myself to the shower, but I moaned as I washed myself, the low, long-sustained guttural noises of a tired mummy, dirty in his coffin, too tired to do anything but moan, too tired to stop moaning, even. Surely the earth contained worse sounds than my moan in the shower that morning, but suffice to say, listening to my moan-noises would not have been the highlight of anyone's day.

Once clean and dressed, I edged downstairs and peeked into the kitchen. Mom and Jeff were at the table together, apparently finishing breakfast. They sat there, upbeat and chitchatting like something from a 1950s sitcom, as if the world couldn't have been righter, as if there had never been a paucity of non-flax-based breakfast options in the house, and the more pertinent question was whether I wanted blueberry waffles or a stack of silver dollars with my bacon and eggs? Which was total horseshit, but anyway.

Since I'd been back, the kitchen had become the hub of dysfunction, so observing a kind of normalcy there produced a reaction in me. I'm sure there were vulnerabilities also at work, but standing just outside the kitchen I felt myself bumping from zombie-blank to manic. Not pleasant-manic exactly, but not entirely unpleasant, either. It was more like I was possessed by a new conviction, and it was electric, as if the new idea that pulsed through me could power a casino for a month. I'd never felt that before, such conviction or its onset. Not just that I wanted something, but that I would have it: Jeff would not leave the house. I was determined to make that happen. Not indefinitely, no need to bolt him down to the kitchen floor, but for the moment he'd stay put. Wheels began to spin. I entered the kitchen and walked toward the table.

It was so obvious. With Jeff in the mix, I could lessen my skulking around the house. Plus, it seemed Mom preferred to keep her mumbo-jumbo private. Those were important considerations, sure, but there was also the business. I don't know why it hadn't occurred to me before. The mushroom enterprise was one thing I could wrap my head around. I actually felt that newfound electricity as it transferred. It replaced the sandstorm in my brain with a bright pink neon mushroom. *Bzzzzz.* I could hear it, feel it tingle and blink.

I launched in, and even though I developed my case on the fly, I was conscious of delivering something that felt well-crafted, even slightly casual, like, Hey, guys, you'll never guess what I was contemplating through the wee hours last night.

I tried to conceal any indications of desperation, but there may have been a pinchful there in the room. I'd ceased moaning, which was a step in the right direction, and the longer I carried on, the better I felt, and the better I felt, the further I swayed the room, including myself. I did my best to wipe away any underlying motivations, and it became purely a business pursuit. *With a little push, Jeff, if you stayed just a few days longer, if we rolled up our sleeves, put in some good old-fashioned elbow grease. We've got to strike while the iron is hot, it's our time to be decisive, do or die, now or never, shit or get off the pot; sorry, Mom.* (Full disclosure—I admit to a *carpe diem* at one point.) In short, my argument was simple: I truly believed we could get our hobbling project up and to its feet.

To be sure, I was a different man than I'd been a few minutes earlier, groaning in the shower like I'd eaten myself catatonic on pot brownies. The change was slightly unnerving, but I embraced it.

I talked fast, probably too fast. Several words in every other sentence came out garbled, almost like I'd been drinking. I couldn't remember half of what I said. I employed an arsenal of idioms, which I'd never done before, and the lot of them felt brilliantly applicable to that morning's pursuit. And yes, my hands swung in the air windmill-style, but I kept my audience at a safe distance.

Mom and Jeff mostly grimaced, so I focused my gaze on the windowsill behind them. They nodded their heads periodically as they took it in. Maybe I looked a little insane. I could commit to a statement like that, though there is a projection-factor that would also need to be taken into consideration.

When I stopped talking, there were two blank faces in front of me. I'd obviously delivered too much, which I understood. But still, I had an objective.

I prefer to think I wouldn't have made a desperate appeal to Jeff's compassionate side if I'd had more time to prepare, but as things were—me, dangling off the side of a building reaching my hand up for help—I was willing to cross over into slightly manipulative waters. My neediness was real. That I can certify. "Jeff," I said. "I really need you to stay. It would mean a lot to me if you didn't go. Will you please stay?"

I didn't leave him options, and I felt bad about that. Jeff spent a long minute considering my proposition. He also provided Mom and me several different face contortions, which would have been interesting to observe if I hadn't activated them. Jeff nodded yes. I felt enormous relief, and I promised myself I'd make it up to him somehow.

There was one other thing, too, and I swear I did not derive pleasure from it, nor was it a toot of my own horn to recognize it. Getting Jeff to stay was the first successful sale I had under my belt. There was a thing, it was now sold, and I was responsible for it. That seemed like something mildly important.

Chapter 29

Later that day, Jeff and I started out close to home with minimarts, groceries, gas stations, etc. We hit any place that sold edibles. Admittedly, there wasn't much of a game plan, but at least we were being proactive and having at it as a team.

We entered those places carrying our plastic shopping bags full of product and headed to the registers, where we asked for the manager. Jeff and I were shy, one or both of us offering a handful of bagged-premium without explanation, as if our story was obvious. It wouldn't have been wholly inaccurate to describe our efforts as pitiful, and we knew it, but we couldn't seem to will ourselves confident.

We hit a dozen spots, and each time, once the managers understood we weren't irritated customers, they waved us away. In an odd coincidence, five of the managers made clicking noises and flicked their hands to shoo us off, like we were naughty kitties. And each time we noiselessly obliged and left more expediently and obediently than a cat would have, which I guess doesn't say much for us.

We finally had some luck at location thirteen, a liquor store called Pop's in Rogers Park. The manager didn't buy anything from us, a Sikh in his fifties, but for whatever reason, maybe sheer boredom, like we were possibly more entertaining than watching another twenty minutes of his freezer aisle on the closed circuit security camera, instead of directing us back to the pavement, he put his elbows on the counter, cradled his chin with his palms, smiled softly, and lazily engaged us.

"What is this, fellas? You come in holding a wrinkly bag of something. I don't know what that is. You want me to buy them? You're fundraising for your softball team? Is it a deductible contribution? Tell me something, tell me what I don't know. Tell me what I'm missing by not having this crumply bag of whatever. Amaze me. It's called an elevator pitch. You've got the amount of time it takes from the first floor to the thirtieth, at which point I step out to chair my board meeting, and you've lost your opportunity. I'm pressing the close-elevator button now." The manager stuck his finger at an invisible elevator panel, then resumed chin on hands.

Jeff and I were dumbstruck. We mumbled a few sentences about the mushrooms, but that's all we managed. We thanked the manager and shuffled off with our tails between our legs. Obviously, we needed a plan, a saleable pitch. We drove to the northeast corner of the city and sat on the rocks looking out at Lake Michigan, the idea being that we could have a nice brainstorming session there, but mostly we watched the waves crash in. It was fairly wild out on the lake, almost angry. The sky was clear, and the water was a deep green.

I watched Jeff squint at the horizon. He may have been wondering what he'd gotten himself into, or how the premium might ultimately impact the lab science and sign language classes he still needed in order to graduate. I squinted myself, to try and see what Jeff saw, but I wound up in dreamland thinking about Dad.

I imagined him draped in practically transparent white cloth. He was sitting on a solid gold litter that was being carried across the sand toward the water by a troop of hefty men in swim trunks. There was another man there, too, in an all-white tuxedo and fancy white patent-leather boots. He could walk on water, and his boots didn't even get wet.

They carried Dad on his litter out into the wet. The water was up to their necks. The man standing on the water gestured for the litter to be lowered. Dad sank down into the water, and everyone swam over to him, touching him and praying.

I tried to picture Dad's face at the moment, but I couldn't, which was odd since I'd fabricated the entire scene. Still, I got hung up by it. Was I imagining heaven? The construction of a moment of salvation of Dad? For me? Ack. I just couldn't take it further than that.

Over the next few days, Jeff and I managed a few meetings of the minds, and the next week, we went back to see the same Sikh manager, both of us wearing shirts and ties. I borrowed clothes from Dad's closet, and Jeff wore mine, the old stuff, like my navy blue blazer with the brass buttons from when I was in high school. Jeff found in its pockets: tweezers from a Swiss army knife (no knife), a wad of napkins smeared with what appeared to be blue cake frosting, seven individually wrapped mint-flavored toothpicks, and on the backside of a church bulletin, a suspiciously phallic drawing of a surfboard and two beach balls.

"Sir," I said, "A terrific new product has recently become available in the area." I held up a bag of premium, and Jeff, standing next to me, gestured toward the bag too, with both hands, like we were presenting a case of car wax on a game show.

Jeff continued. "These gourmet matzutaki mushrooms come from China's Yunnan Province. Situated in the foothills of the Himalayas, the evergreen forests there provide the absolute most ideal climate for mushrooms. Unspoiled, undeveloped, and lush like you can't imagine, it's unlike any other place on earth."

Then me. "For the first time ever, these mushrooms are available to you and your clientele, and because we import the product directly, we are able to keep costs at a minimum."

The Sikh manager's reception was lukewarm this time around. He didn't engage us like he'd done before. Maybe he wasn't as bored that day, or he'd had a fight with his partner that morning before work. Maybe he just didn't like dudes in suits. Whatever it was, to his credit, he endured our pitch, the whole thing, and when we finished, he said, "Guys, that's all fine and well, but so what? How do I even know they're good?" Fair enough, so we gave the manager a bag of premium, on the house, so that he could taste for himself. That got him beaming. Apparently, like me, he was ever-game for a free sample. The transaction was surprisingly satisfying.

I doubt that Sikh manager knows the kind of positive impact he had on our business model, and maybe one day we'll find a way to thank him properly. After we left his store, we began to successfully place premium. Though, to be clear, we weren't yet making any sales. We took a slight detour and instead focused on distributing free samples. It substantially lowered the pressure, which in turn helped us hold our heads a little higher and loosened our tongues.

We printed business cards and taped them to the product, distributed them to potential partners one, two, and three bags at a time. We kept our interactions short and sweet, and each time as we left, we casually mentioned that we were standing by and ready to fulfill orders of any size. That was Jeff's brilliant idea.

Jeff and I felt more like jingle elves than salesmen, but we enjoyed gifting premium—we definitely preferred it to the hard sale, anyway. It got us giddy every time, how a little bag of mushrooms could sprinkle some sunshine on the earth. And other than a tickle in the back of my head now and again that seemed to suggest a borderline irresponsibility with regard to our business plan, in terms of the big picture, it generally felt like we were on a solid course of action. We were planning for the future.

That's not to say there weren't a few wrinkles. A smattering of oddball individuals refused to accept our free samples. In particular, we had issues at the big-fish stores. As if our premium was so freaking toxic, and everyone was suddenly a stickler for the rules—which made me wonder if there was also a chapter in their precious employee handbooks that outlined various techniques for clotheslining customers in parking lots.

In any event, those places asked a lot of questions. They wanted specifics on mushroom origins, documentation of FDA approval, proven shelf life, nutrition facts, etc., which, I mean, we aimed at professionalism, sure, but we couldn't answer those things.

The smaller, classier, family-owned groceries and specialty shops didn't have the same hangups. Those managers were pleases and thank yous as we dropped premium into their hands.

In a week we had nearly half the entire inventory distributed. True, we hadn't turned a dime in profits, and no, there weren't yet any pending orders, but we were getting our name out there, and that had value.

And, more personally, Jeff and I felt really well connected, and it'd been a while for me since anything like that. We were not only strategizing elevator pitches and pushing fungi, but we got beers together and side-glanced the same eye candy. We swapped stories. Jeff lost his virginity to a distant relative in China (he didn't know the DNA score at the time, but apparently she did); I lost mine during a one-night stand in college. Our relationship blossomed in our discovery of shared passions, like ten-cent-buffalo-wing nights, whole milk with one sweetener in our coffee, and 2-ply quilted toilet paper. We even discovered that years earlier we'd rocked out in close proximity to each other at a Hootie and the Blowfish concert in Milwaukee. The world was small.

I showed Jeff Mom's altar once when she was out shopping. I giggled as I poked its various elements with the tip of my finger, which was stupid of me. The sacred did exist and debunking it didn't give me jollies. Jeff didn't show much of a reaction. "Dude," he said, "that's kind of weird." I agreed. I considered offering background on the paper-cutout crystal. I even had an urge to spill completely about Mom, which was probably why I'd shown Jeff the altar in the first place, but at the moment of decision, I opted to jump out of my hole rather than scrape it a few feet deeper.

CHAPTER 30

Dino had been completely off the grid since burying his dad, which was fine by me. Minus Dino, Jeff and I were happier and more relaxed, and I suspect we covered more ground. Jeff and I sometimes gave each other a look of commiseration about it, but neither of us had the heart to say it out loud. It felt ominous even, so we celebrated quietly. At unpredictable times, like sitting in traffic, walking out of a gas station, loading the dishwasher, Jeff and I would silently acknowledge that things were good, that we were good, that this was all much better than before, in part thanks to Dino's absence.

In truth, I hoped Dino would vanish like a snowdrift melting in the rain, which may have been harsh, but still. I didn't want him back in our lives, not even for the duration of a phone call.

But all great feelings ultimately disappear if they aren't first smashed to pieces. Dino resurfaced. Thankfully, he didn't physically appear. Instead there was a large padded envelope that arrived by certified mail. Jeff and I opened it at the kitchen table, and inside were two sets of Chicago Bulls season tickets, plus a post-it note: *Everett, To wine and dine clients. —Dino.*

"Those must be at least a thousand bucks a piece," Jeff said.

"At least," I said. "What the fuck?"

Jeff shrugged.

And yet it still wasn't quite motivation enough for us to contact Dino.

Later that night Dino appeared again, this time in an email that said he'd retained legal counsel for us, for when it was time to "dot the i's and cross the t's." He provided no additional information, just that one-liner email. It raised eyebrows, but Jeff and I supposed it wasn't an entirely bad idea. We didn't reply to the email.

The next day Jeff and I got another email from Dino. *Everett, you mentioned windbreakers at some point. I think it's a good idea. What color? And how about a logo?*

It seemed an inheritance was in the mix, and Dino was dipping into it in the patented Dino-style. Rather than advise Dino in these matters—instead of doing the responsible and kind-hearted thing—I maintained the route of less communication, or, more accurately, no communication.

Another package arrived the day of the windbreaker email—packages, actually, plural. Nine boxes of books, all on mushrooms. Cookbooks, identification guides, gathering manuals, etc. Even a children's book, *Little Larry Lives in a Giant Mushroom,* ages 2 and up, which was either a joke or a mistake, or if not, held some significance that was beyond the collected abilities of our minds.

Admittedly, building up a little know-how with regard to the premium did have its logic. That night as Jeff and I drank beer in front of the television, I flipped through one of the cookbooks and read the names of dishes to Jeff: chanterelle empanadas, stuffed mushrooms with pork and cilantro, pickled mushrooms, beef and mushroom pot pie, meaty mushroom lasagna, chorizo mushroom queso dip.

"Dude, you're making me hungry," Jeff said.

I wiggled my eyebrows at him. "Want another beer?"

"Gracias," Jeff said.

Jeff tipped back his beer, and I went to the kitchen for two cold ones.

When I came downstairs the next morning, Jeff was sitting alone at the kitchen table watching television. When he saw me, he waved. He put four pieces of bread in the toaster, two for each of us. He didn't ask how I'd slept; he didn't do anything more than get the toast going, but I appreciated it. I poured myself a cup of coffee, then walked over and topped up his. It was an unceremonious act—no thank-you or otherwise from Jeff. That was the kind of rhythm we were in.

Usually, we were both quiet in the mornings, together but very much moving in our own kind of sealed pods, but that day I could tell Jeff had something on his mind. He waited until we'd buttered our toast to get into it.

"Did I ever tell you about the time my parents and I saw this Xuan Gong show in Milwaukee?"

He most definitely had not. Jeff and I didn't talk much about the Gongers, and when we did, it was mostly Jeff listening to me spout off about whatever new ridiculousness Dino had leaked to me. I always figured the Xuan Gong just wasn't very interesting to Jeff. "I don't think so," I said.

"A few years back, not even that long ago, this Chinese performance troupe had a show in Milwaukee, which doesn't happen very often, I mean a Chinese show in Wisconsin. They had TV commercials and all, pretty crappy quality, but they ran during the news, so, you know, it was sort of a big deal. My parents got all excited about it, and so did their friends— Chinese, I mean. Everybody was all crazy to get tickets."

"And it was a Xuan Gong show?"

"That's the thing. They called it a spectacular, a traditional Chinese music and dance spectacular, and on the commercials they had guys doing acrobatics and whatnot, big swords, kung fu and whatever. It looked pretty cool, actually."

Jeff took a sip of his coffee, then went on. "So everybody gets tickets, and even I'm kind of psyched to go. It was in a fancy theater, too, not, like, a middle-school cafeteria, but a for-real theater where they have the ballet and symphony.

"Anyway, we get all dressed up, and my mom makes me wear a tie and everything, and she gets her hair done. It's that kind of party. We get to Milwaukee, and the performers are outside the theater in full costume getting everyone all charged up, like at the circus. We get into the theater, and it's mostly Chinese in the crowd. Everybody's digging it, but the show starts up, and it's fine and all, but each of the little stories they tell, like for each dance or whatnot, they're all actually stories about the Xuan Gong."

"Whoa," I said.

"Yeah, exactly. Ten minutes in, and people in the audience start talking out loud. Some of them get up and walk out, and the tickets weren't cheap. I don't remember how much they were, but not cheap. Anyway, it was crazy, and more and more people are just walking out, some people shouting at the actors on stage as they leave. But the performers kept going. Like, the show must go on."

Jeff laughed, but I could tell that he'd been thinking about this a lot. I wondered how long.

"I looked over at my parents to try and see what they wanted to do. I was definitely ready to walk out, too. Not that it was so awful, but, whatever. It's not like I was turning Xuan Gong just from seeing the freaking show. My parents didn't move. They didn't even look at each other, just sat there like statues, and so I did too. It was totally crazy."

"You stayed for the whole thing?" I said.

"Yeah. And the last little section of the show, they had this mother and daughter in a park in China, like in China today, and they freaking get beat up by the cops. It was totally crazy. As soon as it was over, my dad looked at my mom and me and nodded to the door. We were up and out of there. People were clapping. Jesus. Totally crazy."

"What did your parents say?"

"So, we go to the car, and I could tell my dad was super pissed, but he didn't say anything. We get on the road and basically don't talk at all. After maybe an hour or so, and my dad had been sitting totally straight-faced the whole time, my dad just breaks out laughing, laughing so hard. And my mom and I start laughing, too, uncontrollably. We didn't say anything to each other, just laughed, I mean practically crying. That was it."

CHAPTER 31

Jeff and I went out for wings on a Thursday night, and, yes, they were delicious. But as I was pulling out from the Chicken Shack parking lot, I suppose in part because of chicken wing sedation, I got disoriented, and I again forgot which side of the road to drive on. I chose a lane and looked over at Jeff for a reaction. I did that instead of asking for help. Apparently, the wings had transported Jeff to a tranquil place too, because it took a few seconds for his eyes to widen into two Frisbees, but they did. He jammed his foot into the passenger side floorboard, trying to phantom-save us. That triggered my reaction, and I swerved us into the right lane.

"Dude," Jeff said. "What're you doing?" Jeff was worked up pretty good, and for that I was sorry.

I managed a short, uncomfortable laugh and was figuring out how to explain this phenomenon to Jeff when I heard the electronic pulse of a police siren, saw flashes of light in the mirror.

My level of freaked-outness was I think commensurate with the situation at hand. I figured I would offer the officer the truth—it was the best I could do. I pulled off the road into the parking lot of a dry-cleaners and put the car in park.

I'd never been pulled over before, but Dad was, once. I was around ten years old, and we were on our way home from a wedding. I was groggy-tired in the back seat because it'd gotten late. The wedding was for the daughter of a business associate of

Dad's, and Mom and I didn't know anyone there. I remember the red and white Polish flags everywhere at the reception, which was held at a community center/bar over an hour from home.

Mom and I spent most of the night together while Dad hung around at the bar talking with the guys, I suppose networking. I remember eating Tic Tacs at the table and watching Mom and Dad dance to the last song together, which made me sad since Mom had otherwise only danced with me.

It was on our way home when Dad got pulled over.

"Fucking-A," Dad said. It was the only time I ever heard Dad drop the F-bomb like that. It scared me.

The cop came over, and Dad rolled down his window. He asked for Dad's license, etc., then he asked Dad if he'd been drinking. Mom was horrified. She tried to hide it but couldn't.

Dad was respectful but certain with his language, which is, incidentally, how I suspect he conducted business. "I have not been drinking," Dad said. "I'm bringing my family home from a wedding."

"And you didn't drink at the wedding? No cocktails?" the cop said.

"Not when I'm transporting my wife and son," Dad said.

The cop bent down and looked at us. He stepped back and looked at Dad. "How about a breathalyzer and you can be on your way?" the cop said.

Dad said, "Absolutely not."

"No?"

"No," Dad said.

"Please step out of the car," the cop said. And that's when I lost it, major waterworks. I couldn't help myself. I'd watched Dad tipping back beers all night. I'm not sure if it was the fact that I knew Dad was lying that did it to me, or if it was a response to the thick cloud of doom that'd swept into our little ecosystem there in the car, but, either way, and even as a tyke, I knew things looked grim, and that worried me stupid.

The cop must have heard me. He bent down and looked into the back seat. Then he looked over at Mom. "Ma'am," he said, "Have you been drinking?"

"No, Officer," Mom said. "No, I haven't."

"All right," the cop said. He let out a long breath. "Here's what we're going to do. Your wife is going to drive home. God, I can smell the booze coming out the window from you. But I'm going to forget about it, so you can get your son home. Everybody agreeable to that?"

I hoped so badly that Dad would just say, yes. He could be confrontational sometimes. But in this case Dad submitted, without comment, of course—I mean, he'd been breathing in that same toxic cloud there in the car with us. It would have been the act of a complete idiot to have done otherwise. Dad opened his door, Mom hers, and they did a quick switcheroo.

It was a quiet ride home, except for my sniffling, which didn't subside until I was in my bed, lights out.

Back to the predicament in the parking lot at the dry cleaners: the flashing lights were filling up the DeVille like some cold-war psychological stress test. The cop came to my window and asked for my license, etc., which I gave to him. *Edward Metz,* his bronze name tag read. Officer Metz. Patrolman Metz. He looked about my age, short brown hair with either some pomade or natural grease keeping it just so. Metz told us to sit tight and took my documents back to his cruiser.

"God, why were you driving all crazy like that?" Jeff said.

Hearing the disappointment in Jeff's voice—there was some anger there, too—stung me harshly. I was ashamed to admit the truth.

"Sorry," I said. "I got mixed up somehow."

Jeff and I sat in silence waiting for Metz to reappear, and when he did, he had a little pen flashlight that he wiggled into my face, and into my eyes, and then into Jeff's face and his eyes. Granted, it could have been and wasn't one of those four D-cell jobs, but the thing had me seeing sunspots.

"You boys been doing some drinking tonight?" he said.

"No drinking," I said. "We're just heading home from dinner."

"Where do you live?"

"A few miles north of here, but he's from Oshkosh," I said, pointing over at Jeff, which I immediately regretted. "And, I just got back into the country, so that's why I was driving a little funny."

Metz walked around the backside of the car to Jeff's window, and I could see his little flashlight searching the back seat while he made his way. Jeff sat motionless, and when Metz was at the passenger door, he pantomimed rolling down his window to Jeff. Jeff complied.

"Oshkosh, eh? What brings you down here? Have you been here long?"

I could tell Jeff was flailing around inside his skin, but he acted pretty cool. We hadn't done anything wrong, after all. "I came down for a funeral, my friend's dad. I've been here for a few days, will probably head back tomorrow or the next day."

"Right," Metz said. "And you haven't been doing any drinking? How about drugs? Either of you have any drugs in the car? Any alcohol, drugs, weapons, or explosives in the car? Anything you want to tell me about?"

"Nothing like that," I said.

Metz nodded his head, then stepped back from the car a few feet. He said, "Both of you put your hands on the dash where I can see them." Metz pressed the button on the walkie-talkie strapped to his chest and spoke into it. He radioed in his coordinates and rattled off some numbers. He also requested backup.

"Officer, what's the problem?" I said.

Metz undid the strap on his holster, but he didn't bring it out. "Just sit tight," Metz said in a not altogether unpleasant way.

I wondered if I'd left some contraband in the backseat from when I was camped out in the DeVille? A beer can? Maybe a *Hustler?*

Within probably ninety seconds, though to me it felt more like half an hour, two squad cars came screaming toward the dry cleaners. Every surface in the area was flooded with strobes of red and blue.

The cops surrounded the car and instructed us to, "Get out. Get down on the ground. Hands on your heads. Spread out. Wider. Now hug the ground." I felt cold metal, heard handcuffs clacking around my wrists.

"Any weapons, drugs, or sharp objects on your person?" a voice said.

"No, nothing," I said. The whole thing felt out-of-body, even when a pair of hands was digging through my every nook and cranny.

Once they'd patted me down, I turned my head up and around as far as I could in order to inventory the scene. The cops were about ten feet away. Metz's nose was deep in a bag of premium. He offered it to another sort of overweight cop with a buzz cut and sunglasses around his neck, who inhaled, and did this super-inflated head-nod thing, like with that nod, he hath royally dubbed the case airtight, that jackass. It stunk like whenever Mom clued into some serious horseshit of hers.

Next there was shouting. "Bingo!" said a cop who was leaning into the trunk of the car. The other cops scrambled over for a turn to look.

Metz came over to me. "Today's not your day, pal," he said. He shook a few caps of premium onto the ground near my head and pulverized them with the toe of his shiny black shoe. "And enough in the trunk to set you two up for a long while," he said.

"They aren't drugs," I said, suddenly infuriated. "They're matzutaki mushrooms. They're for spaghetti and cream sauce."

Metz appeared confused. He squinted at the bag of premium in his hand, bent his head down and went in for another whiff.

"They're piney smelling. Kind of earthy, too," he said. Then I watched something odd. Metz glazed over for a moment, I think in consideration of some newfound value in himself, that despite the chaos of lights and all else married to a drug-bust-in-progress, that in that unlikely moment, he found himself successfully articulating the bouquet of some edible, I suspect for the first time in his life.

It was sort of intimate, but I wasn't much in a position to appreciate our shared moment. Mostly I felt defeated. Words continued out of my mouth, but I was practically whispering. "I'm telling you, it's not drugs. They're matzutaki mushrooms."

Metz left me facedown on the pavement and gathered the cops together in a circle where they again inspected the premium. I wondered if the aura of this group was being hidden by the flashing lights—or if *perplexed* had activated red and blue flashing halos around them.

Officer Metz, in what could probably be considered moderate to highly unprofessional haste, tossed a dried stem of premium up into the air above his head. He watched it, aligned his shoulders, and caught it in his mouth. The other cops roared, and one of them jumped in front of Metz, twisting and turning his hands in front of Metz's face.

That's when I figured we weren't going to get hauled into prison that night. They released us and returned our premium, minus the bits Metz ground into the asphalt and the stem he'd chomped out of the air like a lizard. "I'm not going to give you a ticket for reckless driving," Metz said, "So there's your tiny silver lining in all of this."

Jeff and I got in the car, and we watched the various cop cars drive away. "What a bunch of bullshit," I said.

Jeff didn't answer, but then he started laughing, uncontrollably, comatose to cracked-out in the blink of an eye. "The fucking premium, man!" he said. "Never doubt the power of the premium!" Jeff was delirious, slapping the dashboard and wiggling around in his seat.

I tried to laugh with him, tried for some of that shared reaction, but I didn't have it in me. Jeff just kept on with it, maybe to keep from crying, I don't know.

That night as I tried to will myself some shut-eye, I found myself thinking about the outdoor restaurant in Pingnan on one particular Sunday evening. Xiao Mu, Mr. Dragon, Williams and I had a decent beer buzz going. I remember that we were using toothpicks to mine meat from the shells of stir-fried snails, and I had a thought that seemed important.

I tried to explain it to the guys, but I had only my shit Chinese to use because Edwards was too drunk to translate. I was getting nowhere, so I borrowed a pen from the waitress and using a dictionary, I wrote the sentences out in pin yin on my napkin. The guys watched me curiously.

"Two things scare me," I finally read to them. "One, I am not living the life I am supposed to live. Two, I am living the life I am supposed to live, exactly as I'm supposed to live it."

Mr. Dragon had no clue what I was talking about. If anything, his eyes offered some mild appreciation of the time and care I'd taken in preparing whatever it was that'd come out of my mouth. Edwards, with his tiny head resting comfortably between his knees, didn't register much. Xiao Mu, however, he lit up like I'd delivered something profound. He refilled our beer glasses. "Okay," he said. Xiao Mu raised his glass—he even cleared his throat—then stared off into the night, in seeming reflection—"Wow," he said, "You speak-eh very good Chinese."

CHAPTER 32

Jeff went back to Oshkosh eleven days after Dino's dad's funeral. As soon as he was gone, I missed him. I missed my friend, and not only that, but I became further convinced that Jeff had indeed been some kind of temporary antidote to Mom's kooky.

Without Jeff, the house again felt like it was cooking something up, like the whole damn thing had transformed back into a giant crock-pot and would soon be boiling at a low roil. It was a hunch and not more than that, but I felt it, that there was something, and whatever it was, it was on its way.

That imminent, unknown thing, its force was strong. The anxiety it produced in me was substantial. For one, it knocked the routine of my bodily functions all out of whack. That impending doom also decimated what little interest I had in tackling anything on the home front. I found myself back in the DeVille, driving aimlessly around town again, but with even less purpose than I'd had during my stint as a fake shopper. I really only had one objective and that was to spend as little time as possible under the same roof as Mom.

Behind the wheel, I focused on the business. That'd worked well before, and I figured there was nothing horrible about a healthy transfer of energies. Plus, mushrooms didn't swear by hypnotherapy or prescribe breathing exercises, which I appreciated.

So, yes: product. As for fungi, we were nearly dry, and I didn't need a PhD in mycology to understand that premium doesn't fall from the sky and neatly seal itself into baggies.

I was stuck at a red light in Oak Park when I decided it was my turn to take the plunge. I turned the car toward home, and when I got there, I headed straight to the computer and surfed travel sites for a plane ticket.

It was the longest I'd been among Dad's effects without pillaging, which was some tiny bump of a milestone. It had something to do with possession. At that point, Dad's computer felt approximately eighty-five percent ours and fifteen percent Dad's. It was the dawn of new ownership.

In an uncharacteristically impulsive act, I click-purchased a ticket, a last-minute low-price fare, and emailed the guys. I considered not including Dino among the note's recipients, but, that sneak, since he'd gone and gotten that lawyer on retainer, full disclosure seemed the more prudent way forward.

Not five minutes after I sent the email, Jeff called and offered to go in my place. Jeff's grandmother's health had unexpectedly plummeted, he said, meaning they needed family there ASAP, not only for care-giving, but in case her estate was to be divvied up, among other things, and neither of Jeff's parents, to their immeasurable horror, could do the trip for another six days. I told Jeff he should forget about mushrooms and just go to see his grandmother. Jeff suggested we go together. I wasn't entirely game for yet another death, for yet another funeral, but I agreed. I could do that for Jeff. Fine, done.

The phone rang again just after I hung up. "Hey," I said, figuring it was Jeff with another something to iron out, but it wasn't. "Everett," Dino said, "how are you?"

I would have screened the call if I'd been able to—there was also the option of hollering "wrong number" in a foreign accent—but in some ways a surprise reconnection was the best it could have gone. Close-your-eyes-and-rip-off-the-Band-Aid-style.

Dino also offered to go in my place. When I asked him why,

he said, "No reason, except that I was good at it last time, plus I've got frequent flyer miles."

"Didn't you just use those?"

"I've got more."

I could smell the horseshit through the phone line, but I didn't dig. I just explained that Jeff was going because of his grandmother, and that my ticket was nonrefundable.

"We'll all go," Dino said.

Fuck. I knew Jeff would be disappointed, too. "Nah, but, well, I guess that's okay," I said. "We'll all go."

"Great, but I've got to leave earlier than you two. I'm on the first plane that has space."

"Why? What's got ants in your pants?" Dino so effortlessly took the transparent and made it dark and spiky.

"Why is because I can't deal with being at home right now."

"Not for Xuan Gong?"

"That doesn't matter."

"Whatever. You want to meet in Jeff's hometown or head with us from Kunming?"

"It would be helpful if you could get in touch with Vice Principal Pu again." He said it plainly, but I knew immediately. That'd been his sole purpose for calling.

"I don't think so," I said. Dino didn't respond. "Are you even going to meet up with us?"

"Why else would I be going? At his grandmother's. I'll be in touch. See you soon." Dino hung up.

There was a substantial distance between the words that came out of Dino's mouth and the place where his mind now resided. He'd achieved new perspective, which felt poisonous, even remotely. I wished there was a way to dissuade him from taking the trip, but I knew better. Any efforts in that direction, short of simple directives at gunpoint, would have been wasted time and energy.

CHAPTER 33

The morning of the day before I left for China, there was a note from Mom waiting for me on the kitchen counter. *Everett, I'm out running errands, but I have something important to share with you. Can you please meet me in the living room this afternoon? I'll be home at 4 p.m. Love, Mom.*

It felt sort of like a death sentence, which is maybe melodramatic, even if there was a time and place of execution and all. At least it meant Mom was out of the house for the afternoon, which was a kind gesture and approximate to a death-row final meal. Mom gone meant I could do laundry and pack without having to slip between shadows, but her absence only went so far. In some ways it felt like she was trudging right alongside me as I pressed forward with the day, because as I did, I couldn't help but simultaneously imagine the buckets of hogwash waiting for me on the horizon.

In addition to normal, pre-trip activities, I also spent some time sanitizing my bedroom in case Mom decided to rifle through my things for old time's sake. Or if Mom was able to fend off the sweet allure of the snoop, there was always the possibility of becoming an airplane-crash statistic. So I tidied up a bit.

It wasn't contraband I was worried about. Other than the porn, I hadn't acquired much since I'd been back that was wholly unspeakable, not really. My room was a mess with everyday items. The problem was their sum total. If someone took the initiative to examine those things, if they tried to fit the puzzle pieces together this way or that in order to create a profile of their governor, they might wind up with a final portrait that wasn't altogether flattering. Purged items included: eight dirty plates of varying circumferences, a depleted squirt bottle of moisturizer from underneath the bed, fourteen empty beer bottles, a bare paper towel tube, five plastic cups, eleven empty soda cans, individual paper towel sheets balled and scattered on the floor (a roll's worth), two pizza boxes, a JC Penney catalog (conspicuously worn at the swimwear/bra section), five coffee mugs with brown stains at their bottoms, and my collection of *Mad* and *Cracked* magazines, which stacked four feet high when they weren't loose across the floor.

I was making my bed when I heard Mom at the front door. It was the first time I'd tucked in the sheets since I'd been back. It was gratifying to have a clean room for once, though with my China bags mashed into the closet along with other floor debris, I couldn't claim a totally flawless transformation.

Maybe because of the order I'd achieved in my room, and also because I was leaving for China the next day, I found unfamiliar courage in myself at that moment and headed down to the living room without delay.

It was an austere space at that point, as per Janice Sugarbottom's instructions, and felt a little like a hotel lobby — just two leather love seats on either side of the coffee table, two rubber trees in a corner, and a ceiling-heightening vase fluffers had put on the mantel that wasn't actually a vase but the brass umbrella stand that'd never once been moved from its spot next to the front door.

Mom yelled to me from the kitchen. "Sit tight, I'll be there in a minute." She didn't sound high-strung. Maybe it wouldn't be so awful. Possibly she'd found a condo. The optimist in me hoped it might even be some innocuous life advice. Rub aspirin on skin tags, colon-cleanse once a year, sprinkle butterfly dust on your pillowcase to prevent migraines, etc.

Mom took a long time, and I had no idea what she was doing. And although I'd started out calm, sitting there became increasingly unbearable. I looked at the umbrella stand, which was in a good spot there on the mantel. I'd never inspected it closely, and I wondered if I would have paid more attention to it over the years if I was the size of a thumb. A man-thumb, not a baby-thumb, though I suppose at birth I would have been quite tiny. That size, adult-thumb size, with all the appropriate adult-thumb sized anatomy, to scale. Imagine that, and I'm saying proportionally accurate. Jesus, just to get across a tile-grout ravine. The whole freaking planet would be an obstacle course. Would I be able to locate a needle small enough to sew clothes? To weave together some moccasins for my cute little feet? On the plus side, there'd be savings. It'd take weeks to finish a banana.

Mom finally arrived. She had the silver coffee set with her, which she put down on the table. She poured two cups and slid one to me. We never used those things, and shining as they were, Mom must have polished them up for the occasion. She probably used a particular tube of polish, which was mostly unremarkable, except that from time to time it would mysteriously appear in a different drawer, all throughout the house, for my entire life, that same antiquated tube, and it was often the one item keeping a drawer from closing properly. I wondered if old silver polish can go bad, and if it can, if "go bad" was a euphemism for turn to poison. I had cotton mouth.

"Very fancy," I said.

"You know," she said, "Tucky has shown me a lot about my life, things that I didn't know. I've been receiving hypnosis therapy. I think I told you."

"Yeah," I said. Then, like a good kamikaze, I sipped my drink. The coffee tasted sour, but not deadly. When I put the coffee back on the table, I saw it had a colorful oily top layer to it.

"I tell things to Tucky when I'm under hypnosis. Tucky and I have uncovered things from my subconscious."

"This coffee tastes a little chemical," I said. I pursed my lips, smacked them lightly. I thought the coffee should have been helping my cotton-mouth, but it wasn't.

"This is serious. Please, hear me. We found that I was abused growing up, by my mom," she said.

"Grandma?"

"Yes."

"Sexually abused?"

"Yes."

"Oh, mom. And you're realizing this now, because Tucky extracted it from you under hypnosis?"

"It's not exactly like that."

"Do you think it could be true?"

Growing up, Mom's parents were the only family I got to know well. They stayed with us a few times a year and they always brought me gifts, a simple but effective measure. Mom was generally happier when they were around, and they almost always visited when Dad was on a long trip, which I'm sure was no accident.

Grandma was thin and wore a shoulder-length, jet-black wig. I remember she nitpicked and was outspoken, which brought out the crazy in Mom, but even so, when my grandparents were around, the house filled with a kind of warmth.

What I remember most about their visits were our extended dinners, routinely several hours long, which in retrospect should have bored me to pieces, but they didn't. Grandpa was built like a lumberjack, tall with a massive belly. During our meals, he would ask me serious questions, even when I was very young. He talked to me like I was an adult, and wanted to know my opinion on politics, fashion, education, sports, etc. He'd chuckle at things I said, but he never laughed at me.

At the dinner table over the years, I remember singing for my grandparents, and I otherwise hated to sing. I made mixtapes in anticipation of their arrival, and Grandma and Grandpa would dance in their chairs if they liked a song. I drew pictures for them. I even modeled the cherry-tree costume that I never got to perform in because I sliced open my leg the night of the first-grade school musical. I presented my scar through the shredded brown corduroys so that they could see how well I'd healed, and I certified the mend via somersaults across the kitchen.

I was in fifth grade when they died, Grandpa first, even though Grandma was the likelier candidate. Grandpa died, and then sort of out of the blue, Grandma followed a few weeks later. I remember Mom cried so much that year that at points I thought she might never stop.

I was, of course, young when they went, and so I knew only a portion of the whole story, but at the same time, I wasn't an infant. I'd logged some time with them. At the very least, I was old enough to sense the mood when we were together, and it was good.

And, yet, what if? Jesus. As much as I couldn't imagine it, I had to allow for the possibility that it was all true, and I did.

Either this was the nastiest of Mom's transgressions so far, or Mom really was a victim of sexual assault. Both possibilities signaled that we were officially stepping into new territory.

"Why would Tucky tell you that? Do you believe him? How exactly did he phrase it?"

"I can see this is upsetting you. Try and take this a little at a time."

"If Grandma abused you, what's to say she didn't abuse

me?" I was angling toward logic and reason, even if there was some self-interest at play.

"Ill, it makes me completely ill to think about that."

"If that were taking place, I think you would have protected me, even if it was subconscious." Which was true, I think she would have.

"Of course, but I don't think you get it. These are suppressed memories from my childhood. Even I don't understand them entirely. There's something else too."

"What?"

"When I was very young, I was also abused by my grandfather. It's difficult to understand, I know. But together we can try."

I didn't know how to counter. It seemed so farfetched, but, again, what if? "Mom, if you don't understand, why would you buy into it?"

"Because Tucky has no reason to misguide me."

"I'm not so sure. Don't you think you'd have had a reaction? Protected yourself, even if you didn't really understand why? Did you ever have any of that going on?"

"I don't know. I'm still trying to figure it out."

Mom's delivery of this new information seemed sincere. I appreciated that, I truly did, and that made me very sad. She was in a no-win situation. She was either a fool for loving her abusive family or a dupe for believing in Tucky, the man who'd single-handedly improved the quality of her existence twofold, which I think he had somehow, though I hated to admit that to myself. There just had to be a way to find an equilibrium with it all. Balance, like Mom said all the time.

I could actually see Mom tearing apart during our conversation. "Listen," I said, "I believe you, but I also doubt Grandma did anything to you. They were good people. I don't know what to make about your grandparents, but it seems very strange to me that you don't have any memories of these things. And I don't think someone could do those things, and you'd still be able to love them afterward. I don't think people work that way. I don't think you act like a victim." In my mind, I began to wonder if Mom actually did behave like a victim. I didn't think so, but still.

"That's what makes it so complicated."

"That's what makes it sort of hard to believe. I mean, what would Grandpa have been doing all that time?"

"Tucky said that he may have had a part in it, too. Maybe even beyond passive enabling."

As much as I wanted to believe Mom, it felt like too large a conspiracy to simply unfold like this. Plus, in a strange, very twisted way, Mom in the throes of her dilemma gave me hope, that in Mom there still lived a divide between her acceptance of all things Tucky and her ability to reason on her own. It was evidence that the old and new Mom hadn't completely merged, that the brainwashing and reeducation hadn't entirely consumed its new host. Maybe Mom could still come back from this. But the larger questions remained. Why was Tucky doing it? What did he have to gain? And was there any truth at all to the claims Mom made?

"I want to believe you, Mom, but revealed under hypnosis? I'm not sure about that."

"It does seem hard to imagine." I could tell Mom wanted to be hopeful.

"And even now, can you remember it? Anything at all?"

"Actually, no, I can't. But Tucky said I wouldn't necessarily." Mom looked like she wanted so badly to be able to announce that what she'd just shared with me was in fact a truckload of the steamy, but as much as she wanted to, she couldn't do that.

"I don't get it," I said. "Why would he even tell you? It's not like there's something to be done. What's at stake for Tucky?"

"But that was his point exactly, that I wouldn't be able to move on until I've processed it." I could see that Mom was now out of words.

"What do we do?" I said. "What's the plan?"

"I'll continue therapy."

"And?"

"Nothing gets fixed. With luck, I process the experiences."

"But that will mean you don't remember any of it, and you'll process it under hypnosis, too. Like it never happened, except he told you it did."

"It does sort of feel that way."

I got up and sat down next to Mom on the loveseat. I said, "Maybe I shouldn't go to China." I mostly meant it. "What Tucky's doing isn't right."

"I didn't tell you because I want you to stay home. I told you because I thought you should know, maybe needed to know. I'm dealing with it in my own way."

"I want to help if I can," I said, but there was shame in saying it. I wasn't actually interested in falling into line at the back end of the Tucky parade. All I really wanted to do was get up from the couch and head straight for the airport, sit in safety at the gate for the next twenty hours until they called my boarding group.

We sat silently until Mom started to cry, at which point I looked for an escape. I wasn't completely without a heart, but it was difficult to empathize. If I thought it was possible, I would have grabbed my snorkel right then and swum through that pool of shit until I located those few nuggets of truth.

I got up from the loveseat and surveyed the living room. I used my sleeve to rub a fingerprint smudge from a window. Mom sniffled on the couch. I wandered the room and ended up at the threshold to the kitchen. I continued through it, poured two glasses of water and turned on the television, I suppose to break the silence. I brought Mom her water, quick-scratched up and down her back, then retreated upstairs to my bedroom.

There was something else, too, something I realized as I crawled into bed. It had me fighting back tears, was powerful and undeniable—Mom was all alone in her chaos. She no longer had friends. Tucky, yeah, but fuck Tucky. I mean someone on the exterior, wholly biased toward Mom, a sounding board that always ended a rap session with reassurances. A voice and mind to tell her everything was going to be okay and that no matter what, the sun would rise and set the next day. I didn't qualify either, even if I'd wanted to. I was too far entangled in the bird's nest of it all.

It was heartbreaking to think Mom was as lonely as I was, or even worse, that she was lonelier, which she may well have been, though it wasn't a competition, and I had no interest in getting my hands on the yard stick that measured those kinds of units.

In the short time before I left, Mom and I didn't talk about hypnotherapy again, or much of anything, for that matter. Together we could ignore giant elephants anywhere—a family tradition—so we pretended everything was hunky-dory. A dozen times I asked Mom how she was doing, and she gave me what I wanted to hear, a perky, "I'm well, how are you?"

Mom offered to take me to the airport, but I insisted on a cab. I feared what an hour of one-on-one in the car might dump on our laps next. When it came time to leave, I said goodbye to Mom on the sidewalk in front of the house. We hugged, and I assured her that everything was going to be okay, even if I didn't entirely believe it. She nodded, and while she didn't cry while I was there, I sensed imminent waterworks.

I ached for Mom, I truly did, but at the same time, my sense of self-preservation was stronger than it'd ever been. It'd ballooned up in me when Mom told me about the abuse and got strong enough at that exact point that I was able to recognize that that flabby muscle of mine had been bulking up, little by little, ever since I'd gotten back from China, like it'd been doing bench presses each time Mom tried to peddle me some of her craziness.

End result, I was guarded in a new way. However, my movement toward self-preservation didn't preclude any of my desire to help Mom. I remained desperate to have her back to normal, for her to be fixed, but it was complicated. However, my feelings were complicated because they somehow conflicted, not because they weren't clear-cut. Maybe I'd started orienting myself in a different way.

Jeff and I met inside O'Hare at Terminal 1, Gate 32. I was so relieved to see Jeff that I hugged him, which I don't think he expected, but he took it in stride. Jeff had an instantaneous calming effect on me, which I didn't really acknowledge until then. I didn't unload what'd gone down with Mom the day before, but, just being in Jeff's presence, it somehow almost felt like I had. I was glad to be leaving that world behind for a while.

Jeff and I sat near the gate, both of us silent. I looked down at the floor and noticed a continent of a stain on the carpet in front of us. I asked Jeff what he thought about it. "Too big for a coffee or pop," I said. "Maybe there's a leak in the roof."

Jeff took pity on me. "It's big," he said. Then he looked around, and got up. "Going to duty-free," he said. Who could blame him?

Sitting there, I didn't have the ability to concentrate. Reading was out, and not that I'd done anything strenuous, but my body was happy to be at rest. So I just stayed where I was and sat staring blankly, essentially giving my body and mind a few minutes to further their transition to marshmallow.

I noticed a pigeon inside the airport. It was sitting impossibly still on a garbage can near a window about twenty feet away. I observed it for five minutes, and it didn't move. I wondered if it was scared motionless or if it had learned stillness for survival. At one point a toddler with curly blond hair also saw the pigeon, and on unsteady feet, the boy slowly made his way toward it. The pigeon remained stoic. The child got close, within about a foot. He reached out his hand to touch the pigeon. The bird flapped its wings aggressively, but it didn't go airborne. A few loose feathers hung in the air and drifted to the carpet. The boy ran cackling back to his parents. I wanted to smile but didn't.

The pigeon was perched on the same ledge of the garbage can when we got up to board the plane, and as Jeff and I joined the slow procession of passengers moving down the jet way, it dawned on me that I could help Mom. I had a way, but of course by then it was too late to do anything in the immediate. It'd have to wait until I got back, but I would do it. Mom didn't deserve that misery, no matter how it'd arrived. Helping Mom would be the first thing I did when I touched back down in Chicago. Maybe, finally, that would be the catalyst Mom and I needed to get our fractured lives on the mend.

I suppose that was hope, even if it didn't energize me the way some hope can.

Chapter 34

It took me approximately 3.7 movies to fall asleep on the plane, and not more than a few minutes after I did, my adrenaline woke me up, eyes open and mind alert in an instant. Something wasn't right. I smelled something. There was movement three rows up, older men on both sides of the bulkhead were squeezing out of their seats and hurrying toward the bathroom. They were each fumbling with something in their hands. Then another guy scurried past me and down the aisle. I saw he had a cigarette and a lighter with him.

Men were smoking outside the bathrooms. Ostensibly one spirited smoker couldn't take it anymore and lit up, which excited the fellow smokers. They came running, à la Pavlov. I smell smoke, therefore I smoke.

It took all eight coach flight attendants, and they were actually very polite if not too understanding as they instructed the men to put out their cigarettes. I laughed while they stubbed them out. Some of these guys were probably in their eighties, and yet every one of them bent their heads down, following their fingers, for one, maybe two, very quick last drags before dropping their cigarettes into the plastic cup ashtrays.

Just as the wheels connected with the tarmac in Shanghai, Jeff got anxious in a way I'd never seen. We were barely slowed down, and Jeff took off his seatbelt. His eyes got wide, and he stood up. He started hummingbird-tapping the back of the seat in front of him.

"Dude?" I said. He looked down at me and grimaced. "Relax, we're here. Everything is okay."

The loudspeaker came on and a voice asked Jeff to sit down, but he didn't. I touched his arm, and he recoiled. "Hey, what's going on?" I said.

Jeff was crying. It was no doubt the last thing a flight attendant would want to deal with after a fourteen-hour flight. By the time she'd jogged down the aisle to us from her breakaway seat, Jeff was frantic. She attempted nice, and she attempted stern, but Jeff would not sit down.

"Jeff," I said, "What's going on? We're safe. We're almost to the gate."

I repeated the same thing several times. I stood up, put my hands on his shoulders and forced his ass to the seat. Once down, Jeff's body lost some of its tension. He turned to me. "My grandmother just died," he said.

"What do you mean?"

"I just know. I've never felt anything like it before."

"First thing is to find a pay phone. I doubt there's anything wrong. We all get a little funky after long flights. Relax. We'll be off this thing soon, and first phone we see, we're on it."

I hoped my pep talk would get us through the next twenty minutes, but Jeff still looked crazed. It didn't bode well. I wondered if it was possible, if Jeff's grandmother could actually have died.

As soon as the plane hit the gate, we mashed our way down the packed aisle toward the exit. Jeff and I operated in true asshole fashion, which we punctuated by dismissing or altogether ignoring each of the several dozen dirty looks and comments given to us along the way. It worked, though. We were nearly the first to immigration. I let Jeff go ahead and waited in line behind him.

I've always gotten paranoid at passport controls, no matter the city or country. I did even before I became a smuggler. The anxiety that comes to me as I stand in those lines never fails to produce heart acrobatics in my chest. On that day, I could have used Jeff the rock much more than the version of Jeff that I had. Plus he seemed to be taking a really long time at the counter.

I checked my visa, even though I'd inspected it fifty times already. It had three months left on it. I slipped it back in my pocket, but then three months felt impossible. I couldn't have still had three months. I checked again. Three months. I triple checked, and Jeff, he was still at the counter. He'd been standing there for five minutes. I began to sweat from heart palpitations. I thought about our return and the mess I'd be in ten days when I had the mushroom-plush toys in my possession. That didn't help calm my nerves.

And still the immigration agent continued to ask Jeff questions. At least ten minutes had elapsed. People behind me in line started making noises and sidestepping to alternate counters. The immigration worker picked up her phone. Jeff wiped his face with the back of his hand, and I felt relief. It suddenly made sense. Jeff must have explained the situation. They were calling his grandmother. My blood pressure began to regulate itself.

The woman was on the phone for several minutes. I tried to get Jeff's attention. I waved, then called over to him. "Jeff. Hey, Jeff."

Jeff shook his hand behind his back to shush me. I behaved for a minute, but I called over again, "Hey, what's going on? Are they calling your grandmother?" This time Jeff didn't acknowledge me at all. That didn't sit well with me.

The woman finally hung up the phone, said something to Jeff, and pointed to the opposite end of the immigration hall. Two uniformed officers were heading our way. I said a tiny prayer that they weren't coming for Jeff. I didn't know who or what or where to direct this prayer—and it was no time for quiet contemplation on the subject—but saying something seemed better than doing nothing at all. *Whoever might be listening,* I said to myself, *whatever receives prayers like this, please make the officers not come to Jeff.* They went straight to Jeff.

Jeff ignored me altogether as they led him away, which scared me more than anything else. There was trouble, and he didn't want to involve me. Was it for mushroom trafficking? Were they bringing down the whole family? What had we done?

I was freaking out, and it felt like any second my heart was going to burst free from my torso and present itself naked to the world. My passport was wet and crumpled in my hand. The sweat on my back had soaked through my shirt entirely. I took a breath and stepped the ten feet toward the counter where Jeff had just been. I handed my documents over to the girl. She flipped through them, typed some numbers into her computer, and in Chinese asked me if I spoke Chinese.

"*Ting bu dong,*" I said—"I don't understand." Moronic, not only because I did understand, but because any other question was beyond my means, for instance the ten questions she followed up with, of which I understood maybe two words. "*Bu hao yi si,*" I said, "I'm embarrassed, excuse me." Five times I repeated it, so she picked up her phone and told someone someplace something about yours truly. She covered her mouth with her hand when she spoke—apparently she thought I was faking dimwittedness, which was generous of her.

She hung up, looked at me and said, "Your friend is Fa An?" I didn't answer. She gave me a flirty smile and shrugged. It was the same kind of demure gesture my cute high-school students gave me. I realized that this girl was probably not older than twenty. Seeing her do that, the way it revealed a little humanity, relaxed me a bit, got me feeling slightly warm and malleable, gave me a minuscule portion of confidence that everything would be cleared up soon.

I said, "Can I have my passport, please?"

The officer shook her head, then pointed behind me. I didn't want to look. I knew what was in that direction. She was pointing toward the inconspicuous door at the end of the hall, the one that Jeff had just disappeared into. Two officers came out of the door and headed our way. Chances were slim, but I kept hope alive—I can say that about my character in the face of this type of adversity. I remained hopeful until it was actually happening.

Up to that point in my life, I'd always been glad to never have passed through such a door. I eyed doors like that only peripherally or with protection, the same protocol I employ when I look at the sun or a stranger's crotch. I don't have business behind that kind of door, though I doubted explaining that to my two officer-companions would have done much good.

In this case, the mystery of what lay beyond that door wasn't very interesting. It opened to a long hallway with a cement stairwell at the opposite end, which reeked of stale cigarette smoke. We took the stairs up one flight and entered another hallway with about a dozen doors on either side. I could hear conversations taking place in the different rooms as we passed them along the hallway, but it was impossible to make out anything being said. I listened for Jeff's voice but didn't hear it.

We got to our room, a small, dank, windowless rectangular space with a square, unfinished wood table in the middle, and four simple chairs. They shut the door.

"Please sit," the older officer said. His English wasn't bad, and of the two, he carried himself in a more pleasant way. The younger officer, maybe in his mid-twenties, had nicotine-stained teeth, and the curvature of his eyebrows made me fear that my case was the one he'd been waiting for to expedite his rise to power in the Party.

I sat, they sat. The older officer clasped his hands and lowered them to the tabletop. "So," he said, "you claim to be a teacher."

"What is this about?" I said. "Yes, I'm a teacher, *wo shi lao shi*. I taught in Pingnan Middle School in Pingnan, near Hong Kong."

"Of course, we are aware of that."

"Why am I here? I'd like to know why I'm here."

"We have some questions for you."

I wondered what the penalty for smuggling matzutaki mushrooms might be. But at the same time, I figured any case against me would have been infinitely stronger with an actual seizure and confiscation of goods. Why weren't they nabbing us on our way out? Not only that, but I couldn't think of a single shred of evidence linking me to the mushroom business, not that existed in China, anyway.

"Why did you come to China?" said the younger one.

All that time standing in line, waiting at the counter, shuffling across the passport control area, up the stairs, back down the second floor hallway—I'd had several long minutes to manufacture something other than the truth, but it hadn't occurred to me to do so until just then. I was a despicable criminal. "Just missed China," I said. "I wanted to come back and see friends. Travel. Tour. Tourist. I'm a tourist."

"Pshaw," said the younger officer. "Tell us why you are really here."

"I told you," I said, "I'm a tourist here on vacation." Even I could sense the weakness in my voice.

The officers spoke to each other in a dialect. I couldn't understand a single word of it, but I had a response, which was probably stupid of me, but I did. I attempted double-reverse psychology, which was a term and strategy I coined and first utilized my freshman year of college. As best I could, I portrayed the deliberate appearance of someone who doesn't understand what they're hearing; i.e., I feigned casual disinterest, the logic being that no one would bother trying to pick up pieces of an important conversation if they were already fully absorbing its content. Unfortunately, just as it had during my time as an undergraduate, my efforts produced few results. I managed to amuse the younger officer, if anything, but I doubt he was actually clued into the multiple layers of my deception. He may, however, have had some idea of my ploy's overall usefulness.

The older officer said, "May we search your bag?" It wasn't as much a question as it was a directive, and he meant my old childhood backpack, the one that was too small for me to wear that I'd brought with me as my carry-on.

The younger officer looked ready to clobber, so I handed it over. They emptied its contents onto the tabletop. There wasn't anything related to the premium, thankfully. My journal was there, and that gave me the willies, but I doubted they'd be able to decipher my chicken-scratch handwriting, plus, ultimately, there was the yawn factor. Also, I was carrying an item I didn't recognize. Mom must have slipped me a small tub of gummy worms, which the older officer opened, sniffed, and poked with his finger. There were a few pens, a mini-flashlight, and my cell phone. Lastly, there was the JC Penny catalog, which I'd intended to toss out at O'Hare or at some point but never got around to doing—thankfully, I'd trashed the porn in Chicago before I left, but not this. The younger officer picked it up, and it opened quite naturally to those few pages in the middle that were of obvious interest to its owner. I regretted not having incinerated that thing when I had the chance.

They scrutinized and inspected, I suppose in a professional manner, until the officers were satisfied that I didn't have any mushrooms on me. They repacked my belongings into my bag, including my journal and the JC Penney catalog, but they left the cell phone on the table. The older officer picked it up and hugged it to his chest, Lady Liberty-style.

"What're you doing?" I said.

They glared, then walked to the door, twisted the knob.

"Hey," I said. I pushed back my chair and stood up. In a single motion, the younger officer slid his revolver from its holster and pressed it into my sternum. I worried that an elephantine heart-thump of mine might precipitate a discharge. "Empty your pockets," he said, "and sit down."

With the thin gun barrel still pointed at my chest—I think it was a .22—I produced the following: a pack of Extra Big Icyfresh gum, three flesh-colored earplugs (two caked in earwax), a clump of ratty tissue, a pen, eighty-six cents in assorted change, and a junk-mail envelope with Jeff's grandmother's address and phone number written on the outside. Wow, I thought, I truly am the world's worst criminal.

The officer fingered the envelope, and I think recognized the scribble as contact details and coordinates. I put my idiot-face back on and hoped my Chinese calligraphy was, as my former teacher repeatedly told me, so poor it burned the eyes to look upon. The officers took the phone and the envelope, turned to the door and left. I heard a bolt lock slide into place.

I was reduced to basic functions. I tilted my body to the side and released some methane, but there was no relief. I was bloated and severely off balance.

Time stood still in that room. Sitting at my table, I imagined what the future might hold for me, like chow-time chopstick shankings and mahjong in the exercise yard. But at the same time, the equation still didn't make sense, not even if I was deep into an elaborately choreographed sandbagging.

Maybe there were things about Jeff that I didn't know

about. Or maybe our encounter with Officer Metz? Could news like that travel so fast? But no, sharing information on almost-infractions had to have been pretty far down on the list of Sino-American diplomatic priorities. Maybe there was something with Ron. Or Jeff's joke about smuggling drugs, har-har, and I was about to go down in flames with their entire clan.

The officers finally came back, minus my phone and Jeff's grandmother's address. "Men," I said, "we might be able to move this along if you tell me what the problem is. I'm innocent, so I'd be glad to explain whatever misunderstanding there might be."

The officers looked at one another, and the older officer spoke. "Fine," he said. He slammed his fist on the table, which was shocking, yes, but it was also a horribly exaggerated gesture that, if anything, had the opposite effect. The younger officer had been staring me down, but after the fist-slam, his gaze moved to the opposite wall, I think in an effort to disassociate himself from his partner.

The older officer corrected his posture and slowly moved his hands up to his chest. He checked the placement of his lapels, took a breath and said, "Admit that you are here to aid the Xuan Gong, and we will let you go on your way."

I hadn't been mistaken for an international spy, and they weren't looking for drugs or mushrooms. What was good about those theories was that they ultimately wouldn't have held water, not even the mushrooms, not really. What was playing out instead was in fact much worse. With Dino, there were a lot of dots to potentially connect. Of course, they would never find exactly what they were looking for, because it didn't exist, but there was enough damning evidence on the surface to know that Jeff and I were in it thick.

It felt like my blood was barely circulating, like it'd coagulated into the consistency of porridge.

"I'll tell you what I know," I said, "But please, you've got to understand that I'm not in the Xuan Gong, and I wasn't coming here to do anything Xuan Gong to anyone."

CHAPTER 35

They wrecked us. I rambled on for the officers about how unimpressive the Xuan Gong was to me, but they weren't easily swayed. If they truly believed I was Xuan Gong, I was bar none the most spineless practitioner in history. Even so, my interrogation didn't end positively, and neither did Jeff's. We were both denied entrance to mainland China and put on the next flight out of the country to Hong Kong. Our banishment, they said, even without substantial evidence (a phrase I'd used several dozen times during my interrogation), would remain in effect for fifty years, and if we came back any earlier, we'd find ourselves in prison or worse.

We arrived at Hong Kong International Airport in late afternoon. Jeff was finally able to make his call, and it turned out he'd been right. His grandmother, apparently very near to the time Jeff had sensed it, died of congestive heart failure. Over the years, the disease distended her heart. The muscle grew larger and larger while the aorta and pulmonary artery didn't. Eventually it enlarged beyond the capacities of the rest of her body and Jeff's grandmother's swollen heart got so full that all it could do was stop. I wondered if it was a hereditary condition.

I listened while Jeff talked with his parents, and I gathered from Jeff's half of the conversation that his parents were keen on us staying in Hong Kong until they had a next move. They would begin calling in favors to have Jeff's status corrected.

They wanted him in mainland China with the family, and there weren't alternatives. I was worried his parents would face the same wall we had at Chinese immigration, but I didn't say anything. I was horrified of what that might mean.

My body was limp and heavy, and my heartbeat was slow and arrhythmic. I sank against a wall of plate glass and watched Jeff. Jeff, outside gate 23 at Hong Kong International as passengers loaded a plane bound for Singapore, standing at a payphone, calmly talking into the receiver with his face soaked in tears like he'd just been hit with a bucket of water. He was so wet and miserable that it embarrassed me. I tried to fight that impulse, but the wetter he got, the more determined Jeff seemed to be to not wipe his face. I felt helpless. The only course of action I could come up with was to take off my shirt and use it on Jeff like a sponge, but I didn't think that would improve matters much.

I shared that ugliness with Jeff, and maybe that's what was so painful. We were both so weighed down with shame, much more than either of us could handle. But maybe living that moment was in part Jeff's penance, and also mine.

It was Jeff's first time in Hong King, but I knew the city well enough to get us to some version of a safe haven. We needed cheap digs, so I brought us to the Chungking Mansions, a massive seventeen-story multipurpose building in Kowloon. There was never a shortage of entrepreneurs in the area, and in our weakened state we submitted to the first tout we encountered, a giant named Samir who said he was from Bangladesh. He ushered us, lit cigarette in his hand, from the heat of the sidewalk into one of the building's dank entranceways. Stopping just inside, out of sight from the other touts, Samir barked something into his cell phone, and in two minutes we were following into the elevator a very short, very effeminate Hong Kong gentleman with heavy makeup, painted nails, a tank top and sarong skirt.

It was a surreal, but altogether quick and painless transaction.

Our guide's English was very good, but neither of us could understand the guide's name. It was repeated, slowly, methodically, the same thing many times, until half way up the elevator ride, Jeff got it. "Esther?" he said.

Esther lit up. "Yes! My name is Esther! I am she," she said. And from that point, Esther was giggling, giggled as she repeated whatever we said: "Tee-hee, Everett... tee-hee, Wisconsin ... Shanghai, hee-ha ... tee-hee, one or two nights."

Our room was cheap, air-conditioned, didn't appear completely unsafe, and was clean—maybe not hospital-sterile, but I didn't see any hairs on the pillowcases. And Esther was entirely kind and very welcoming. We had a private half-bath that adjoined a large room with two twin beds. Every wall was whitewashed and bare. Granted, in our condition, Jeff and I would have been on board with any quasi-agreeable accommodations, but with this place, it felt like maybe we'd finally run into some luck.

Curious, though, was the guest-house layout, which was on par with the Chungking Mansions. Spaces there remained in a constant state of flux, all the time getting rented, re-rented or leased out, and often wholly reconfigured. We'd entered the guest house area through a steel door off an ancillary hallway on the fifteenth floor, but that might have been a side entrance to their facility, as it led almost directly into our room, and besides the door to our room there was only a twelve-foot darkened hallway that led to a common shower and to one other door that Esther said was the reception. It made sense as a small operation, a single room to rent and another for Esther and possibly Samir to live out their lives. But there were three doors in our room in addition to the main door and bathroom door. They were all without doorknobs and had been painted shut at some point, perhaps multiple times.

Esther left us after giggle-pointing to the mini-fridge. Jeff and I didn't know what to do with ourselves. We were desperate for calm and overwhelmed by a need for things to make sense, but all of that seemed too far off on the horizon. Our beds looked inviting, but we were too jittery for sleep, so we showered and headed back out.

Leaving the guest house, we couldn't find the elevator. The fifteenth-floor redesign became a maze. Esther made it seem so easy, a quick corner here, another there, etc. Narrow hallways and sharp turns enclosed by unpainted drywall partitions looked like they could have been there for years or only a few minutes. One dark area stank like an ashtray, another sounded like a dozen cats were stowed in crawlspaces left, right and above, and all elsewhere was like multiple continents in microcosm: countries, cities, and mountainsides stewing and stir-frying without ventilation—international transport available in the dark walkways, cement board accumulating flavor over time like passport stamps.

Jeff and I grabbed a quick bite, and afterward hit an internet café. It was almost eleven at night, but all of the computers were occupied. I sat on a metal bookshelf while I waited for a free computer. Jeff went straight to a phone.

Despite occasional relief from a few rotating fans hanging from the ceiling, it was seriously hot in that internet café. The other patrons were all men, at least that I could see, and it seemed every corner of the world was represented. Most of the guys had the bottoms of their t-shirts pulled up on their chests and their sleeves rolled up—lots of flesh, and when I sort of squinted, it looked like they were all wearing camisoles. I ordered a cold beer and watched two teenagers play the same internet video game, maybe even against each other.

When a computer station opened up, I was just beginning to

feel slightly calmed down. The beer was relaxing me, Jeff on the phone hadn't yet acquired sloppy cheeks, and being surrounded by normal people whiling away the evening was soothing. But then my email. I had three messages, one from Dino with the subject line *Urgent! Open with a Public Computer! Important!,* one from Peter Green with *Re: yo* in the subject line, and one from my mom, no subject.

My money was on Peter's as the least toxic of the bunch.

Dude, sorry I missed you at Paddy's, I got a flat tire. There's another killer band tonight at Paddy's. You in? How's it?

I've never used the flat-tire excuse. So lame. Flats are like food poisoning, their conveniently quick recovery time, yes, but also for their true frequency. Sure, anyone can relate and sympathize, but actual incidences occur far less than reported. I didn't have it in me to reply. I was without the energy, but more than that, there was nothing simple I could report about my life at that moment. Pleasantries weren't an option, so I deleted it.

I refreshed my inbox to make sure there weren't any other choices, refreshed four times and took a long sip of beer. I opened Mom's.

Dear Everett, would you please call me as soon as you have a chance? I don't want to interrupt your business trip, but there's something important we need to discuss. Please call. I love you. I really, really love you. It's not an emergency, but it's important. I don't know what else to say.

Love, Mom

Jesus. I hoped it wouldn't be, but I had a feeling Dino's could only be worse. Refresh. Refresh. Refresh. I ordered another beer and asked the guy next to me for a smoke. I hadn't noticed until then that he'd been unabashedly surfing porn and saving the images of his liking to a floppy disc, the old machine dutifully copying data at a steady clip. Refresh. Refresh. Then, this:

Everett, all hell has broken loose. Stay out of China and alert the media. I've been deported for alleged Xuan Gong activities. I was harassed and abused during a 37-hour interrogation. I fear for your safety. I am lucky to be out of that country alive. China is not the same place. Tell all of your journalist friends. A sack was put over my head, and I was taken to an abandoned warehouse. This is an international disaster. Be safe and spread the word. I will contact you again once I'm in a secure place. Please don't send your location. I hope you are still in America where freedom is allowed to ring. I can't believe the tyranny, but it is very real.

Delete. Refresh. Refresh. The porn man's computer was buzzing and coughing a picture of sideshow-enormous breasts onto the 3.5-inch floppy disk. The porn man shifted in his seat as if concealing an erection, then his erection was apparent through his slacks. My cigarette fell out of my mouth and landed on my lap, but I didn't want to touch it. Within seconds the porn man reached over to grab it, which was somewhat heroic of him, I suppose, but I leapt back in my seat. The porn man's computer hiccupped, then sounded like it was crumpling soda cans, so the porn man jumped up too, his pecker tenting his pants. Out of the corner of my eye I saw Jeff was back to damp-faced and looking in my direction but past me. Porn man was trying to pry his beloved floppy out of the drive before it became confetti. My inbox refreshed. There was a message from Vice Principal Pu, subject: *No Longer Welcome Pingnan.* I stood there and watched Jeff. My inbox refreshed again and there was another message from Vice Principal Pu, same subject. And a third, same subject. Porn man successfully wrestled his floppy from the drive, but it was mangled. He held it out to me, his eyes looking for commiseration, but I had none to spare. Jeff's left hand was covering both his eyes as if the room had gotten too bright for him.

I drained my beer, then walked to an available phone near Jeff and called home, because, well, why not?

"Hi, Mom," I said.

"I'm so glad it's you. How are you?"

"Do you know anything?"

"Know anything what? What's happening? Are you okay?"

"I'm okay, but they didn't let us into China. Dino got everything messed up. They think we're Xuan Gong."

"Where are you?"

"Hong Kong."

"Hong Kong? Because you're in the Xuan Gong?"

"I'm not in the Xuan Gong. They think I am because of Dino. Jeff, too, and Jeff's grandmother just died. Jeff knew before we could even find out for sure."

"That's something, that's really something. He sensed it. Amazing."

I'd made a mistake. I'd lobbed it right into her strike zone. "Mom, get off that boat," I said. "Enough. I'm stuck in Hong Kong and could do without mumbo-jumbo."

"It's zipped, not another word. Last thing I'm going to say is that you should read between the lines. And you're not going to like this, but I sensed there was a problem. I really did. That's one of the reasons I wrote you."

"Well, couldn't have come at a better time, Mom. No kidding, I needed an email like that about as much as a bullet in the stomach."

"Don't say that."

I sighed.

"I did, I sensed something was out of balance. I guess I was right." The tone in Mom's voice was changing.

"I've got lots of shit to take care of. Everything is okay there, right? I've got to get back to Jeff, figure out how we're going to get out of here."

"Do you need money? Can you get a plane ticket home?"

"That's not the problem, just we have to get Jeff to China for his grandmother's funeral, and we've been banned from the whole country for fifty years."

"Has he called his parents?"

"I told you, he's on the phone with them about two freaking feet away from me."

"I must have misheard you."

There was static on our connection.

"Mom," I said, "the connection's gone bad."

"What? I can't hear you, just keep talking."

Keep talking. I said, "I'll call you back."

"I can't hear you. There's static. Just keep talking."

I took a sip of beer. "Mom? Can you hear me?"

"I can, I can. I think we had a bad connection," she said.

"I should probably go. But you're okay? I wanted to make sure, but there's a lot going on right now. You're fine?"

Mom was quiet, and then said, "There is something else, but it sounds like there's already a lot on your plate. Maybe you can call me back in a few hours once things have settled down."

"It's practically midnight. I'm not going to call you back. Just tell me. It'll be worse to know more bad news is on the way."

"It should wait. I can tell."

"Too late. Please just tell me."

"It's a somewhat serious matter. I need you to be in the right frame of mind."

"I'm not going to hang up until you tell me. Please, Mom. Please."

"Take a few deep breaths for me."

"Mom."

"You won't get off the phone with me, well, I won't tell you unless you're centered and more relaxed. Take a few deep breaths, and do them into the phone so that I can hear."

I huffed into the receiver.

"Please, this is a worthwhile exercise, I promise. It'll help overall."

I took a few audible breaths as I motioned to the cybercafé staff that I needed a fresh beer. "Okay," I said. "Spill."

"I was exploring my subconscious with Tucky this morning, and we discovered some more upsetting information." She paused.

"Yes? And?"

"This is difficult for me. Please be patient."

"Go on."

"I don't know how to tell you this, but it seems I may have done things to you as a child that I shouldn't have. Bad things. Your father and I both did bad things that we shouldn't have."

"What are you talking about?"

"Please," Mom said. She was sobbing on the other end. "It's worse. I abused you as a child."

"So you're telling me that you abused me? And Dad?" I flipped through the file cabinet of my life, each folder containing a different snapshot—showering as a child with Mom, Dad tugging muddy clothes off my young body and marching me to the tub, any possible moment when I could have been a victim—but they all came up clean.

And yet it was the kind of information that had the ability to create doubt. I wondered if I was missing something. Repression and anguish, for instance. Yet, nothing like that had ever crossed my mind. I always wanted approval from Dad, but would that have been the case if he'd abused me? Maybe that's exactly why I needed it. But, no, it didn't make sense. I was, after 40 seconds of consideration, 99% sure that this was unrefined, purest-form Tucky dung.

I heard Mom yelling into the phone, trying to reel me back in. "I'm so sorry. I don't know how I'm going to live with this. If I could change anything in the world, it would be this. I would, but, oh, God, how do you change this?" She was hysterical on the other end of the line.

"You didn't abuse me. Tucky is filling you with lies." I said it with confidence, was mostly confident.

"They aren't lies. I remember. Sort of. Tucky told me details. My God, I'm some kind of pervert."

"This is crazy." I was interested in details, but ... Fuck. I didn't want to deal with it just then. It was too much. "I promise you didn't molest me." I practically yelled it into the phone. It occurred to me that I was standing in the middle of an internet café. I scanned the room to see if anyone, especially Jeff, had heard me. It didn't appear so.

"It's okay to be upset."

"I'm not upset. It didn't happen."

"I'm sorry."

"All right. Jeff's calling me. I've got to go. But remember, you didn't do anything. Really, you didn't. Tucky is full of fucking lies. I love you. I'll talk with you later."

"I love you." Mom let out a pained squeal just before I hung up.

Before we left the cybercafé, I remembered the legal counsel Dino got us. I truly hated to contact him but managed a few lines. *Dino, fuck. We need that lawyer. We're stuck in Hong Kong, accused of Xuan Gong stuff, which is obviously bullshit. We can't get into China, and Jeff needs to because his grandmother just died. It needs to happen. Who's the lawyer?*

CHAPTER 36

Jeff and I got silently drunk at a nearby bar. We also brought a few bottles back to our room. Beer gave us confidence and patience to navigate the Chungking hallways. We eventually found our guest house, and poor Jeff, he'd protested with that shoulder shrug of his, but I barged in anyway, to the wrong room.

There they were, Esther and Samir, naked in the dark, intertwined on the couch watching television and drinking tea. They weren't startled to see us; that or they'd learned to not let a mild surprise precipitate a dumping of hot tea on bare flesh. Their calm, in fact, calmed me, to a fault, and I didn't move. I stood there looking at the naked pair, at that enormous Bangladeshi wrapped around his tiny Hong Kong lover. I watched the various hues of light from the images on the television as they flickered on their skin. It was a sacred place. Within the confines of that small space, those two lived out their lives in peace. Behold the wonder of adaptation.

The next morning, I lay in bed immobilized by a hangover. I wished we'd remembered to turn on the AC the night before. I began wondering about the predictability of life. I attempted to forecast ten, twenty years down the road. FYI, this is something better attempted when a body isn't punishing the mind for a recent assault of toxins.

I imagined Mom never moved out of the house, and

neither did I. Tucky gave Mom drugs that made her immortal and decrepit, like a vampire, which was to somehow atone for abusing her son, and every day she was compelled to apologize to me for the molestations. Mom modified her appeals daily in order to demonstrate sincerity, and I had to endure those sessions with Mom every single day, a little redress of my own for my role in the production, even though I'd certified for myself that Tucky had indeed fabricated the entire saga.

I suppose I fell partially back asleep. I had a dream that I was in prison, not a Chinese prison, but a hardcore federal penitentiary back in the States.

I was still fresh in, but I was there for the long haul. For safety, I kept to my cell, but the other inmates kept waltzing right in, one after the other, helping themselves to my commissary. My stash of Pop Tarts, caramel corn, Snickers, etc. was dwindling fast. And each one of the prisoners, after they'd picked out their treat for the day, told me, in their individual styles, that I'd better keep my supply up, because if I didn't, I'd find out what molestations were for real, and that I might just find out anyway.

Jeff plucked me out, woke me up from my half-sleep. "You up?" he said.

I took a deep breath. What a horrible fucking dream, plus it was further evidence that there was never sunshine to be found in contemplating the big picture after a binge.

I rolled over, facing Jeff. He was motionless and in the fetal position on his sweat-soaked sheets. He looked as bad as I felt. Maybe he was also attempting to crawl out of whatever hideous place he'd taken himself.

"Jesus, man. What are we going to do?" he said.

"Any idea how prison commissaries actually work? I sort of get it but sort of don't."

"Now. Do now."

"I don't even know if our passports work."

"I know."

"We could kill Dino. Or pay someone to kill Dino."

"At least chop off his fucking balls."

"Nah, he doesn't need them. He'd probably thank us for ridding him of sexual desire. He wakes himself up when he has wet dreams."

"I know, but I still think castration is the answer."

We laughed, and I tried to remember the last time both of us had laughed together, but I couldn't.

"What about my grandmother? Fuck."

There was a knock at the door.

I didn't expect anyone to actually come in and so didn't worry about my presentation until Esther and her clickety-clack sandals were making their way across the room, and she was handing me a cup of tea.

"Thank you," I said as I reached for my shirt. "And sorry again about last night."

Esther giggled and dramatically covered her eyes with her free hand. "Not looking, not looking, tee-hee," she said. "Hee-ha, just bringing tea for the party boys." She gave Jeff tea, and said, "Are you boys saying bye-bye or staying one more night?"

Jeff and I looked dumbly at each other, perplexed by even the simplest question. "Not sure," Jeff said, "Can we tell you in an hour?"

"Yes. Drink your tea. It's good for you."

Esther stepped toward the door, and I, without first thinking it over, called to her. "Esther, can I ask you a question?"

Her feet facing the door, Esther twisted her head and upper torso back toward my bed so that she could peek over her shoulder at me teasingly. "Yes?"

"What are funerals like in Hong Kong? What do people do here when someone dies?"

Esther had obviously hoped I'd be asking her something a bit more playful, and for that I was sorry, but as soon as the question registered for her, Esther untwisted from her peek-a-boo pose into something more appropriate. "Did someone die?" she said.

"My grandmother," Jeff said, which surprised me. Not that Jeff appeared to judge Esther, or Samir for that matter, just that he usually defaulted to introversion, especially when stresses set in.

Esther stepped toward Jeff and lovingly swept her long, painted fingernails back and forth across Jeff's shoulder. To put it mildly, Jeff soaked it in. So effective was that human touch in releasing the stored tension in Jeff's body that his head actually lowered two inches closer to his mattress. I could also tell that the interaction was providing Esther a validation of her maternal inclinations, which was brilliant and quite amazing. I was glad for Jeff—and aware of how starved he was for TLC—but I couldn't squash my jealousy. I began to wish that I too was mid-catastrophe, and that there was another female form in the room, also with manicured nails like Esther's, who was deeply concerned about my wellbeing.

Though of course I did have a tragedy, tragedies. Mom had just told me that I was the victim of parental sexual abuse. Even if I didn't believe it, that information was stand-alone traumatic, and I bet sour enough to score me a few long sweeps from somebody's fingernails. *Esther, I hate to burden you with another dark tale.... Esther, my mother just confessed to me that she's a pervert. I pray you're not also a member of that club.... Oh, Esther, you're so kind, I can't help the need to tell you about this horrible and recurring abuse I received as a child, of the sexual variety, that has only recently come to light....* How practiced, I wondered, would a man need to be to effectively produce tears at will? *Esther, my dad died a few months ago, and he was a dirty child molester to his only living son, me. Oh, and did I forget to mention my dead brother? Not even one year old, that's a very sad story as well.*

And so it was, while I sat rearranging words in my mind in an effort to create a perfectly heart-wrenching list of personal trials that would trump Jeff's predicament, I missed an entire conversation, one where Esther offered to bring Jeff to her grandmother's herbal medicine shop in Tsim Tsa Tsui for consultation on paying respects to the recently deceased.

CHAPTER 37

Later that afternoon, Esther knocked on our door. She was very pulled together, had traded in her sarong for a pair of shiny black slacks. She was wearing a form-fitting denim jacket, and her hair was pulled back tight in a ponytail. And other than eyeliner, Esther was free of makeup. She'd even removed her fingernail polish. It was the most traditionally masculine I'd seen her. Still, for strangers, guessing Esther's gender would have probably been tricky.

We headed out. Esther was self-assured on the street, chin up in her muted drag as she led us to Hong Kong Island. Jeff and I combined didn't match her confidence. There was safety trailing in Esther's wake, and purpose.

Approaching the waterfront, the Star Ferries of Hong Kong looked impossibly heavy, as though every additional minute of buoyancy sustained was a small miracle. On all surfaces of these boats was an unimaginable number of thick oil-based layers—top half glossy white, bottom lime-rind green—which added to the illusion of weight; plus, the fog of its diesel exhaust suggested an engine so large that it couldn't possibly be encased in something that floated.

It was just past three in the afternoon, so there wasn't the rush-hour madhouse on board that there could have been. We chugged across Victoria Harbor toward Wan Chai and stood on the lower deck, starboard side. I had my fingers tight on the knobby handrail and observed the city landscape. I watched huge waves glide across the bay and crash into the side of our boat in no pattern at all.

I didn't have expectations for the day, and as we got off the boat I realized that I didn't want or need them either. It was an adventure, the idea of which I liked, especially with someone else at the helm.

"Wan Chai used to be a red-light district years ago," Esther said as we walked along the sidewalk. "I grew up here. This shop has been in my family four generations."

When we got to the building, Esther bowed slightly and gestured with her hands to the front door, which was bellhop-like, but I didn't laugh. I think she meant it as a sincere welcome. It upgraded the formality of the afternoon somehow, which I hadn't expected, but maybe I was the only one who hadn't been taking it so seriously. I nodded in appreciation.

Stepping into the shop was like entering a primordial cave, not so much because of the lighting, but because I could sense that humans had been operating in that space for a long time. It went beyond lived-in and toward something more significant. And although the objects for sale looked like they could have been there for decades if not centuries, it was all very tidy, extremely clean. The jars and bottles on the shelves were perfectly transparent, like their interiors and exteriors got hit with a rag each morning.

Esther's grandmother was six inches shorter than Esther, which put her well under five feet. She was wearing a loose-fitting light-blue blouse and tan slacks, and had short, stark-white hair parted on the left side, bangs flared. She moved briskly from the back room when we entered, marched up to Esther and pulled her down toward her by the collar so that she could kiss her on the forehead.

Esther and her grandmother spoke in Cantonese. We couldn't understand the words, but the shifts in Esther's grandmother's facial expressions were indicators enough that Jeff's story was being relayed.

"Jeff, Everett, please meet my grandmother, Mah-mah."

We shook her hand. I said, "Should we call her Mah-mah?"

"Oh, yes," Esther said.

"*Ni hao,* Mah-mah," I said. Mah-mah cracked a smile. She pulled us, actually tugging pinchfuls of our sleeves, into the back room where she'd been when we arrived, a small, sunlit space, also meticulously clean.

"We'll take tea," Esther said, and the three of us sat down at a circular table as Mah-mah put water on to boil. Esther continued speaking with Mah-mah and occasionally asked Jeff questions. What was his grandmother's name? Li Mei. How old was she? 83. How long had his family been in the U.S.? Nearly his whole life. Was his grandmother loved? Yes, very much, by all.

Next they got the scoop on the premium, also on Dino and the Xuan Gong. Mah-mah shook her head and said people should be left to do what they want.

Esther and Mah-mah continued mining out particulars from Jeff, but my mind began to wander. I considered the possibility of sexual abuse. It weighed on me—behold the command of paranoia—and I'd more or less been carrying out a comprehensive scan of my cerebral cortex since talking to Mom. So far I hadn't encountered any red flags, which is to say, nothing alarming surfaced that was directly related to this particular subject matter (but in the process, I did revisit a few old gems, among them: spying on Mom one Easter as she cried alone in the basement, Dad hollering at me for testing the durability of his giant golf umbrella, and the patented hallway-shuffle routine I employed whenever I dumped in my pants during grade school).

Sitting in Mah-mah's shop, I angled a little differently at

information gathering. I took a swim through my sexual history to see what I could find there, the idea being that an unbiased evaluation of my behavior might provide some insight into whether or not I'd been abused.

Starting at the beginning, I thought about when my alone time first required tissues. It was during middle school, a transition that was contemporaneous to my introduction to porn. So, yes, the soundtrack to my initial sex education had a lot of wah-wah pedal, but more importantly, it allowed me to connect A to B, porn to prowess. The porn itself was ultimately traumatizing somehow—but more to the point, I recognized porn as the catalyst. Way back then, it changed me from stork-delivery enthusiast to man with a hand. I hadn't learned it from my parents earlier in life, and I wasn't further informed until health class years later.

On top of that, I didn't have any abnormal fears when I began exploring my body as a youngster, not more than a vague anxiety about being barged in on mid-process. Barely a teenager, and despite the knowledge of the one-on-one, two-on-one, and other interactions that I observed in the porn, it never even occurred to me that someone might like to assist with my pleasure sessions. It was more like I feared Mom would suddenly open my closet door and, standing there with a laundry basket balanced on her hip, ask me why I was in there, naked and in the dark.

I'm not perverse, either, I don't think. On a scale of zero to sociopath, I'd be in the middle somewhere, one to one-and-a-half pegs to the dark side, at most, but still very much a middle-man.

In general, I've had mild to low-mild success with the ladies, with an unenviable record of repeat customers. Not that I don't try, and sometimes I get lucky. The times I do, it feels lucky, like stars have aligned and that's why I'm allowed that singular attention. I become so grateful and head-spun when it happens that, in the thick of it, I've never bothered worrying about the inevitable, that soon I'll be on my own again and back to square one.

I've got impulses, sometimes more than normal maybe, but I'm not sure if that's true. Yet, for the record, I've never been hungry for the twisted or depraved. On those days when I can't find satisfaction, I'm voracious for the mundane. I foam at the mouth for a few mostly quiet missionary wiggles and not much beyond. Truth is I've always been fairly average with uninteresting desires to match.

Everything that came to mind while I sat at Mah-mah's, my pathetic sexual history, the introspection and analysis, the dredged-up anguish, those things drove home one simple fact: I didn't know squat about sexual abuse or how a victim negotiated the world. Incidentally, I would not recommend this exercise to others, poring over your life trying to determine whether your faults and failures might be the result of possible childhood handjobs/blowjobs to/from Mom and/or Dad or God knows what else.

Nothing to that point had convinced me that I operated as though carrying around a secret dungeon in my gut, where I allegedly stored the awfulness that my mind had tried to erase.

And so I remained confident in my memory. I've always kept everything upstairs. It's a mess up there, yes, but anything of value has ultimately proven locatable for me.

But even as I reassured myself of my virgin childhood, I couldn't help feeling like I'd deposited myself in a pond of shit, smack in its middle. And I knew continuing to explore the road I was on would increase the distance I'd have to paddle before I hit a shoreline, but I, the good lemming, kept on.

I second-guessed Esther and my desire to have her fingernails tease the hairline on my neck. That seemed possibly abnormal somehow. Maybe I was reaching out for the unfamiliar because it was the only entity that felt safe. Or, the likelier, less interesting and more depressing conclusion, that I was actually just that desperate for companionship, and so long as I got it, I didn't give a damn who dished it out. But, yikes, unfurl another layer, and maybe that desperation did ultimately derive from victimization.

My heart felt engorged, as if it was trying to engulf my torso with its mass—like it was willing itself to get so big that a corner of it could creep up my neck and whisper to my brain *Get off this train, man, it's not a good one.* Which I appreciated. I took note of this new dynamic in the relationship between my heart and me.

I widened my scope, took a few breaths as a gesture to my new friend, my heart. My family was out of whack. That I knew, and it wasn't up for debate. I estranged myself from them because of it. Individually and as a unit, we were always substantially off-kilter, yes, but at the same time, our lives never seemed crooked beyond repair, and even though we seldom attempted to do so, I never considered us unfixable, not even Dad.

The small grain of inquiry I'd started with had expanded in the style of a dry sponge dropped in a bucket, and despite logic and reason, it felt like it could absorb even more and get bigger if I let it. Doubt, even baseless doubt, can be so powerful.

Mah-mah flopped a newspaper down on the table in front of us, and the tiny breeze from it caused me to become aware of the nerves on my face. I could feel how tense the muscles in my cheeks and brow were. I was glad to not be looking in a mirror, and when I scanned the room, I saw Esther watching me. She looked concerned, bless her, and she smiled at me, apparently aware that I was popping out of my trance. I managed to smile back, then looked down at the table to watch Mah-mah.

She shimmied a single piece of newsprint from the folds, opened it wide and began to turn down corners—a parallelogram into a triangle and back into a square, many times over, neat and calculated slow-folds, pressing long and firm down each centimeter of every crease.

When she was done, Mah-mah fiddled at corners and tugged lightly at certain spots, but those last adjustments seemed to be more a reflection of her personality than of structural necessity. Mah-mah had created a perfectly symmetrical boat out of the newspaper. It had a four-sided pyramid in the middle, like a sail, and deep pockets between the sail and its sides, like a tugboat.

Esther said, "We will fill it and send it to your grandmother."

Mah-mah stood up and began gathering items from her store. She put them in a canvas shopping bag that had, I saw when I looked closely, the single sultry close-up bottom lip album cover art from the Cure's *Kiss Me, Kiss Me, Kiss Me* on it. Esther saw me eyeing the bag and let leak one of her giggles, really the only indicator of her other life that she'd revealed in front of Mah-mah. I smiled, and although I'm sure Mah-mah heard it too, she acted as if she hadn't—not in a cold way, just as if her head was in the clouds. But maybe that was just as cold; I don't know.

Jeff and I followed Esther and Mah-mah back onto the ferry to Central, where we transferred to another ferry, this one to Lamma Island, which is on the South China Sea side of Hong Kong Island. It was early evening and most of the other passengers on the boat were on their way home from work. Lamma Island is populated by only a few thousand people, I suppose those who prefer to go home each night to the quiet.

It was slightly perplexing that so little had been built up on land so close to the heavy congestion of Hong Kong Island. Lamma Island was lush and undulating, and the village where we arrived, Yung Shue Wan, was tiny. It had been a fishing village, and it was still largely undeveloped, save for an expanse of a dozen stilted seaside restaurants and a few rows of concrete houses that'd been poured into the hillside. No cars were permitted on the island. It was backcountry and moonshine compared to the rest of the city.

The mood was upbeat but all of us were silent as Mahmah and Esther walked us through Yung Shue Wan. At the edge of the village, we continued south on a cement sidewalk trail that traced the shoreline. We passed three beaches, and when we got to the fourth, Mah-mah and Esther stepped off the path. They removed their shoes and started toward the water. Jeff and I did the same. Day was fading, and aside from the towering red beacons that topped the power plant on the northern tip of the island, the scene was idyllic and pristine; tiny waves were lapping at the shore, the sky was a dull orange-yellow, etc.

Mah-mah took a small brown blanket out of her lip-bag, spread it out and emptied the rest of the bag's contents onto it. Then she got on her knees and began arranging the items. She motioned for us to come down too.

The four of us, our eight knees in the sand on each side of the blanket, looked at what was there: a candle, fruit, a small bottle of wine, a wad of imitation paper money, and a bag of dried mushrooms. Last to come out of Mah-mah's bag was a section of the newspaper. She unfolded it and handed a page to Jeff.

Articulating only through hand gestures, Mah-mah instructed Jeff on folding the boat. Her hands created the very same boat with an invisible piece of newspaper in the air in front of her. Each crease, each fold, Jeff executed every nuance, and what patience and concentration they both had. Esther and I as spectators were completely absorbed.

When the boat was done, Mah-mah began to speak. Esther interpreted.

"We will send this boat to accompany a wandering soul on their journey to the after world. This candle is put in the boat and lit to help guide the way. Food and wine are put in to feed your grandmother on her journey. This money is for good luck. And these mushrooms, you and your grandmother like mushrooms, isn't that right?"

"Yes," Jeff said. He smiled, and I suspect he had the same short-lived, sinking feeling I did, that without the premium, we wouldn't have been stuck in Hong Kong doing this in the first place.

"Put them all in the boat," Mah-mah said. Jeff followed instructions. Then Mah-mah got up, we all got up, and walked over to the ocean's edge.

"Light the candle, and when you are ready you can go into the water and let the boat go. Think good thoughts about your grandmother. Later, I will go to the temple and ask the monks to pray for her."

Jeff nodded, took off his socks and rolled up his pantlegs. He lit the candle, arranged everything on the deck just so, in balance, and entered the water. Esther, Mah-mah, and I stepped into the water up to our ankles, but Jeff made his way out farther and farther, until he was almost up to his waist, about twenty feet out from where we were.

I began to worry that the boat would take on water, that it might sink. I imagined tiny sailors, breathless as they bailed the paper vessel with rusty coffee cans, a lone lamp on the tip of the mast lighting their futile pursuit, peg-legs then torsos sinking with the pulpy hull as the sailors contemplated their final thoughts.

Or even worse, that the soggy clipper would beach itself before Jeff even had a chance to wade back to shore.

But it was as positive an outcome as we could have hoped. Jeff released the boat, and it sat sturdy there in the water. It allowed the tiny waves to kiss it, to make it dip and bob, but the boat stayed right where it was. Its longitude and latitude didn't alter, and Jeff, hands on his hips, surveyed from above.

It slowly, over several long minutes, floated a few feet out to sea, but only so far that it was just out of Jeff's reach. Then again it was as if anchored. The boat didn't move from that spot when Jeff started backing away from it, back toward us. It hadn't moved when Jeff got to shore, or by the time we had the newspaper and blanket back into Mah-mah's canvas bag. It was still stuck in that spot when we dusted the sand from our feet and had our shoes back on. The flicker of the candle seemed to be in the exact same location when it was just barely still in view, when we reached the first turn in the cement path on our way back to the village. We stopped there for a moment, all aware of the gravity of that curve in the trail. Jeff waved to the boat, and we headed back to the ferry.

CHAPTER 38

Jeff fell right to sleep when we got back to the guest house, but I didn't have the same cathartic down comforter to crawl under, so I went out.

First, I hit the cybercafé to check my email, which felt risky, but I did it anyway. There was some nonsensical barf from Dino about how our lawyer wasn't a good candidate to take on the case because he was also on seventy-five-year sabbatical from China. Dino said the injustice of our predicament was now his top priority.

Dino, I wrote back, *no lawyers. Don't do shit. Do nothing. Forget I wrote you. Forget it all.*

Dino supplying zero help wasn't surprising. In fact, I found solace in the predictability of it, and in a roundabout way, his unreliability soothed me. That was my mood. It'd been a good day. That was just one component of the composite. All the various little things and the way they fit together provided relief, even if I didn't fully understand how or why.

I decided to observe and celebrate that relief by heading for drinks at an expat spot I'd been to in Soho (south of Hollywood Road). The bar was about halfway up one of the largest escalator systems in the world. Open-air, it squirmed between buildings and over busy streets from the financial district near the bay to primo real estate farther up the hill. In all, there's nearly a kilometer of escalators and people-movers, which always impressed me.

I zigzagged my way to the bar, went in and took a seat. I ordered a beer and surveyed the scene. I was very clearly the anomaly among the lithe and wealthy clientele, but I didn't care. The beer did me decent, and the environment, although much stuffier than I'd normally plop myself into, had me feeling more civilized than I had in a while.

Part of me wanted to spill it all, every last detail, and at that moment I felt prepared to tell it to anyone unfortunate enough to engage me. But even if that didn't happen, if there would be no release like that, at the very least I planned on getting ripped, like I'd been the night before, and that'd be a fine enough cap on the day.

I sat alone for about an hour until a young woman came in and took the barstool beside me. She had gnarly blond dreads and a giant backpack. Her shirt was dirty and her cargo pants were zippered to shorts. Weathered but not altogether unattractive, she wasn't wearing a bra, which I admit interested me on a number of levels. I looked forward to sneaking peeks and silently etching the details of her form into my mind over the next little while, so I was slightly startled when after a few minutes she turned to me and said, "Hi. I'm Fawn." She was American.

"I'm Everett."

"Also from the States?"

"Chicago. You?"

"Sort of a long story, but originally from Vermont. Now I'm traveling." Fawn began playing with her tongue ring, poking its stainless steel bead in and out between her lips.

"How long?" I managed to say. Maybe thirty seconds had passed, and already my marker was gracelessly banging around in my pants.

"As long as the money holds out, at least two more months, but not if I stay in Hong Kong. Dude, this place is expensive."

"Tell me about it," I said. The words came out of my mouth awkwardly and made me feel horribly out of practice. "And here, let me get you a drink."

She slammed her remaining beer and ordered us two more.

Fawn wasn't very different from the other backpackers I'd met in Asia. She'd hit the regular circuit, Thailand, Vietnam, Cambodia, and was heading into mainland China next, where she was considering getting a teaching job. "It's a good gig," I said, "as long as you don't expect to go home with any money. That's the thing."

Fawn reached for the backpack at her feet, unzipped two zippers, and took out a credit card.

"See this?" she said.

I did.

"Know what it is?"

I shrugged no, and looked a little closer. E-Funds, a MasterCard. "A credit card," I said.

"FEMA debit card. They're subsidizing my trip."

"FEMA card? Like Hurricane Katrina?"

"Not like Katrina. Katrina."

"You were in New Orleans during Katrina?"

"Yep."

"And you're using your FEMA card to travel around Asia?"

"Yep."

"Didn't some guys get busted using their FEMA cards at a nudie bar?"

"I don't know about all that."

"I think so."

"Doesn't matter. It's my disaster relief, for all the soggy shit I left behind."

It wasn't lost on me that Fawn was doing real damage to a large-scale government program meant to help people. Fawn is like gunpowder and a bullet for the critics of federal aid and that mattered to me, but in that moment, it didn't matter enough to steer me off my course.

"Is your family in New Orleans?" I said.

"They've never been there." Fawn said it like I should have known better.

"So where's your family?"

"So where's your family?" she said, mimicking me in a super-cold way.

I pretended she hadn't just done that. I hoped she hadn't twisted a faucet and increased the flow of crazy to her brain.

"My family is in Chicago, my mom," I said, extra upbeat and positive.

Fawn put her FEMA card away and slugged back the rest of her beer.

"Want to hear a story?" Fawn said. She was back to cheerful again, even flirty. "I'll tell it if you buy me a beer."

I ordered drinks and Fawn told me a mostly unbelievable story about leaving New Orleans. She told me she has a kid she hasn't seen in years. She got sick after she gave birth, lost a lot of weight, but the doctors thought it was postpartum depression. She got sicker. They ran tests and diagnosed her with terminal stomach cancer. That night, the night of her diagnosis, she jumped ship; abandoned her baby and the rest of the family in Vermont. She went to New Orleans, where the plan was to party her way through her final months.

On her fourth day in New Orleans, ninety-six hours into her bender, she had what she called a moment. She'd just plucked a half-eaten hot dog out of a garbage barrel, she said, and as she sat on the curb building the courage she needed to eat that hot dog, a woman approached her. She told Fawn she could see the sick in her. She said she could cure it.

Fawn moved in with this woman and slept in a hammock in the backyard. She got off the sauce and drank some gnarly herbal concoction all day.

After three weeks, the woman told Fawn she was cured. Fawn went to a clinic, and the doctor there gave her a clean bill of health, said there were no traces of cancer, no evidence cancer ever ate away at her. The doctor thought Fawn had made up the whole cancer story; at least that's what she told me.

Katrina came four days later. Fawn battled the storm from the hammock, or so she said, and used a bogus address to get her FEMA dough. Then she ducked out to Asia. She still hasn't talked to her family since she left Vermont. "They probably think I'm dead," she said.

Every word of Fawn's story could have been complete horseshit. Or not.

At one point Fawn bent down, and with her head just below the bar, she spit on the floor. She looked up at me and smiled, as though she hadn't just spit on the floor. She took my hand and led me to the dance floor. Michael Jackson's "Human Nature" was playing, and Fawn began to wiggle and twist. She noodle-danced and spun around like we were at a hippie festival out in some meadow, and every nuance and movement of her arms reverberated on her bra-less chest, which challenged my chivalry, but I wasn't complaining.

I employed my only available dance style, which approximates to the hand and hip movements of a mechanized toy drummer. I kept my body rigid and my arms out front, fists tight, and adjusted the speed of my drumming to the rhythm of the music.

Thanks only to Fawn's breasts, we weren't the complete eyesore we could have been, but it didn't matter. It was dancing without repercussions. Fawn danced like someone equipped to skip town and not look back. I'd aspired to that when I first left for China, but I never had the heart to truly fuck-all and move on.

Like a hungry zombie, I fed on Fawn. Tasty Fawn and her middle finger to the world were temporarily inside me. She gave me something more or different than courage. Maybe it was the synergy of it all, too, the day and week and past few months all contributing—but no matter the recipe, together Fawn and I spit on the floor all night, spit on the floor with our dancing, with whiskey shots, even Fawn's big nipples poking through her shirt was spit on the floor.

And I was better than okay with it. I felt wonderful. No, Fawn never heard about Mah-mah or the Xuan Gong, about molestations or Mom's crystals, but I was fine with that, too.

Fawn came back to the guest house with me. She didn't have anywhere to stay, plus the obvious. It was very late, and I had to wake Esther up to get an additional room for us, which apparently did exist, a windowless room the size of a closet with a single bed. The three of us barely fit inside without someone on the mattress.

We closed the door, and Fawn and I collapsed into each other in drunken love-humping. I hoped at some point she'd go down on me with that tongue ring of hers, but she didn't, even though I was very generous myself—Fawn had a wild bush and tasted like armpit.

We fucked, and I didn't use a condom. I came inside Fawn, and just as my heart began to mellow, when I no longer feared cardiac arrest in that small room, I began to cry. Fawn thought it was a reaction to the sex, as if joyful tears were all I could manage after my first visit to her pleasure-universe. She said we could do it again, but I wasn't interested. I cried harder and stuck my face in her dirty, matted hair. I breathed it in and sobbed myself into a drunken sleep.

Chapter 39

The next day I woke up with another killer hangover, and that love nest of ours was cooked up hot, kimchee-style. There was condensation on the walls, and we were rank, our bare skin red and raw.

There was no delay to Fawn's departure. I watched as she blinked her eyes awake, and seconds later she was clambering out of bed and getting dressed. I raised myself for the farewell, but that was the extent of the fanfare. We didn't exchange emails or phone numbers, and when I hugged her goodbye, she whispered to me that I yelled in my sleep all through the night. Then she was gone.

I went to find Jeff. It was barely seven in the morning, but when I entered the room, Jeff was sitting on the edge of his bed. He was staring at the opposite wall, fully clothed with his shoes on. He had a bottle of water in his hands that he hadn't yet opened. Jeff appeared as though he might have been sitting like that for a long time. He gave me a strange look but didn't ask where I'd slept the night before.

"My parents are coming to Hong Kong," he said.

"That's good," I said, and I sat down on my bed. Jeff looked awful—cleaned up, yes, but also cracked into quarters on the inside. I didn't want to look at him, and instead I found myself staring at his bottle of water. Jeff followed my line of sight to his hands, and lobbed it over.

"You sure?" I said. Jeff shrugged, asking, why would I ask?

"Thanks," I said. I gulped down half of it. "What happens when they get here?"

Jeff looked so young right then, as if he now understood less of the world than he did on his first day of kindergarten. "We'll bribe our way across."

It was plausible, just a matter of cash into the right hands. But then what? "Getting out might be more difficult," I said. I didn't want to be alarmist, but, fuck.

"I don't know," Jeff said. "My parents think it will work, and, well, they know much more about this kind of thing."

Jeff looked nervous. Who could blame him? "It sounds risky," I said. "Maybe you should wait for some other options."

Jeff shook his head no, and I understood the gravity. It meant Jeff himself had very little to do with the decision-making. I found myself holding back tears—probably leaking into Fawn's hair half the night didn't help that cause any.

"You should go home," Jeff said. "There's nothing for you to do here." Jeff's voice was shaky. We were both on the verge, and neither of us was interested in a blubbery transaction.

"You should come with me," I said. Jeff shook his head again. Waterworks were on the way, so I grabbed a towel and draped it over my head as I dug in my bag for fresh underwear. I headed to the shower.

I packed up my things, and as I was leaving, I told Jeff to call me when he got home. I also told him everything was going to be okay, and though I hoped it would be, I had serious doubts. As we hugged, I willed myself conscious of the moment, of that goodbye to my friend. I wanted to be able to remember it. "Take care of yourself," I said. Jeff's body shook against mine, a brief tremor, then he sniffled, pulled it back in.

"You too," Jeff said.

I had no idea when I would see Jeff again, if ever.

I couldn't face anyone, so I didn't say goodbye to Esther and Samir. Anyway, I'd offered a nice *fuck you* the night before when Fawn and I woke them up at four in the morning, which was too bad.

I stepped out into the sticky Hong Kong mid-morning air and realized I was alone. I didn't feel lonely exactly, just lighter, like I'd traded in the cement boots I'd been wearing for a pair of flip-flops. There was sadness there too, but I didn't feel guilty, not exactly. That's just how it went down.

That sunlit airiness in me didn't last, unfortunately. As soon as I began to sweat, which wasn't a block away from the Chungking Mansions, I began to itch, down below. My mind immediately produced a single explanation for the burning, that Fawn had given me warts, herpes, and the clap, those three most definitely, and I allowed for the possibility of other transmittables as well.

It got worse with each step. I tried to convince myself that it was just crotch rot, on account of the heat and humidity and all that walking we'd done the day before. But, no, it was worse than crotch-rot. I wondered if crotch-rot was contagious. I decided that yes, it very likely was. And, anyway, what the hell was up with Fawn's giant bush? What'd she have hiding in there? It seemed to matter.

I recognized the onset of a new sensation in my heart, too. It felt like a heap of salt-water taffy, like I could watch it through the window: my heart in the taffy tub with the stainless-steel arms, my heart getting pulled edible and delicious, to be bought up, gobbled and gone.

When I got to the airport, I booked a ticket to O'Hare via LAX and had just enough time to grab a cycle of Amoxicillin and bottle of calamine lotion at the airport pharmacy. They were at least something, a little reassurance, two tangibles to remind me that I'd taken steps to prevent the shriveling of my manhood, eventually into dust, in the recycled airplane air that no doubt exacerbated the dick-to-dust disease Fawn had gifted me.

I didn't sleep on the plane, but I wasn't twitching strung-out-junkie-style either. I did not bang my head against the seatback. I was instead anesthetized by my hysteria, motionless during fits of nausea and mini-panic attacks. The flight became an odd little purgatory. I tried thinking of Dino but couldn't picture his face. I tried thinking of Jeff, of Esther and Mahmah, of sticking my willy into Fawn, but I always returned to the same place, which was nowhere and everywhere at once.

I was in horrible condition by the time I finally stepped out of the airport and into the bright cold of Chicago. I felt so full, and full of so much. My body did what it could. It purged a portion of the available, but there was little relief. So much gas came out of me, but I was constipated at the same time. I chiseled and dragged from my nose large snot-oysters, and they kept coming, like a mama oyster had laid a few hundred eggs up there. My undershirt was sopping wet. It felt like I hadn't stopped sweating since I left the Chungking Mansions. Plus, over the course of the flight, I'd successfully drained the entire bottle of pink calamine lotion into my underpants.

I wished I had somewhere else to go. I wished Jeff had an apartment nearby, and rather than what he was actually occupied with at that moment, he was instead sitting on his Papasan chair playing video games, waiting for me. That would have been nice. Even just to grab lunch or a beer—some immediate alternative to Mom, but there wasn't one.

Chapter 40

I'd been gone less than a week, but things felt different. I'd changed, though I wasn't exactly sure how. Moving east from the airport in the back of the cab, I rolled my window halfway down. The rush of cold on my face felt good, even if the driver gave me crazy-eyes. But I didn't roll it up. It felt important to exercise what I was beginning to sense as newfound authority over myself. Even that small act of disobedience seemed to matter.

The house looked the same as we pulled up, but I again had a strong sensation of transformation. The door was unlocked, and I walked inside.

Mom must have heard me. I barely had my bags past the storm door, and there she was at the top of the stairs looking down at me. She'd been crying, was still sniffling a little, but she was also smiling, an awkward smile I'd seen just a few times before, where her mouth-curl conveyed curiosity, maybe even some hope, and I think a bit of humiliation.

She didn't come down to me. She stayed where she was, so I dropped my bags and started up the stairs to her. Mom still didn't move, so I bounced a little faster. When I got to the top, I hugged her.

Mom cried, pulled back from me even, but I didn't let her. I pressed my face into her shoulder and said, "There's no way you did those things. No way."

Mom nodded her head, but I couldn't tell if she was doing

it in agreement with me or not. She whispered, "Truth is the only way forward."

Well, so that was that. Mom was apparently unchanged, which didn't exactly inspire me to dance the Roger Rabbit there in the second floor hallway. If anything, I revisited an old thought of mine where I tried to constrict and mash the insanity from Mom's body. But it wasn't a very strong desire, and I only thought it for a moment. And, after I had, I realized that, in the end, I wasn't much compelled by it at all.

I didn't respond to Mom about truth being the way forward. Standing there, I began to understand that for me, the nonsense had in many ways gone stale. It just didn't gut me the same.

After checking email for word from Jeff, which there wasn't— my inbox had no new correspondence—I showered, and, clean again, I slipped out the front door. I didn't think Mom heard me. She was in her room meditating, or if not meditating, she was engaged in some other activity that required the accompaniment of a Pan flute.

I parked across the street from Tucky's dojo. The barber's pole out front reminded me again of the poor frosted-tips stylist at the hotel in China, and that put me in a funky mood, but I tried to remain focused as I got out of the car, as I pulled the dojo door open and entered.

I didn't anticipate it, but just inside, Tucky was right there, leaning casually against the front counter. He waved to me. "You're Everett?" he said, as if expecting me. He stuck his arm out for a handshake.

"You know, this old plate glass front window is a hazard," I said. "If it broke, huge daggers of glass could impale someone. It could kill them." I wasn't sure from where it'd come inside me, but I appreciated the tone it set.

Tucky reached out and took my hand in his, kept our hands

interlocked, even, and he waited until I'd made eye contact with him before he spoke. "What can I do for you?" he said.

I wondered if it was the barber pole, that somehow when I get within a certain proximity of barber poles I have the ability to act out in atypical, un-Everett ways. I leaned my face in close, deep into Tucky's personal space. "Why are you filling my mom's head with those things?"

Tucky answered calmly, casually, like we we'd just spent the last half-day sitting next to each other at a pig roast. "It's not like that at all. I share with your mom what she shares with me under hypnosis. It's important stuff."

"But none of it is true. Nothing." I leaned in a little closer. My nose was just a few inches from Tucky's. He was letting me look directly into his eyes, which was unnerving. Our faces practically touching was creating an intimate moment, and very briefly I felt like I should be kissing him. I got dizzy. I steadied myself by ranking the level of bloodshottedness in his left eye. 5 out of 10, with one long red river of a blood vessel streaming damn near the whole thing.

"I wish I could agree with you," Tucky said. "But as I've come to learn, rebirth sessions can, and often do, reveal the most deeply suppressed emotions and experiences. Real experiences, not imagined."

It was the first I'd heard of a rebirth session. "Rebirth?"

"Yes, it's one of the types of therapy your mother and I are working on."

I tried to imagine the components of a rebirth. I pictured a canal, a bright light, etc. But it wasn't for me, so I jumped ship. "Are you qualified for that?" I said. "For any of this?"

"It's not an actual birth. There's more to do with what's called connected breathing. No pauses between the inhalations and exhalations." Tucky took a long, relaxed breath to demonstrate; whatever fear I'd managed to cultivate in Tucky was vanishing.

"I know all about rebirthing and connected breathing," I said. "What you don't seem to get is that it's ruining her. You're ruining my mom," which was the truth, and, realizing that we were still holding hands and had been since I entered the store, I rolled my shoulder back and swung my arm so that the tips of my fingers created a theatrical arc through the air. That got a reaction from Tucky, finally. He took a step back.

"I'm doing no such thing." Tucky backpedaled slowly, and I moved forward.

"That stuff didn't happen. No way."

"It's her past. I'm helping her come to terms with it."

Tucky sidestepped so that the corner of a large wooden table separated us. I glanced down at the tabletop's contents—some textiles, soft reds and turquoise, and several skinny tree branches poked into floral foam that had shiny jewelry and whatnot hanging from them Christmas-tree-style. I stepped around the corner of the table, and when I did, the top of my hand grazed and toppled a tower of bamboo whistles.

I was again next to Tucky. He moved, and I followed. We weren't running, but our pace had quickened.

"Have you ever been sued?" I said. Then, still in pursuit, I reached across the table and plucked a tree branch display from the nearest foam brick, for a weapon. The branch was nearly weightless, and the way all those trinkets shimmered in the light, it wasn't as menacing as I'd hoped. I tossed it on the floor, which was satisfying, so I snatched up the next nearest branch and flung it down on the floor, too. One after another, I felled all of Tucky's tree branch displays, and when I looked at him to gauge his reaction, to assess how many ticks away from a battle royale we were, he was wearing that same docile expression he'd had on when I came in, which was infuriating, but also sort of a relief.

"You can't sue for this kind of thing," Tucky said. He'd

gotten to the opposite side of the table from me, gained a leg up while I was occupied with the branches.

I stopped, he stopped. I reached down and grasped the tabletop with both hands, bent at the legs in preparation to overturn the thing.

Tucky watched me delicately. He didn't look angry or afraid, just dumb, and maybe borderline sympathetic.

"Why not sued?" I said. My imagination moved toward the violent. I could see it clearly, leaping across the table and hammering Tucky with my knees and fists.

"Because it's consensual," Tucky said. "But more to the point, I'm helping your mom, not hurting her."

In my mind, Tucky was down on the floor like yesterday's buzz-cut discard, and I was on top of him playing the drums on his face with two handfuls of the bamboo whistles.

"Stop telling her those lies, man. It is destroying her." My voice cracked, but I remained in table-spilling position.

"They aren't lies."

"You're destroying her. Destroying."

Tucky thought for a minute, and another battle scenario arrived to me. This one involved me, head down and palms at my shoulders, pressing Tucky across the store battering ram-style, finishing with Tucky airborne through his plate glass window.

"I wish I could help you, but there's nothing I can do," Tucky said. "I think it's time you let your mom live her life. That's what she needs now more than ever, to process her past and proceed as an individual. Not as a wife, not as a mom, but as an independent spiritual being."

I was very focused on Tucky and what he was saying, and perhaps overly tense in my table-toppling position, but no matter the contributing factors, I certify to having received no warning signs for what I next offered to the conversation. It was audible and became *put-put-put* when I tried to stanch it. I hoped it sounded like the noise a shoe can sometimes make, when it hits certain surfaces at certain angles.

"Well?" he said.

I looked for a twinkle in his eye, a slight turn in his lips, anything indicating gas-recognition and so, excuse to thrash, but there was nothing. I tried to maintain the course. "Even if there's something behind what you're saying," I said, "Why the crystals and rebirths?"

"Maybe you'd be interested in a session to better understand?" He seemed to be part asking and part telling.

"I don't think so."

"Yes, maybe that's it. That might help resolve some of this."

Gas aside, it felt like I was deflating, which was a new and disturbing sensation. Something very strange was happening to me. There were aspects of Tucky's offer that almost seemed sensible, and when I realized that, it felt like there was an instantaneous compounding of all the nonsense that had accumulated inside me. And somehow that gathered ridiculousness became simultaneously uncontainable and scattered, almost like it'd vanished, but not via the slow release of a puncture hole, or even matter escaping from a large rip or tear. It was more like the membrane that had been holding it all in magically disappeared, and its contents followed suit just a heartbeat later.

My head was truly spinning. I couldn't make sense of what had just happened to me. I started toward the dojo's front door to leave. I think I heard Tucky call after me and again offer a rebirth session, but I didn't turn around. I wasn't sure what he said, actually, or whether he'd even called after me at all.

The goddamned tattletale must have called Mom when I left, because she was waiting for me when I got home. She didn't say anything, just hugged me and gave this knowing look of hers, as if our nonverbal connection actually communicated volumes, which was horseshit, but anyway.

That encounter with Mom was brief, and afterward, Mom retreated to her bedroom, and I took cover in mine. I turned off all but a nightlight and got between the sheets, I suppose to set the mood. I planned to have at a little practiced breathing, the rebirth kind.

I'm not sure what I hoped to accomplish by dipping my toe in that river. I was somewhat open to the possibilities, whatever they might have been, plus I was curious. That said, I knew nothing about the actual process, just what Tucky had told me when I was at the shop. So that's where I started.

It turned out that connected breathing was more difficult than I'd thought. Iiinnnoouuttiiinnnoouutt, etc. I tried to calibrate my efforts with an imaginary ping-pong ball, which I thought was resourceful. I balanced it on the nozzle of my human-bellows. It hovered softly above my mouth, and I let it sink back to my lips, over and over again. At least that was the idea.

I had some mild success. Maybe the calm lowered my blood pressure a bit, but in the end, I just wasn't cut out for that kind of thing. Even in my mind, the ping-pong ball kept rolling off the bed, and not just that, but I kept having to gasp for air, and I doubted there was a chapter on that in the rebirth manual.

I thought about Mom, too, during periods of rest, while I monitored the progress of my invisible ping-pong ball across the carpet. She hadn't left her room either, which was strange. I didn't know what she could be doing in there for so long. I knew she was in there, though, which is to say the ambient tunes were abundant, as was the sage stink.

Chapter 41

A little before midnight, just as I was beginning to enjoy some variation of repose, I heard a high-pitched squeal. I rolled out of bed and peeked out my door. The house was thick with aromatic smoke. I didn't see any flames. That was good. Then Mom was yelling at me from the other side of the house. "It's okay," she said. "No fire. The sage got a little out of hand."

For no good reason, I grabbed an embarrassingly tight t-shirt from deep within the China pile and tugged it on, and I went out to help. I rolled the desk chair from Dad's office into the hallway to underneath the smoke alarm. The chair had a tilt feature, which had loosened and made it unstable, but I got up on it anyway, extended tippy-toe and fanned at the smoke detector with a July *Midwest Living*. It rained postcard inserts briefly.

I fanned double-time, but the alarm kept screaming into my ears. Plus, the chair I was standing on had really started to shake. It was tweaking out, as if I'd yanked it from Dad's office while it was smoking something speedy, and the dope was now coursing through it at Mach 2.

At that moment, it occurred to me that there were other things I could be doing, that the world was full of infinitely more pleasurable pursuits than the one I was presently engaged in—but me, I wasn't complaining.

I finally took the damn battery out of the smoke alarm, which helped, but something else happened, too. From my position there in the hallway, high up on that shaky chair, I had an unexpected opportunity to observe Mom. I watched her hustle from one room to the next, heaving up windows, and as I did, I recognized a new heaviness in her movements, and I could sense that it wasn't a reaction to the sage-smoke episode we were experiencing. It seemed like Mom was carrying a different kind of weight, not like there was a new heavy on top of the old heavy, but more as if the new heavy had swapped out the old.

That interested me, but I couldn't put my finger on more than that. Maybe I should have dug a little deeper, invited Mom for a beer to unwind, share a few post-smoke alarm chuckles, and in the process execute a little reconnaissance. That would have been a wholesome aberration from our everyday dysfunction, and given all that had just gone down, maybe even possible for us. But by the time the smoke had cleared and we had the windows back down, I'd had enough for the night. I peeled off the ridiculous t-shirt I was wearing and crawled back into bed for some nesting.

A few hours later, in the middle of the night—at 3:42 a.m., to be more precise—Mom came knocking on my door. "Can I come in?" she said. "Are you asleep?"

I pulled a pillow over my face. "Yes," I said.

I meant, yes, that I was sleeping, but Mom came in. She removed the pillow covering my head. I kept my eyes closed, and when I opened them, Mom's face was right there, maybe twelve inches between our noses, which was shocking. She was tear-soaked, but glowing.

"I have great news," she said. Mom was bursting. "I didn't do anything to you, thank God. And I wasn't abused. Not like you think."

Not like I think? Mom was elated, but I was at the other end of the bell curve. "Yeah, I know," I said. "It's complete bullshit, glad you finally see that." I was getting claustrophobic. I felt around on the bed for another pillow for my face.

"Well," Mom said, "It's not all bullshit, not exactly. It was me in a former life. It finally makes sense. I did go through those things, I did do those things, but it was in a former life."

There was a pillow between my legs that I considered for my face, but once I've delegated a pillow to my thighs, I don't like to change it up all willy-nilly. "A former life," I said.

"It makes complete sense. Don't you get it?"

"Not really. Who told you that?"

"Annette, an advisor I've been talking with."

"A friend of Tucky's?"

"No, she's a psychic, the real deal. We've been talking the past few hours. I've never had this kind of clarity."

"Is she here?" I looked over Mom's shoulder and out the doorway for Annette. I also allowed for the possibility of Annette as an apparition; Annette floating around the hallway looking bored as she waited for Mom to finish up with me.

"No, we talk on the phone."

"A phone psychic."

"She's on the other side of the city, so we have to talk on the phone."

I didn't have a response.

"I was meditating and found myself drawn to the newspaper, to a certain section, and there was an ad for her services. I called, and she explained it all."

"Seriously?"

"I didn't have to tell her anything, she knew it all. 'Honey,' she said, 'it is true, but it was a former life. You can rest easy.' Isn't it wonderful?"

"Great, Mom, great." Desperate times, desperate measures. I yanked the thigh-pillow out and over my face. It was hot and damp, but it suffocated well.

"Please look at me," Mom said. I sighed but moved the pillow a little. I could see Mom, but it still protected the lower half of my face.

She was still hovering above me. "I'm sorry," she said. Mom blinked, which produced a single tear. It collected, big, then broke free and fell through the air toward me. I felt the wet on my forehead, where it'd landed. I got somewhat repulsed by that dewdrop of Mom's. I had an urge to wad the area with paper towels, or pump a few globs of hand sanitizer on the spot.

I tried to remain focused, to keep a grip on the larger picture, and mini-teardrop-crisis aside, it was the moment I'd been waiting for, at least a version of it.

"I'm so sorry I put you through this. I am truly sorry," she said.

The information came into me a little at a time, Mom's weird apology-baptism thing. Like it was syrup and I tilted my head sideways, the information streamed from its landing spot on my forehead, crossed my brow, and entered into my ear where it began to slow-coat from the inside.

"I'm sorry," Mom said again. She must have sensed the syrup effect.

"It's okay," I said.

Mom reached toward me and combed through my bangs with her fingers. What I'd craved, and finally receiving it, I in part got sad. A few fingers in my hair wasn't an outrageous demand.

"And know what else?" Mom said.

I shook my head no.

"I forgive you."

Apparently those last words were the clincher for Mom, because saying them enabled her smile to do the impossible. Her mouth got bigger and wider until there were so many teeth, so much of the gums on display right there in front of me, that I actually got scared. It was a cartoon-nightmare set of choppers, capable of the unimaginable. That popped me back to claustrophobic in a hurry. It didn't just feel invasive, the fingers in my hair, Mom's proximity, etc. it felt more like Mom was engaged in a hostile takeover of my domain.

"Forgive me for what?" I said. It felt like I was shouting. I might have been.

"For not believing me, but I know it was a tough pill to swallow."

"You said you molested me. Now you forgive me for not believing you, even though it was never true?" I was incensed. I grabbed opposite ends of my pillow and pulled it down hard around my whole face.

"Let it process," she said. Mom gave a few love-pats to the top of the pillow, like it was my head. I couldn't see her, but I imagined Mom, in her exhilaration, dancing out into the hallway. She might have used a single happy finger to pull my door closed, and that finger's euphoria, contagious and spreading, had Mom in full-flare jazz hands as she moonwalked to her next task, whatever that might have been, whatever might have logically followed the completion of this, her most recent activity, which she could now check off her to-do list.

I, on the other hand, was immobilized and wanted to think and feel anything other than what I was. I didn't think it was possible, that Mom could have really rubbed out all of her uncertainties. It made me doubt all of my own doubts.

I considered storming out of the house—beelining for the DeVille, and then who knows where—but without even the power to pull myself upright, the bed defaulted to as good a place as any to stew in my personal Dutch oven with all the odd flavors and their complexities. I was numb and motionless, save for whatever my heart was up to. The chaos in my chest was unreal, like if the angry revolution carrying forward in there could have somehow been harnessed by the right militia, no coup would have been out of reach.

I tried to derail my mind with distracting thoughts, but I couldn't manage, so I instead worked on occupying myself with tiny physical activities. First I pinched the flesh on my knees and elbows, really clamped down hard. That provided some short-lived amusement. After that, I measured my fat index via two handfuls of belly, which was no ego boost and only ate up about eight seconds of the night. I had a go at masturbation, which I should have known I was in no mood for, but anyway—failure there also did little for my self-esteem.

I'm not sure what starbursts in my mind inspired what I did next, but there in my bed, I began experimenting with the removal of various types of hair on my body. At first, I tested the amount of pressure that follicles in different areas could withstand, but that quickly graduated into outright yanking.

The top of my head wasn't so bad—easy to pluck and not very painful. My sideburns proved trickier, because of their length, and when I managed to get a few out, it carried a totally decent sting, which I noted. I figured pubic hair would also provide a good bite when freed from the skin, like sideburns, but their removal didn't do much for me. It was the same with my leg hair and arm hair, and also the hair in my armpits—none of those extractions proved very satisfying.

Then I got a terrible itch in my nose, an itch that felt like a feather was being pulled back and forth from the nostril to the back of my head. I dug in and scratched, to some relief. It occurred to me that the itch was actually a sign, as if my body had sensed my pursuit and wanted to assist. I tested the theory, pinched a nose hair between my thumb and index finger and yanked: brilliantly excruciating.

I set aim on cleaning house, both sides. I tugged coarse hairs out, one after the other, and sprinkled them off the edge of the mattress and onto the floor. I kept expecting the sting to diminish after each hair I removed, but I can report that it didn't. I yanked and cringed, over and again, until there wasn't a single hair to be found inside my nose.

Simultaneous to my engagement in those activities, I was aware of a weighty feeling drifting around in my head. I kept denying it entrance, even though it wanted in, badly. It was big enough, it seemed, that if I allowed it access, it had the potential to snuff out a lot of the monsters I'd collected the past few months; check out those blue skies. It was the possibility of Mom finally being cured, that she'd gotten her hands on the antidote and taken a drink.

But for that, I'd have to accept that it didn't matter what road she'd taken to get there or who she'd rubbed elbows with along the way, and that felt like a risky settlement. Then again, maybe it wasn't too far-fetched. Maybe it was a final turning point, the bookend to our turmoil. And, in the end, maybe that was the thing that mattered the most.

Chapter 42

I assume I slept during the night, but if I did, it wasn't much. It made for an odd feeling in the morning, the moment I became conscious that my eyes were open. It was as if I'd been asleep, as if I was just waking up, except that it was hard to say for sure if that's what was happening, if I was truly transitioning from sleep to wakefulness. All through the early morning I imagined vivid scenarios and visited memories in my mind, as if in a dreamland, but I wasn't dreaming, I wasn't asleep, and in the dark it didn't matter if my eyelids were open or shut.

I could have done without that confusion. It felt like it set a bad tone for the day. In any event, from which state I arrived at my moment of awareness was irrelevant. I got there, to the point where I understood that I was me in my bedroom, naked on a scratchy, bare mattress, also that I possessed the ability to adjust myself from my horizontal position. It took me many slow minutes, during which I produced a variety of sad-elephant-type noises, but eventually I rolled off the bed and onto my knees. I pulled on a pair of shorts and the too-tight t-shirt from the night before, which I still had some mysterious magnetism toward, and went to Dad's office to check my email.

I had one new message, but it wasn't from Jeff. The sender was Red Can Market, and the subject read *MUSHROOMS*. I got tingly, which surprised me. Regardless of all else, it was news enough to contact Jeff again. I was deliberately limiting the number of emails I sent—like he needed my constant nagging and worrying on top of it all.

I opened the email.

Dear Sirs,

I received a package of your mushrooms and found a large dead cockroach inside with the mushrooms, a cockroach the size of a mouse. Is there a reason I shouldn't contact the health department?

My reaction was strange but powerful. To be sure, I couldn't have cared less about the alpaca-fuckers at the Red Can Market. I remembered the place. They vended organics exclusively, and this slow-talking, squirrely guy with a soul patch made me swear our premium was 100% organic, which I did. In truth, our fungi may very well have been organic; at least, no one ever told me it wasn't. Anyway, I seriously doubted there was a cockroach the size of a mouse in with their premium. Jeff and I packed those things ourselves.

No, my reaction was to something much larger. Before opening that email, I was proud of myself for building the courage I needed just to raise myself out of bed that morning. On its own, the mouse-cockroach allegation was insignificant, but when I put it in line with everything else, it became exhibit Q, another piece of evidence that a higher power might have been out to get me, to get both of us, Jeff and me. And I had no idea what we'd done to deserve it.

Being the target of a higher authority was worrisome. I also knew it was a fairly crackpot conclusion, but still. I was wrapping my head around that as I attempted to write to Jeff, just to say hi and check in on him again, and I couldn't seem to get the words where they belonged.

It felt like over the past few months I'd become increasingly unsure of everything I did, and now, in the place where I'd arrived, my mind and all it drove was constantly gummed up by uncontrollable hesitations. Except when I realized that,

I was admittedly also aware that not all of my cylinders were operational, which may or may not have been symptomatic of the status quo, but anyway.

I tried to power through it. I sat at the computer, but the longer I toiled away at the construction of a few very basic sentences for that email to Jeff, the more worried about him I got. It was a cyclical and debilitating process. I felt so helpless. Plus, I think there was also fear in the mix. It was way down deep inside me, but big. I was afraid to hear back from Jeff, afraid of what news he might deliver.

I searched for Jeff on the internet, first his given name, also its diminutive, in English and pinyin, then all versions with the following search terms in different combinations. *Xuan, Gong, Dafa, grandmother, plush, family, optometry, Hong Kong, accused, alleged, smuggling, bribe, dui, imprisoned, executed.* Nothing hit, which didn't provide relief, and when I finally stepped away from the computer, I realized that the exercise, while begun in earnest, had taken me to a different, even darker place. I considered the possibility that the task I'd just carried out was borderline-masochistic.

I rubbed my hands on my face and deep into my eye sockets. I knew, too, that there was more still. In just a few hours we would have our first open house, so that was also tacked into the equation, and it bobbed around with everything else I had floating around upstairs. I took a deep breath, which transitioned on its own into a deep-ocean kind of sound: ailing humpback whale in D minor.

A shower occasionally helps me rinse off the crazy. I stood under the water for some time before I even picked up the soap. It did help, and I took some deep breaths as the water dumped over my face. Amazing what hydration can accomplish, I thought to myself. Then I remembered the activity in my nose from the night before. I carefully stuck my soapy pinky finger inside my nostrils to wash the areas clean, which seemed important. It stung badly, and not in a satisfying way. I made a tiny basin with my hands and let it fill up with water, and I dunked my nose into it, to at least get the soap out. That helped.

I picked up the shampoo bottle and decided to indulge in a short *xi fa* scalp-scratching session, which I enjoyed, even as giver and recipient. Once I'd emptied approximately a quarter of the shampoo bottle into my hair, and I'd found a rhythm with my fingers, I began to brainstorm how Mom and I might continue our discussion from the night before, which in some ways felt like the most impossible of all propositions up to that point. I think that was in part because of how withdrawn I felt, despite my central placement in the thick of it. There was also the possibility that Mom was already past it completely, thanks to Annette. And if that was the case, it was no small miracle, and of all the miracles out there, Mom's was definitely of the delicate variety, like the very intricate and miraculous way Mom had been pieced back together could get shattered back into a million pieces just from someone breathing on her wrong.

It took about five minutes of the simultaneous-counter-clockwise-circular-sideburn portion of my *xi fa* treatment to convince myself that my conversation with Mom from the night before didn't require rehashing. I had nothing more to contribute, not really, and even if I did, it was not enough to motivate me toward another sit-down with Mom.

I persuaded myself that we were edging past the crazy and back into familiar territory, and I worked the logic over in my mind until it became fact. We'd have a fresh start of it all, and from that point on, Mom and I would proceed together and ignore crazy's lingering bits, and crazy would hopefully return the favor.

I toweled off optimistically.

I was upbeat but a little scattered still when Janice Sugarbottom arrived. Our place looked sharp for the open house, save for what Janice called "spices gone wild" throughout the second floor, referring to the sage-smoke fiasco the night before. The charming three-bedroom colonial home of my childhood was fluffed. The eat-in kitchen was scrubbed. Plastic fruit rested in a wooden bowl on the butcher-block countertop. Fresh white towels hung in its 2.5 bathrooms. Every surface in the semi-finished basement had a fresh coat of paint, which Janice took a moment to reflect on, as she'd done a handful of times throughout the process. She reminded Mom and me that our basement was one of the most challenging assignments she'd ever given her crew, which was total passive-aggressive dog crap, never mind how she'd again skillfully glossed over my own efforts with regard to the scrubbing and whitewashing of our catacombs, but anyway.

Just inside the front door there was a card table with a poinsettia, a stack of business cards featuring Janice's smiling face, a sign-in sheet, two pens, and a greeter/security detail; i.e., a teenage girl flipping through an issue of *People*.

Mom and I had to scram during the open house. I told Mom I had to run a few errands, and Mom said she'd hang back out in the garage.

I'm not sure what exactly compelled me, but it felt like an important moment. I felt hopeless and directionless, which was maybe how Mom and Dino once found themselves—a drunk's rock bottom or something, when it almost doesn't matter whose hand it is, so long as it's pulling you up from the darkness and into a different place.

I was sort of like a robot, and I had an objective. I got in the car and drove straight to Tucky's. I parked, trotted past the barber's pole, and into the shop.

The place smelled awful, like Tucky had borrowed some

hobo's fifty-five-gallon burn barrel in order to cook up a few bricks of goat-shit incense. A far cry from sandalwood or lavender, this stuff made the air musty and sour, though I admit to some quality in it that was unmistakably from the earth.

Tucky or someone had straightened up since yesterday's visit, re-stuck the branches and such, but I didn't see Tucky. The shop was empty. I sniff-followed the stink to its source, to a door at the back of the dojo. I knocked three times, but there was no answer. I turned the knob and walked in.

Opening the door released even stronger odor, and it was at least fifteen degrees hotter just beyond the transom. It was darker too, lit only by candles and three droning propane camping lanterns that hung from hooks in the tin ceiling. Stepping inside was borderline otherworldly, but my senses adjusted. The room was about ten by thirty feet. There was a worn black leather sofa in the middle of one wall and a desk and chair in a corner. A dream catcher the size of a hula hoop and a large tapestry hung on opposite and otherwise bare walls. There was an Afghan rug on the floor with a giant, triple-sized pink beanbag at its center.

My mind flooded with snapshots of the activities that could take place in a space like this; most of them were sexual, and nearly all utilized the beanbag. I wondered if the room was soundproof. I had other questions, too, but didn't get to them. Tucky appeared, as if by magic, through a door that'd been obscured by the tapestry. He was holding a scratchy wool blanket in his arms and was a doe in the headlights when he saw me, but he kept cool. I was intruding, clearly, but that didn't bother me.

"Quite a setup," I said. He nodded in agreement. "Did my mom tell you about Annette?"

"She did." Tucky walked to the middle of the room. He tossed the blanket on one end of the couch and sat down on the other. He crossed his legs, intertwining them impossibly, like ivy growing on trumpet vine. Tucky gestured to the beanbag, and I accepted, air hissing from its seams as I sank down.

We sat in silence looking at each other. I was oddly comfortable in that strange room. The whir of the lanterns, the heat, and maybe I was growing used to the pollution-stink in the air—it was a bizarre but effective recipe.

It was soon clear that I wouldn't win any staring contests. Tucky looked like he could, and probably had, sat on that couch just as he was for many hours at a time.

"What do you think?" I said. "The former-life business."

Tucky was expressionless, but he also somehow projected sympathy. The transaction felt very honest, even though we'd communicated almost nothing.

"I think your mom is finding her way," Tucky said.

"But does that mean it's true? I mean, true like she didn't do anything to me? Like her parents didn't do anything to her?"

"Sure," he said, "why not?" He was practically upbeat about the idea.

"Doesn't that ruin everything? Some psychic changing it all with a phone call?"

"It's not about that. It never has been. It's about your mom finding herself, pursuing her life as her true self. First is finding what we need in life, then we figure out how to get it. That's the goal, the end; how to establish a meaningful existence. It's different for everyone. For your mom, she's working hard at it. She's making good progress."

"What about me?"

"You've got to do the same thing. Like I told you, I'd be glad to schedule a session."

"No, I mean what about my mom and me. Do I fit in?"

"Of course. Absolutely."

"Why would you say she molested me?"

Peace for me was drifting. Tucky's may have been too. "She

told me," he said, "it wasn't the other way around. I never planted ideas in her head. I only help her uncover what's already there."

"I was never abused. I'm 100% sure of it. I can't say about my grandparents, but I doubt it."

"I don't know what to tell you; maybe there's something to the former-life idea, or maybe she fabricated those memories as a manifestation of her deepest fears, which has been known to happen. Yes," he said, like he was really starting to dig that new train of thought. He spoke faster, got all excited. "Something along the lines of your mom being so focused on not hurting you, as you grew up, and now, especially as she bears down for this completely independent journey of hers—which she needs to do, I hope you agree—that while on that journey, she's struggling with the idea that she needs to make choices for herself, based on her needs foremost. And that can be a real, well, mind-fuck."

Mind-fuck. That was an interesting way to put it. I felt mind-fucked. I possibly felt mind-gangbanged. Right then, I might have been hearing some parts of what Tucky was saying, and that made me slightly uneasy. I thought it should have been the opposite.

For some reason, at that moment I recognized a medium-high level of intoxication in myself, like I was in a trance or under a spell. I wasn't afraid of the feeling, necessarily, and it wasn't altogether unpleasant, but it was unfamiliar. Maybe it was that unfamiliarity that caused my unsure-footedness, what tripped me up and got me to recognize my altered state in the first place. I almost didn't want the feeling to go away, and it was. I was losing it, but it felt like I should wade around in it a little longer, learn more about what it offered, find out if I ought to try and reenter it.

"Does it have to be so painful?" I said. "Is that normal?"

"There's no one way. Sometimes it gets ugly. It doesn't have to, but sometimes it does."

I started to doubt that there'd been any actual alteration of my mind. Maybe I'd given Tucky too much credit, like all I'd done was swallow each of the pills he'd dosed me. But, in reality there was a part of me that wanted to believe in it, that what Tucky offered was real, that I could actually get my hands on something. Its source didn't even matter.

"It's time," Tucky said.

"For what?"

"That's it."

"That's it, what?"

"My client."

I heard knocking at the door. I had no idea how long somebody had been knocking like that.

"Everett," Tucky said, "my client is here, I'm afraid."

"Am I under hypnosis?" I immediately felt stupid.

He laughed, but not in a condescending way. "No, you're not under hypnosis."

Tucky went to the door, opened it just a crack and whispered that he'd be right out.

"I'm sorry to cut this short, but," he said, and he gestured at the door with his thumb.

It occurred to me to get up from the beanbag.

"My offer stands about a proper session. We'd see results."

I slowly rolled off the beanbag and onto my knees, stood up. "I'll think about it," I said. I gave Tucky a handshake. "Thanks," I said, and I left.

I didn't know what I wanted, but the question was fair. I knew I didn't want what I had, and I suppose that's a starting point.

CHAPTER 43

When I got home, Mom was taking refuge in the garage. I didn't tell her where I'd been. I handed her an iced coffee I'd picked up for her on my way back, ostensibly the product of my important errand.

The garage was our final frontier of chaos and disorder. I began sorting through a mound of several dozen overstuffed garbage bags. Some were full of trash, even old trash, like kitchen trash from who knows when. Others weren't as obvious: sweaters, drop cloths, shoes, a croquet set, etc.

In the center of the garage was an oil spot that'd grown wider over the years. It was black and textured from the dirt and debris that got stuck to it. Mom was sitting on a rocking chair that was positioned in the middle of the darkened area. It was an odd place for her to have plopped herself. When I looked at her, if I squinted, it was almost like we had a tar pit in our garage, something straight out of La Brea, and Mom was floating on its surface.

I imagined there were eons of accumulation beneath her, amoebas, a pterodactyl, even a tandem bicycle from more recent times. I didn't fear Mom would sink down with those things, however, and recognizing that reasserted Mom's strength for me somehow. Mom held some kind of invincibility just then, which filled me with positivity, even though I knew it was a very weak crutch, since all she was really safe from was the imaginary sinkhole I located in the garage from squinting, but still.

The chair Mom was sitting on had been in my bedroom most of my childhood. Maybe that's what inspired the tar-pit fantasy. It'd almost always been broken, too, the left arm missing or barely attached. Even broken, I'd always liked that chair. It fit my backside well, egg-and-spoon kind of thing.

Mom was thumbing through a box of kitchen utensils on her lap. "Would you ever use this?" she said, waving a lemon-juicer at me.

I gave Mom this confused look, like the suggestion that I might ever juice something was practically offensive. I told myself to curb it. "Probably not," I said, "but thanks."

Mom dropped the lemon-juicer by her feet and dug back into the box. "The home stretch," she said.

I squinted again, but the tar pit had vanished. The garage was just old and dirty again.

"How about this?" Mom said. She pointed a rusty pizza-cutter diagonally toward the garage door. Mom looked ready in case we were attacked by whole pizzas flying at us rapid-fire. Shifting gears, I cupped my hands in a ready-to-catch position, but Mom didn't throw it, which was probably for the best. I shook my head, no, and Mom dropped it on her garbage pile.

"You don't actually believe that stuff anymore, do you?" It surprised even me to hear it come out of my mouth. That hadn't been a part of my plan for the morning, not that I had much of a plan.

"I'm still working through it," she said. "Want to bring me a garbage bag? Here," she said, moving the box a bit higher up on her thighs, "Spread it over my knees."

"I think we should take Tucky to court. Sue him," I said. I positioned the garbage bag for Mom.

"No, nothing like that." Mom pulled a turkey baster out of the box. "This is the turkey baster your dad bought when my mom insisted on it to cook turkey properly. Do you remember that? Dad got so steamed. Into the dark abyss it goes." Mom smiled at her trash bag setup, slid in the baster.

"I think I'm out of the mushroom business," I said.

"How about a yard sale? Raise some funds," Mom said. "What would you pay for this fork? Ten cents? A nickel? It'd take a lot of forks."

"How come we never fixed that chair? I'd take that chair."

Mom started rocking. "It was your grandfather's, on your dad's side. You used to sit in this chair for hours. You'd go quiet. I'd wonder what trouble you were up to, come up to your room, and there you'd be, next to the window, legs crossed, just rocking away like some kind of little Buddha. Your dad loved this chair. He used to sit in it and rock you to sleep when you were a baby."

That was news to me. It was a warm image. "Why didn't we fix it?"

"We did, probably a dozen times, but it kept breaking. Dad couldn't bear to throw it away, so it came here."

"I don't remember it ever being fixed."

"It was broken when we got it. It's probably always been broken. Dad tried to fix it, one of his first and only home repair projects. He was never good at that kind of thing, but he wanted to fix this chair. He was back and forth to the hardware store, and he'd come up from the basement grinning. 'Fixed it.' But it'd break again. I guess that chair never wanted to be fixed."

"Maybe I can fix it."

"It's all yours." Mom rocked a few more times, but she didn't get up. I sort of thought she would. She tossed the now-empty box from her lap onto the mountain of garbage bags. "Hand me another?"

I heaved a garbage bag of linens onto Mom, then hunted around for the arm of the rocking chair. I guess, like Dad, I had no idea how to fix it, but I'd at least need the missing arm, that I knew. I started rummaging through some boxes.

"What are you doing?"

"Looking for the arm."

"It's there." Mom pointed at the back wall.

The tip of it was poking out from behind a snow shovel. It was in a canvas bag that also contained rocking-chair-mending supplies: four different wood glues, a hammer, screws, clamps, epoxies, nails, tacks, and a screwdriver.

"Lean forward," I said. I attached the canvas bag to a spindle with masking tape.

"I'll get up," Mom said, though she didn't even gesture to raise herself, which I thought was funny, and also very Mom-ish.

"It's on," I said.

Mom leaned back, resumed rocking. "Oh, these are nice," she said, holding up a fistful of white fabric.

"What?"

"Hankies."

"Hankies? I don't want used hankies."

"They're clean. Very high quality."

"Is it so strange to not want used hankies? Or to not want hankies in general?"

"They're your dad's."

"Pass."

"Into the abyss."

We sorted through garage contents that way and at the same gait for the rest of the day. Occasionally we stumbled on hidden treasure. Most notably, I was reunited with my collection of Garbage Pail Kids; we solved the mystery of Dad's stolen bicycle; I was heavier a dozen hankies, under light protest; and Mom again had her long-lost sandwich baggie of broken family jewelry that she'd accused a jeweler of losing, which she found in the pants pocket of a pair of slacks at the bottom of a storage bin.

Also, I was happy to record in my internal daily log that Mom hadn't presented to me or the world any of her specialized loony or kooky, nor had she interpreted numbers in a fashion that couldn't have been duplicated on a calculator. Those things were significant to me.

When it got dark outside, Mom and I called it quits for the day. We headed back into the house. Janice Sugarbottom was waiting for us at the table where the young girl had been sitting. She looked pure-devilish.

"We got an offer," she said, "Fifteen thousand over asking price."

I should have been happy, and I was, but there was something else at operation there, too.

CHAPTER 44

Later that night, I was getting a beer from the kitchen, my fifth of the night, and I noticed a cardboard box in the refrigerator's crisper drawer. I could see, even through the foggy plastic, that it was a piece of mail, unopened, a cube about a foot each way, which was a strange thing to have cooling down to 35° there in the crisper drawer.

I reached to extract the box, but that damn drawer, it never slid on its tracks right, not for my whole life. I had no clue what kept it stuck like that for so many years. Apparently my patience with that crisper drawer had depleted, because I yanked it hard, harder than ever before, and when it finally loosened, it was accompanied by the sound of cracking plastic, but, hey, in terms of first-world tragedies, not to mention with the house sold, the death of that crisper drawer hardly knocked the earth off its axis.

The package had been sent by certified mail, to Dad, and apparently arrived sometime during the open house. Probably that teenage girl who'd run our little circus that afternoon hadn't known what to do with it, like she needed it disappeared, but once she'd signed for it, there were obligations, and so stuffing it in the bushes out front and forgetting about it wasn't an option, so she put it in the crisper drawer, which, well, I could imagine arriving at a similar place if I'd been in her shoes, not to mention that at that moment the bushes out front seemed as decent a place as any to stash the busted crisper drawer. Any which way, I doubted there'd be anyone as understanding as me on the back end of that transaction.

In theory the package wasn't such a big deal. Dad had continued to get mail periodically, but it was mostly junk, to Dad or *current resident*. But a package like that, wrapped up and sent under lock and key via the USPS, handwritten address to boot and arrived from someplace I'd never heard of, Glide, Oregon; well, those elements suggested some extraordinariness.

I made a quick executive decision. Rather than consult Mom, I grabbed a paring knife from the drawer and incised the tape the length of the box.

Packaging peanuts spilled onto the counter and floor as I dug inside and removed its contents: a receipt for $240 from Glide Imaging, Inc., two DVDs (handwritten on in marker, *Master* and *Backup*), and six 8mm film reels, the brother and sister reels to the one I found in Dad's closet.

Master and *Backup*, I guessed all of the content fit onto a single DVD, and that—determining the quantity of what I held in my hands—became my first pursuit. I brought the two discs into the family room, put *Master* in the machine, and pressed Play.

I watched the first ten seconds. It was a wedding, old-timey sepia hue like the other reel, and I watched as a sequence of bridesmaids and groomsmen paraded down the aisle of a church, but that was all I watched, just those first ten seconds. I pressed Open on the DVD player so that I could swap in *Backup*.

I wasn't sure why I did that, why I couldn't or didn't view beyond that first snippet. Of course part of me wanted to have inhaled and processed the entirety of the content all at once and in an instant, but the bigger part of me was sheepish about it, or if I wasn't intimidated exactly, I was something, and that something inspired me toward slow and deliberate movements, I think as a way of managing the situation, which admittedly felt unmanaged, as per the insane thumping in my chest and the sudden sweat-saturation of all fabric on my body.

Backup had the same bridesmaid and groomsman taking their same calculated steps toward the same altar as on *Master.* I hit Stop and switched the discs again. Incidentally, I was careful not to view the *Backup* footage any longer than I did the *Master.*

Logically speaking, if the discs were identical—which it appeared they were—theoretically I could have watched *Backup* and seen the same content as on *Master.* But with *Master* available—and the original from which all duplicates were and would be created on hand—why move forward with anything but *Master?*

And such was my thought process as I put *Master* back into the DVD player.

I watched the first ten seconds and pressed Pause at that same spot in the wedding. Right after I did that, I kind of looked over my shoulder and scanned the room, as if half-expecting a few dozen people to be gathered there, shaking their heads in collective judgment. It was an unusual sensation, which for whatever reason made me thirsty. I ducked out to the kitchen to get something to drink.

Standing in front of the refrigerator with the door swung open, I couldn't make a decision—not that it mattered; distraction is distraction, no matter its stripes. I was directionless. Beer? Orange juice? Milk? I wondered, when was the last time I drank a glass of milk? Many moons. I poured myself a giant glass of milk.

When I was younger, I used to drink ridiculous quantities of milk and jump up and down so I could hear it slosh around in my stomach—not that I was much interested in doing that right then, but anyway. I brought the glass to my lips to take a sip, and a sour smell wafted up into my nose. I took the jug out of the fridge, and indeed, it was about ten days past its prime.

Gnarly. I put the jug back, but I also had an impulse to give myself a milk mustache.

Yes, I was aware of a funny-something happening to me, the reversion to childhood or what have you, but it felt more correct to entertain it than squash it away, so I did. I stood at the counter and pursed my lips around the rim of the glass, so as to not allow any of the spoiled dairy to leak into my mouth, and I tipped the milk at my face. I did this repeatedly, and I worked to perfect my milk mustache by checking my reflection in the door of the microwave, sip-view-wipe, repeat. I had a decent technique in development when I was interrupted.

"What's all this?" Mom was standing in the doorway. She didn't appear totally shocked by the scene, which suggested to me that she'd had a few minutes to take it all in, to process the 8mm film reels on the counter and the scattered packaging peanuts. She'd also likely observed several rounds of milk-mustaches, so, yes, another gold medal of mine for Mom to hang proudly on the wall.

I dumped the milk in the sink and discreetly wiped my mouth and chin with my sleeve. "Dad had some old home movies converted to DVD," I said. I pointed at the broken crisper drawer. "They were in the crisper drawer."

"I know about those," Mom said. "Your dad had one made a few months ago. It's around here somewhere. I meant to give it to you." Mom didn't say anything about the package materializing in the crisper drawer, which I thought was odd, but maybe she too was no longer thrown off by the unexpected. "Well?" Mom said, which meant *What are we waiting for?* I nodded my head in agreement.

I kind of stepped in front of Mom and scurried ahead of her so that I'd get to the family room first, then I plopped down on the couch. "It's all queued up," I said. Mom gave me a funny look, but I didn't care. I guess that was what I'd been waiting for, for Mom to press Play, though I wasn't sure why. I really didn't have a single reason to be afraid of watching the DVD. My reaction didn't quite make sense to me, but that's what it was.

"The first ten seconds or so are the beginning of a wedding," I said, "just people coming down the aisle," which I suppose was to suggest that Mom didn't have to start it from the beginning, and she again gave me this puzzled look. I decided to shut my mouth. Mom pressed Stop on the player and started it from the beginning.

Mom didn't know whose wedding it was, but as we watched, she started to identify subjects. She'd say it was so-and-so, my grandparents mostly, other distant relatives, etc. But the weird thing was how very still Mom kept. She wasn't stoic exactly, and whatever was underneath her neutral expression wasn't negative, not that I could tell. It was more like she was deep in concentration, possibly enthralled and captivated to the point of paralysis. And it came. "That's your dad," she said. There he was, six or seven years old and fresh from a dip in the pool. Dad was skinny, a runt, really. He was dancing around poolside, trying to wiggle the wet off himself. The camera zoomed in on his face, and his lips were dark from cold. A pair of man-hands entered the shot from the left and wrapped him up in a towel. Dad closed his eyes and let the towel and hands shake him softly.

I glanced over at Mom. She couldn't take her eyes off the screen. Fast tears were dripping down her face, and then I lost it too, except I also had these puppy-dog whimpers and huffs, which, well, I didn't care, and neither did Mom. It was all about us, and it had nothing to do with us at the same time. That contradiction offered some kind of permission.

The family reunions, the parties, the camping trips, the dinners in diners, etc. We watched Dad and others carry on with their more or less ordinary lives, and it had us in a trance. In that state is how we passed the rest of the evening.

The sum total of that very shaky archive was profound. I can go as far as to say that the cathartic properties of that moment for Mom and me filled up our family room like wet smoke. It was big, and it was not of the mumbo-jumbo variety, which I dug supremely. To be sure, for Mom and me, I was glad.

Mom and I had a righteously transcendental experience. We fell headfirst into that footage. But for part of me, there was something about the Dad there that didn't align with the Dad I now had in my mind. It may be even fairer to say that the Dad on screen and even the Dad from my childhood, those Dads were a different Dad than the Dad I'd been shaping in my mind over the past few months. I had good feelings, slightly complicated feelings, but overall good feelings. That's about as far as I got in my deconstruction that evening.

That night as I tried to fall asleep, instead of thinking about Dad's home movies, I couldn't stop thinking about Jeff. Jeff in prison. Poor Jeff, not quite American enough for the foreigner treatment, and not Chinese enough to disappear if he needed to, and he would need to. I was worried about him.

I hoped that he'd had a stroke of luck somehow, and it dawned on me that he ought to try and get to this one particular island in the South China Sea. I'd heard about a place, a state-run addiction treatment center on an island off the southern coast. I began to imagine that's where Jeff was now making his home—that what Jeff's family connections got him was placed on that island instead of in the slammer.

The treatment center occupied the entire island, and it was a humane facility, not a prison or labor camp, although it employed some unorthodox strategies, like addicts running around the island completely naked, doctor's orders, in some bizarre, bohemian detox experiment. The patients grew dreadlocks and worked their organic farm, and for group sessions, they lazed around on the beach.

Jeff growing dreads and taking 'er easy, that was the picture that took shape in my mind.

It was dumb, but I wished a few things for Jeff for while he was there. One, that he had confidence in his naked body. I'd never seen *it*, but I wanted Jeff to be spared insecurities on that nudist island, no matter what.

Second, I wished for the island many young, beautiful, fully-recovered pothead women who would be defiant enough to sometimes doll themselves up for Jeff, but who were altogether level-headed beyond that single indiscretion. Those women would appreciate the kind of person Jeff was and ultimately love him for it.

I even imagined Jeff on that island a few years down the road. He'd established a copacetic polygamist family. He happily weeded in the organic garden. He'd brokered with island officials for a mango orchard.

I'm not sure why, but I also pictured Jeff with a set of bongo drums, and he was always either playing them or had them strapped to his back. He'd become a legend in island drum circles and started them often, though he accumulated the most time drumming on his own.

Every morning at sunrise, every evening at sunset, Jeff could be found with his bongos sitting on top of a particular boulder at the water's edge. The boulder had no business being where it was, there on the beach with no other boulders. It was a slightly cylindrical boulder, and he scaled its steep face by wedging his fingers and toes into its few, tiniest of holes. And there on top of the boulder he beat on his drums while he looked out over the expanse and contemplated the cosmos.

Imagining Jeff on his island in the South China Sea did provide some comfort, and I managed to get some sleep, but in the early morning, I woke up startled.

I'd had another dream, and in it, Dad came to me.

I was a passenger on a small jet that had to make an emergency landing in the streets of downtown Chicago. I watched out my window as we whizzed between buildings, taxied, and eventually stopped on Lower Wacker Drive. The passengers unloaded, and I walked alone toward the river and stopped at a small alcove on the riverfront. It was quiet out, nighttime, not too cold with a light snowfall.

A cab pulled up—apparently there was a street connected to the alcove—and Dad got out. He didn't recognize me right away. I hardly recognized him. He took an old-school external-frame backpack out of the trunk and set it down in a puddle of slush, then leaned in to pay the driver.

Dad was scruffy, like some kind of drifter, probably around forty years old, and he had shoulder-length brown hair that he kept pushing behind his ears. He was plump; not heavy like I'd known him, but beer-belly fat, skinny arms, loose chin. There was still a lot of youth in him, and he looked happy.

Dad pulled a half-smoked cigarette out from his breast pocket, took a few drags, then dropped it to the ground and stomped it out with his foot. He picked up his backpack and began digging through it. I noticed strange objects dangling from the frame of his pack, like a giant spatula, a snorkel, flippers, and a rubber Jimmy Carter mask.

"Hey," I said. Dad looked over and waved. He knew who I was. "I just got dropped off by a jet, right here on Lower Wacker."

"That ain't right," he said. Dad sounded country. He took a cigar out of his backpack and lit up.

First I thought Dad should have been at home with Mom.

I thought maybe he was there to meet another woman, but that didn't seem likely. He was too grubby and disheveled for that. Plus, more than anything, Dad looked completely purposeless standing there, or maybe fairer to say, Dad didn't appear to have an agenda, in a pothead-vagabond kind of way.

"What are you doing here?" I said.

"I'm smoking this total-crap cigar." He was slow-swiveling his head, taking in the surroundings. He had this excited look on his face, like he didn't know where to go or what to do first. "It's been so long since I've been down here," he said. "I hardly know where I am." I'd never seen Dad so wide-eyed.

"What are you talking about?" I said. "You worked five minutes from here for thirty-eight years."

Dad shrugged, looked around some more. He was giddy. We stood there watching the snow fall. I heard partying from some bars in the distance. I could even see the light from a few of them. I was a little nervous asking, but said, "Do you want to grab a beer?"

"Why not?" He picked up his backpack, and we headed off. As we walked, I tried to gauge Dad. Was he happy? Relieved? Surprised? I couldn't tell exactly, but Dad was smiling and looked freer than I'd ever known him to be. I was happy, too.

It was a friendly kind of mood, a couple of pals out for beers.

I woke up just as we were stepping into the bar. I wanted back in that dream, badly, to see what Dad and I would talk about, where we'd go after our drinks. Just to spend a little more time with him.

That dream, it just wasn't the kind of thing my mind could ever make up. I've never had those creative juices. I didn't know what it was supposed to mean, but it felt big.

CHAPTER 45

When I checked my email in the morning, I had messages from Ron and Dino, but still nothing from Jeff. Ron wanted to know if I had any new information. "I'm real fucking worried about that guy!" he said. I told Ron that I didn't know anything, and that I too was worried. Truth is, fuck, I was so worried about Jeff, but I wasn't sure what I could do. *P. S. Have you ever heard of that drug rehab island off the southern coast of China? Any connections there?*

As for Dino, he didn't ask about Jeff, but no surprise there. His note was written in a cryptic, paranoid style, as though anything revealed in that email was potential ammunition for his imprisonment, and maybe it was, I didn't know. Dino said he wanted to talk things through. For me, that meant dissolving the enterprise, and although I had no doubt the conversation itself would be intolerable, the transaction seemed unavoidable.

Dino asked me to meet him at the Daley Center Plaza the next day at noon. He already had an engagement there around that time, he said, and it would be difficult for him to meet the rest of the week. Fine, done. Our house wasn't exactly spitting-distance from the Daley Center Plaza, but at least it was a public space; that, and we'd have lunch options. I told Dino I'd be there.

I sent one other email that morning, to Amanda Marlowe, the librarian from my old grade school. I found her address online, and I asked her if the substitute teacher position at her school was still open. It felt new and interesting to do that.

The sky was threatening rain when I stepped out of the subway station at Lake Street, and as I took the stairs to street level, I found myself walking next to a man who reminded me of a fellow teacher from Pingnan, Yisan Ming.

Yisan Ming taught history at Pingnan, and we only spoke once, during Xiao Mu's birthday party at the Sichuan hot pot restaurant. Had I known Yisan spoke English so well, I would have taken him out for beers months earlier. He spoke English better than almost anyone in the school, including the English teachers, but apparently he was even better with history.

Yisan told me that he grew up in a small *xiang ba lao* coal mining town in Gansu Province, but they were farmers, not miners. He had seven brothers and sisters, and they were all back home on the farm still. Yisan was the only one in his family who'd left his hometown.

We drank at the party, and there was a lot of karaoke. Yisan sang mostly old folk songs from his childhood, and I sang "Yellow Submarine," twice.

At the end of the night, I asked Yisan if he'd like to get dinner sometime. I was a little nervous asking, like a first date. Yisan smiled and invited me to sit down with him on the couch.

In a low voice, he told me that this dinner was also a kind of quiet farewell party for him. He was leaving Pingnan in a week. I asked him why, and he said because of family.

His wife was pregnant with a second child, he said, and Principal Xi had caught wind of it. Principal Xi called Yisan to his office and gave him an ultimatum. Get rid of the baby or lose his job. Yisan chose, and so he and his family were moving back to his hometown—out in the sticks, where the one-child policy wasn't enforced.

I must have had a pained expression on my face because after Yisan had finished telling me his story, he turned to me, put a hand on each of my shoulders and gently shook. He smiled wide and said, "I'm having another child!"

When I got to the Daley Center Plaza, it took me a minute to figure out what was going on. Several hundred protestors were gathered. Nearly all of them were wearing something yellow or red, and they had banners and posters, "Bring China to Justice for Genocide"; "Stop the Killing, Free Xuan Gong in China"; and "One World, Equal Human Rights." Then I saw Dino. He had a red t-shirt on over his oxford and tie, and he was holding a clipboard. Mei was standing next to him, the woman from Lake Butte de Morts. She was squeezing a megaphone between her knees.

I absorbed from a distance. It appeared that Dino had achieved minor celebrity status in this circle. One after another, people shook his hand and asked him questions. Dino was the answer man and exercised substantial clipboard consultation—from my perspective, the clipboard itself didn't do much. It was just another one of his meaningless props. Mei was busy with index cards and must have distributed and collected a dozen in the few minutes I'd been there. They were a team, yes, but of the two, and for this odd circus, Dino seemed more the ringmaster.

A young guy was sucking on a cigarette near me, obviously an observer, so I asked him if he knew what the deal was. "There's some high-up Chinese official visiting today," he said, "along with the Chinese Foreign Minister from the Consulate. These guys showed up to protest. What is it, Xuan Gong? I don't know, some Chinese thing. They've got pretty sick pictures up over there—burn victims, organ harvesting and whatnot."

I looked at my watch. It was a quarter past twelve. This party was just getting started, which meant Dino had done it to me again. Clearly he wanted me here for this, but he was too chicken-shit to ask—not like I would have come if he had, but still.

No one, not even Mom, can cultivate crystalline moments of rage in me like Dino, but at least it was short-lived. The seething got interrupted—my stomach with an allegation of famine, like it had the last time I was with Mei and I dreamed up that clandestine chicken-wing tiki bar. Jeff would have dug that place. I wished I'd told him about it. Maybe I still could. Poor Jeff. And, not to make light of Jeff's situation, but I held little hope for my own predicament, either. I foresaw no food that afternoon. It wasn't the kind of shindig Dino could jump ship on, and to be sure, Dino scrutinizing my decimation of a turkey pesto panini would not have contributed to the greater effort. I waited for my stomach to quiet down, and headed over to them.

"Hi," Dino said, "thanks for coming." He was acting all serious- and professional-like, which, fine, he was free to do anything he wanted, but I wasn't buying. He tucked his clipboard into his armpit and stuck his palm out for a handshake. We hadn't shaken hands since we first met in China. "You remember Mei, don't you?"

"Mei, hi, good to see you," I said.

Mostly I was nauseated by the scene, by Dino's confidence and his apparent triumph in this new field. There was jealousy there, too, somewhere, but more than that, I didn't like it because I had the inside scoop on their new prince. That's what made me queasy. I'd seen Dino go down in flames too many times not to know. And, yes, there was always the possibility that this time things would be different. The tiny humanist in me even hoped for Dino, that he could avoid yet another of his patented face plants, if for no other reason than the world could do without another. But, in the end, those things meant nothing. I knew Dino's scorecard from the earlier innings, and that's not the kind of thing that just gets erased overnight.

Anyway, it didn't take more than a minute or two with Dino and I was able to predict how the day would shake out. I was immediately glad that I'd made the trek. That said, catharsis didn't arrive because I was finally up close and personal with the Xuan Gong conflict and the convergence it activated. It was something much more personal.

Studying Dino at that moment, all pulled-together in his khaki slacks with the pleats, that ridiculous clipboard and the way he licked his finger every freaking time he flipped a page, the whole damn ruse guaranteed Dino's transformation for me, and that forever cemented a distance between us, the permanence of which was evident to me right away.

The Dino of earlier times was gone, and while he may not have been the loveliest creature in the forest, I at least understood him. I could wrap my head around the Dino who obsessed over low-dpi boobie pictures from the internet. I even sympathized with the dude who slept off benders curled around a squatter toilet.

Dino had traveled so far and so quickly on his new road that it would be impossible to bring him back—not that I wanted to, not that he wanted me to, either. And it didn't matter what went down in a month, a year, or at the end of his life, for now Dino had his focus, his distraction, the thing that occupied the space in his mind that illness and death bore into it.

It was feasible that the Xuan Gong could mend fractures in Dino, in its strange way, seal them up like caulk, and if it did exactly that, probably it was okay. But with something as offbeat as the Xuan Gong, there was a good chance its practices would only burrow new cavities in his heart and mind, one after the other, and in the end dump him off even emptier, even needier.

It was a sticky proposition with a lot at stake, and I reacted. I made a decision that afternoon, and being there even for that short time gave me full confidence in it. From there on out, I would have nothing to do with Dino. I would wash myself clean of the man.

Dino and I had been through a lot together, so it was significant to understand it was our final goodbye. I found myself completely unemotional though, and that felt cruel, so I attempted a moment of reflection on the good times. I tried to pinpoint a few things that I might miss about Dino's company. I didn't come up with much. I wondered if maybe my subconscious was keeping me disengaged in order to streamline the breakup. It could have been any number of things, not that it really mattered. I drifted into a pragmatic mood.

Ever since my interrogation, I'd fantasized about seeing Dino again, what I'd say to him and how I'd position my hands around his throat, but standing nose to nose with him at the Daley Center Plaza, as I contemplated our farewell, no words came to me. I had no impulse to claw his face. There was nothing. I had no further business with Dino, period.

Except there was Jeff.

"Pretty decent protest," I said. Then, a little louder, I said, "I still haven't heard from Jeff. He's basically MIA, could be in prison."

Mei and Dino both shook their heads. "It's a tragedy," Dino said, as though he had attained full detachment from it all, like he wasn't and never had been to blame. "That's exactly what we're protesting. The Chinese government has been carrying out atrocities for too long, and without consequences. They are violating basic human rights."

Dino looked down at his clipboard and checked his watch. He appeared to be making some kind of calculations in his head, as if something was about to happen. I thought *bomb.* I scanned the landscape for the nearest safe cover, also for anyone sporting a vest of C2, but in doing so, I actually found calm. Those gathered were old and young, and of all skin colors, as docile and unintimidating a group as I'd ever seen. They were united there in the Plaza simply to get their peaceful protest on. That was all. They weren't terrorists.

"Can I count on you?" Dino said. "Can I get you a t-shirt and a poster? We need your help."

I felt disconnected from myself as I took in what Dino said, even a little light headed. It was like I'd stepped into the murkiness of a hallucination, similar to how I felt in Tucky's dojo. I didn't answer Dino because in that surreal context, I didn't feel like I had to. I just looked around at the protest, at the Picasso statue, at the low-hanging, thick clouds—fine worm-hunting weather, but lousy picnic forecast.

"I want to tell you more about what happened to me in China," Dino said, ignoring my silence. "I need your help with that too. Spread the word, alert the media. Can I count on you?"

"Truthiness. Sympathy. Acceptance." I said. It was screen printed on the back of a red t-shirt a woman near us was wearing. I pointed at her with mild interest.

"Are you listening?" Dino said.

I wasn't, not really. I wondered what was so attractive about the Xuan Gong. All those people, and apparently millions more, so fully committed to such strange behavior, and in Dino's case, the transition was practically overnight. Did all practitioners devour its doctrine like that? Did abstaining from cupcakes and all variations of sexy-time actually relate to universal human voids?

But at the same time, I didn't think there was anything really scary about Xuan Gong practitioners. Clearly it was a bizarre undertaking, but they didn't seem to hurt anyone, except maybe themselves. Apparently, their leader has even claimed he can fly, but even then. And yet there existed so many hideous and unbelievable stories about the Chinese government's clampdown on the Gongers—labor camps, torture, organ harvesting, also gory and elaborate pseudo-Xuan Gong protests orchestrated by Party henchmen, etc.

So many of the accusations were so outrageous that it was almost impossible to believe any of them could be true; that said, I've never doubted that versions of the horrible did exist. Disruptions of any kind threaten the power structure, and the harder one entity is willing to lean against the other, the greater potential there is for things to get dangerously out of hand.

I'd tried, to an extent, but never understood the Xuan Gong. It was always difficult for me to know which end was up and who was on the level when everyone acted so off-the-wall all the time. No one ever seemed entirely credible or righteous, so I never found a good way to engage the situation, not that I necessarily wanted to.

For me, I was more on board with what Mah-mah in Hong Kong said about the Xuan Gong, that people should be left alone to do what they want. That seemed as good an answer as any, something to live by, even.

And with that, after our brief conversation, it was time for my curtain call. I was ready to sidestep my way off the Daley Center Plaza.

"Want the mushrooms?" I said to Dino. "I vote we give them all to Jeff when he gets back."

"This is beyond mushrooms. Do what you want with the mushrooms."

"Terrific," I said. Then, with sincerity, I said to Dino and Mei, "Good luck with all this." I shook Mei's hand. I raised my arm for a final high-five from Dino, but he didn't bite. I guess he preferred to maintain handshake-professionalism in front of his disciples, which I could understand. I obliged, and that was that. I turned around and walked toward the subway. Dino may have yelled something as our distance increased, but I didn't hear what it was, and I didn't turn around to listen.

I had a new idea—two ideas, actually—before I'd even gotten to the subway. The first was to get a gyros sandwich for the ride home. Admittedly, the bold flavors that waft from a gyros can practically melt graffiti from a train window, so, no, in terms of fellow passengers, I wouldn't have described it as a noble food choice, going with the gyros. But I was feeling slightly invincible post-Dino, like what really mattered, just maybe, was that I was hungry, in particular for a gyros, and if I desired to eat that gyros while I sat on a train, that's what would be.

The second idea had a bit more depth. I hoped it was the kind of thing that would get Mom and me cruising in a new direction.

I purchased a gyros, then stopped at a payphone. I called home. I don't know why, but I think Mom was surprised to hear from me. I asked if she had plans later that day. She didn't, so I invited her out with me.

"It's a date," she said.

CHAPTER 46

I went straight to the bathroom when I got home, to brush my teeth and otherwise, on account of the obvious and with regard to the gyros. Incidentally, the gyros was delicious and didn't incite a riot in my train car, though I was primed to deliver insanity in the event that it did.

I began gathering what I needed for my excursion with Mom. I'd unknowingly inventoried and tracked most of the items since I'd been back from China—not my most recent trip, but the big return—which was strange to consider. I never could have predicted then what Mom and I would soon be setting out to do.

I put those things into an old briefcase of Dad's, closed the lid and clicked its two clasps secure. There was a wicker basket in the foyer, courtesy of the fluffers, I suppose. I removed the giant plastic fern from inside and replaced it with a blanket, a bottle of wine, a wine opener (foresight occasionally comes to me), and two glasses.

Mom was giggly and waiting for me in the kitchen. "What in the world?" she said.

"You'll see."

We got into the car, and I drove us north along the lakeshore, past the university, past the ornate Bahá'í Temple, and north still to where the road curved gracefully, as I'd remembered. It was calm there, which was no coincidence. The houses were enormous, and as the properties got increasingly expansive, the road drifted lazily to accommodate the layout.

At a point, we'd driven for so long and gone so far north that I began to fear we'd passed it and might never find our destination, and I had no plan B. There was hardly a plan A. I was edging toward turning back when I saw the entrance to Forest Shores, a quasi-public beach access flanked by the very exclusive, very private Forest Shores Marina.

Mom scrunched her nose and did a sort of mock highfalutin' wiggle in her seat, which made me laugh. It was closed for the season, but the gate was open. We drove in and followed the road down to the water. It weaved between the landscaping and trees in that familiar serpentine design.

Ours was the only car in the parking lot. I stopped the engine. Stepping out, the air felt cool and damp, and everything was completely still. It was almost dark. Not exactly ideal beach conditions, but the rain earlier in the day had subsided, and what few clouds remained hung low in the sky. I wondered if the night might eventually reveal stars. Fine worm-hunting weather but lousy picnic forecast, I thought to myself.

"I never," Mom said. I could tell she was digging it, but she had no idea why we were there. Even me, I'd only been to Forest Shores once before, and as for the excursion, aside from a few plans in the works, I was more or less winging it.

"Do you remember coming here?" I said. I thought that might help bump things a little more dramatic.

"Maybe. What were you thinking?" Mom seemed up for anything. She stood with her hands clasped at diaphragm level and her back arched. That was her new, slightly-modified casual pose. No matter how healthy and correct it may have been, for me it still came off as deliberate, and so, unnatural. But it worked for Mom, and while it didn't inspire anything vis-à-vis my own hunchback-slouch, I no longer had the impulse to force her shoulders back to pedestrian-crooked. That was a small something, I suppose.

"When I was ten, Dad brought us here after church for a regatta," I said. "We saw the sailboats, and he showed me how to rig them."

"I remember that," Mom said. But she wasn't very convincing, and I could see that for her, at that moment, bending the truth, even for my benefit, was making her anxious.

"Let's have some wine." I got the basket and Dad's briefcase out from the trunk. "He was so excited," I said. "I don't have many memories of Dad like that, happy, teaching me things. 'This is the jib, this is the main sheet, this is the rudder.' He had his life jacket on the whole time, even when we were on the beach. I guess it's just that he was so happy. That sticks out to me."

"That's a nice memory," Mom said.

Mom was right. What I'd just described to her was a terrific image, but it was, in fact, only part of the story, and so I knew for certain that Mom had absolutely no recollection of that day. The skinny was this: both Dad and I were invited to join some sailing team, but for whatever reason, at the last minute, they couldn't or wouldn't take me along. Dad and the rest of the crew sailed off without me. I was devastated and cried for hours. I cried like I can't remember ever crying.

I'd banked on Mom not only remembering all of that, but I also hoped she could fill in some of the blanks for me. That was one of very few plans I had for our evening together, mother and son rehashing some misery. It was why I'd driven us way the hell up there in the first place.

I felt stupid and petty and miserable in my selfishness. It'd been completely forgettable for Mom, so it probably should have been for me, too. It was a pathetic move, and what made it worse was that I had no idea what I actually hoped to accomplish by it, or what I wanted it to fuel.

I became momentarily very unsure of myself. I suppose

I'd had a loose assumption that just being in the location of that ultra-sour childhood experience would reveal something obvious and poignant. It hadn't.

Or, maybe that was exactly what it was doing, just not how I'd imagined. I don't know. At the very least, it'd changed our course. I opted not to give Mom a refresher on sailing-day activities. So, yes, there was a tangible deviation, and a change had occurred.

I tried to shake it off and hoped some mobility would help the cause. I led us across the hardened sand toward the water and found myself thinking about Dad, and, more specifically, I thought about the Dad from my recent dream, on account of his somehow having reached out to me while I slept. That was the Dad I had future business with.

There on the beach, I switched my feet into autopilot and willed myself a head trip. The ease with which I did this was such that an outsider, someone without any clues into my background, might even have thought that I possessed some long-sharpened talents that allowed me to do such a thing, but the reality was the complete opposite. In truth, I wasn't quite sure how I did it. But exactly how or what facilitated it was inconsequential. What was important was the act, that I channeled myself into the haze.

Dad and I were sitting inside the bar having beers. There was a nautical theme to the place—a lobster pot in the corner, old buoys and crusty nets hanging from the ceiling, etc. Twenty years earlier, I'm sure the place was charming.

I looked over at Dad, and for the first time I saw he had a tattoo on his forearm. It was creeping out from the bottom of his shirtsleeve. I could only see a portion of it. If I'd been pressed to guess, I'd have said what I saw looked like skinny little frogs legs. But, I decided to wait to ask Dad about the ink. I wanted to cut to the chase about the sailing day.

"This was a long time ago," I said, "Do you remember sailing at Forest Shores?"

Dad got this funny smile, but in a good way. "Sure," he said. "What a blast." Dad had an unlit, half-smoked cigar in his mouth.

"Why didn't you take me with you? All day you kept saying how great it'd be, and you left me on the beach."

"Man," he said, "That was such a bummer. The tightwad whose boat it was had some insurance liability thing about youngsters on deck. Dude didn't even tell me, not until we were casting off. That dickhead. But you were with me, pal," he said, "with me the whole time." Dad pointed a finger at his chest, which was hokey, but we were a few beers deep by then, so, you know.

"Do you think I'm whiny?" I said. Unfortunately, the question came out of my mouth very whiny.

"You're the whiniest!" Dad said, and he laughed. But then he squeezed my shoulder, which felt very intimate and was a warm gesture. I felt good. I felt loved. Dad dipped the tip of his cigar into his beer like it was cognac, popped it back in his mouth. "On that note," he said, "Want to slip back to the alley and smoke a doobie?"

I appreciated the invitation, but I passed. There were a few years when I partook frequently, from the end of high school until partway through college, but after that I mostly wasn't interested. Importantly, though, ever since, I've been able to wrap my head around the scene.

Mom bumped me with her elbow, middle school flirting-style. She laughed and said something, but all I heard was "briefcase."

"What?" I pulled myself back to the beach.

"I said, you're like some kind of private investigator with that briefcase. I love it."

I chose a spot close to the water's edge and spread out the blanket. Mom prepared to sit down on it, understandably, but I stopped her. "We need this for supplies." Mom made a funny face but dropped to her knees beside the blanket, like I had.

I opened the wine and poured for us. "Cheers," I said. I took a sip, and buried its base into the sand.

I opened the briefcase and gently shook its contents onto the blanket. "I learned this in Hong Kong," I said. Mom took another sip of wine. She was surveying me more cautiously than I would have guessed, but I knew she'd be all right.

First there was the fedora. It'd gotten flattened during transport but popped back to form with two light punches and a pinch. I put it on my head. The fedora, now paired with the briefcase, did mumble something investigator-ish to the world, though to what end, I have no idea.

Just then, for the first time ever, I actually liked the fedora. Even earlier in the day, when I'd packed it in the briefcase, I admit to a vague portentous image of it Frisbeeing into Lake Michigan, but I now realized a personal affinity for the hat. Maybe it was because I understood a bit more about Dad. I think he might have been trying to gift me some of his eccentricity.

I liked the hat, but that didn't suddenly make it super-cool or anything—I wasn't about to fuse it to my scalp—but it had some new value. I would keep the hat. Dad probably had another one in his backpack that he wore on special occasions. I'd do the same. I took it off my head, plucked out its peacock feather, and placed them next to each other on the blanket.

Next, I took the newspaper in my hands, yellowed newsprint I'd found in Dad's filing cabinet. I used it to make the boat. Mom seemed interested in my folding and jiggling of corners, but at the same time, she conspicuously eyed the other items on the blanket. In particular, she seemed zeroed in on the crystal there, the one I'd stolen from her. She didn't say anything, but it looked like she was taking mental notes, which was a fine reaction—better than throwing a fit, anyway.

I tried to do Mah-mah proud with my handiwork. The end product wasn't exactly symmetrical, but it appeared seaworthy.

I put the crystal in the boat first, port side. Mom didn't balk.

Next I counterbalanced the crystal with the faux jade dragon Dad bought me in Chinatown all those years ago. As I fiddled with its placement in the boat, my mind floated back to the bar.

Dad sat down, having just smoked his joint in the alley. He was totally ripped and could barely keep his eyes open.

As if Dad knew exactly what I was up to, he said, "Some folks, man, they've got different strokes. It's cool. Your mom wanted you to have that. Plus, that day in Chinatown, that was a great day in my life. I planned it for months."

"You did? I thought it was last minute."

"No way, man, that was, like, one-on-one time. Predestined or predetermined, pre- what? Premeditated, man, yeah. As good as it gets."

Dad stared at the wall of booze in front of us on the other side of the bar, possibly in contemplation, or else in absentia, but then an idea seemed to hit him. He reached down to his backpack and undid the twist-tie that attached his giant spatula to the frame. He held it toward me, a bit in awe and also curiously, like it was some beautiful scepter that he hadn't yet had the opportunity to determine whether or not held magical properties. Never mind that it needed a scrubbing. "Would you ever have a use for this?" he said.

Even if he was very quickly edging toward total obliteration, I was grateful to communicate with Dad, especially with things having changed as they had.

Next was the dough I scavenged from Dad's pockets. I fanned out the colorful bills and held them up for Mom like in an old car commercial from my childhood. I said, "Where you always save more money." Mom smiled. I hoped the wad was still impressive. Full disclosure: what I had there wasn't every single last bit of the cash, but it was a good chunk of it, to be sure. I rolled the tender into a tight tube and snapped a rubber band around it. Into the boat.

I had a waxy banana from the unappetizing bowl of plastic fruit Janice Sugarbottom had used to stage the kitchen. That went into the bow and stuck off the end like a fat yellow pulpit.

When I'd tidied up my room in preparation for my most recent trip to China, I found an empty film canister in one of my old contraband-cubbyholes. I used to store weed in that canister during high school. I figured Dad would appreciate a little doobage, even if it was just trace amounts.

"Very thoughtful," Dad said. He emphasized each word with a shake of his spatula, but it slipped out of his hand and dropped to the floor. He didn't make a move to pick it up. He just left it there. Dad looked a little defeated and seemed to be getting confused.

I poured the film canister full of wine and pressed the cap back on. It went into the boat, port-side in the stern.

To me, the fedora feather looked like it would get lost on deck, so I poked its quill through the tip of the paper mast. It looked like a flag.

The candle I brought was a foot long and the diameter of a dime. It was from my baptism, and I'd found it on my bookshelf between the pages of an otherwise unopened bible. It seemed like a pertinent addition, but looking down at the crowded ship, I realized a birthday or tea candle would have been more practical. Mom recognized my dilemma and gently took the candle from my hand. "Can I try?" she said. She wrapped the base in a bit of the yellowed newspaper, and she lodged it between the sail in the middle and the wad of cash. Into the boat.

"What else?" Mom said. She looked pleased to have contributed, which was good.

"That's everything."

Mom reached into her purse and took out her journal. She scanned through the pages looking for something, then stopped and turned to me. "You can read this anytime you want," she said. "It's not secret. Really."

I shook my head, no, as though it was an appalling suggestion. Mom went back to thumbing through the pages. She found what she was looking for, tore out that page, folded it into a tight triangle and tucked it underneath the banana at the bow.

"Almost forgot, be right back," I said. I got up and jogged to the car. Moving across the sand at approximately cow-trot pace, I thought about Jeff. I imagined that I could see him at that moment. Jeff was also running, more of a frolic than for his life. He was barefoot, making his way along the tide line on a pristine beach at that paradisiacal drug-rehab island in the South China Sea. Like they were my own, I could practically feel the granules of sand as they slid between his toes and gave way underneath his weight.

I got to the car and opened the trunk. There it was, the last bag of premium, half-stuck in the spare tire well. I'd seen it when I put the briefcase and basket in before we left the house. I wondered why I hadn't grabbed it when I first saw it, but no matter, it wasn't a point worthy of consideration. I grabbed the premium, slammed the trunk, and headed back to Mom.

With Jeff on his beach: I wouldn't claim that I willed myself into another hallucinatory chitchat, like I did with Dad. It wasn't as if I woke up that morning with a new ability to zigzag between times and dimensions or anything. All I can say was that whatever interaction I was having with Dad may have illuminated for me a new capacity to imagine. That was all. For instance, in that most recent Jeff-dream, and the sand between our toes transaction within, I wouldn't have been able to substantiate the truthfulness of my vision, or that what I felt was fact. For the sake of simplicity, I probably would have been most comfortable suggesting that it was a pipe dream.

I fell down to my knees at the edge of the blanket. Sort of out of breath and kind of high-pitched, I said, "Dad liked mushrooms, didn't he?"

"He did," Mom said.

The package was practically weightless. What a scam. I nestled the premium in between the jade dragon and the gunwale.

I had a horrible thought, that maybe we should have been sending out two boats, one for Jeff. But no, there weren't enough facts gathered for something like that.

"He would have loved to help you with your business," Mom said. "Did it occur to you that you were following exactly in his footsteps? Funny how that works."

Dad had his head down on the wooden bar top. He was fighting to keep one eye open, but apparently he was still listening, or at least trying to. "Hell, yes," I think he said. Whatever it was came out garbled. I lost him—one silent breath transition into a peaceful, low snore.

And, actually, no, I hadn't thought of it in those terms, following in Dad's footsteps. I had to admit there was some truth to it, and thanks to recent events, it was a bit easier to swallow than it might have been.

I began to imagine that I had a son, and that he was on a beach sending a paper boat into the blue for me. It created a sudden, mild crisis, which was compounded by my son. What demons was he battling as he folded together my vessel? Was he sending out anything peculiar or special for me? Had I been good to him?

"Hey," Mom said. "Lighten up. You just lost three shades. It's okay to be like Dad. I know you fight it like hell, and you have your reasons, but it's okay. You're not him, and you're all him, no matter what. Same with me. That's how it goes."

I touched Dad's arm to see if I could bring him back, but he didn't move. I said, "Dad," directly into his ear, but he didn't answer. I shook him by the shoulder. Nothing. His body went up and went down. The snoring poured from his lips. The barkeep gestured at Dad and gave me a look like, Hey? I shrugged unsympathetically, like, Hey, it's your bar.

I heard seagulls calling from the direction of the marina, and when I looked out over Lake Michigan, there weren't stars, but I could see a thin, gray crescent moon. I took off my shoes and picked up the boat.

Standing there in the bar, I wasn't sure why I got so impatient with Dad—as though I hadn't seen the coma en route, or I thought he could snap himself out of it at will. And it wasn't like that short, mildly substantial interaction was causing a dependency to grow or anything, I just wanted to keep it going a little longer, that was all. I pulled up Dad's shirtsleeve to check out the tat: Marvin the Martian. Like Dad said, different strokes.

Everything was secured in the boat, and I asked Mom to send it out. She said we should do it together, but I said no, that I thought it was more appropriate for her to do it, which was true. Mom rolled up her pants legs, like Jeff had. She waded out and released the boat.

It must have caught a crosscurrent or something, because it cruised on out of there like we'd attached horsepower to its underbelly. Or maybe Dad, who was admittedly looking pretty needy for tangibles those days, somehow pulled strings to expedite delivery, which was, well ... but anyway. If he had, that would have been pretty okay in my book. Maybe manipulating the system a little isn't the most egregious crime against humanity. I could go along with that. I might even endorse it, if, for instance, it helped Dad get a handful of tangibles for his journey, even just a few things so that at least his heart could rest easy for the duration of the ride.

Acknowledgments

Immense love and gratitude to all of my family. My core: Courtney, Alex, and Helen. My amazing parents, Bob and Prue Burke. My loving brothers and sisters, nieces and nephews: Alex, Stacey, Anna and James; Steve, Katie, James and Elizabeth; Adam, Kelsey, and Silas; and Chris. And my extended family, who advised and supported and read for me, Tom and Lily, John, Allison and Murray Burke. Jim and Pam Cochran. Our beloved Sue Cochran. Rich, Casey, Chelsea, and Reid Searles; John and Ann Searles; Mary Ann and Ted Weiss; and all of the others.

Enormous thank you to my wonderful friends who've supported this project and me. Rachel Gitelson and Doug Nilson, Nora Kahn and Dave Walters, Kathy Kahn, Frank and Erin Gidcumb, Aaron and Victoria Himes, Anders and Jelyn Franzon, Rich Liccardo, Andy and Whitney Baker, Jeremy and Briscilla Greene, Jeff Hazlett, Thomas Zwergel and Tracy Walsh, Peter and Liz Dangremond, Phil and Cecilia Hoskins, Josh and Eve Engelman, Marc and Lindsay Whitman, Joel and Kate Currier, Rich Gleason, Josh and Feryal Peterson, and these fine folks and their families: Jamie Dowd, Seth Potkin, Adam Hershman, Heath Levine, Mat Scheller, Fred Gibney, Drew McWilliams, Brian Field, Eric Menard, Chris Weiler, Tim Carpenter, Matt Wieler, John Winters, Ryan McKinley, Thatcher Woodley, Eric Sharfstein, Marty Alberts, plus all of my other Union friends and UMass friends, and many more.

And my colleagues, my mentors, my friends: Mikhail Iossel, Jeff Parker, John Goldbach, Terese Svoboda, Padgett Powell, Sam Lipsyte, Holly Clayson, Wendy Wall, Jules Law, Jessica Winegar, Megan Skord, Jill Mannor, Jennifer Britton, Susan Manning, Laurie Shannon, Rachel Webster, Kasey Evans, Kathy Daniels, Susan Lee, Brad Zakarin, Jeffery Renard Allen, Fiona McCrae,

Binyavanga Wainaina, Dawn Raffel, Chris Bachelder, Nina Barrett, Anne McPeak, DW Gibson, Shane Dubow, Steve Newman, Todd Israelite, Arthur Flowers, Emily Gilbert, Sara Černe, Hamilton Poe, and many others.

And of course, a huge thank you to Marc Vincenz and all of the good people at MadHat Press: Thank you!

About the Author

THOMAS BURKE received a BA from Union College and an MFA from the University of Massachusetts at Amherst. *Eastbound into the Cosmos* is his first novel. He has contributed work to *Tin House, The Rumpus, Playboy, Hobart Pulp* and *St. Petersburg Review,* among other places. He has taught at UMass Amherst, the Newberry Library, and Northwestern University, where he is currently assistant director of the Kaplan Humanities Institute. Formerly Burke helped direct the Summer Literary Seminars in Russia and co-founded its sister program in Kenya. He is the recipient of the Eugene Yudis Prize for fiction, a fellowship from the UMass Amherst MFA Program, and a residency at Art Omi's Ledig House, among other honors. He lives in Evanston, IL with his wife and two children.